ARCHER

<u>Dedications</u>

This book has been in my head for years, but I never
took the courage to write it because of its nature.
My wonderful wife, Ciara, gave me all the
encouragement I needed to write it on hearing the plot.
So here it is…..

Sleep my friend and let it be,
Dream all night, no reality,
Wake at dawn and face me then,
You start to live your life again.

Live each day as it were your last,
For life is short and I come fast,
Live your life without a care,
For you won't cheat me, just you dare.

Too many souls have sealed their fate,
They scream and howl, but it's too late,
Tumbling through my darkest black,
No life to live, no turning back.

Grow too tired to end the fight,
Come the day you feel the fright,
Dread the day you feel my breath,
Look long and hard, for I am death.

Adrian Hirst – aged 20.

Chapters

Prologue

A perfect, beautiful summer's morning! The streets were quiet at this early time and the old man loved to walk slowly with his Blackthorn walking stick down the old stoned path, aware that his senses seemed to be heightened with the lack of the usual street noise. The old three storey Italian shops were still and the mannequins displaying designer clothes in the windows stared past him as he sauntered by. Dawn's light was that in-between time of night and day and the speckled clouds were starting to be bathed by the sun as the birth of a new day began. The only sound to break the silence was the chorus of bird song as they sang out their different tunes, calling to each other yet keeping an eye out for danger.

He really enjoyed this time. Devoid of human activity, save for himself, he bathed in the solitude and took his time as he walked purposefully along the path. He believed it brought him closer to God in his mind's eye and at times like this, he could have a deep conversation with him.

Suddenly he stubbed his toe on an uneven paving stone and stumbled. He lost his balance, despite trying to save himself with his stick and fell forward onto his hands and knees. He stayed there for a few seconds, fumbled in the pockets of the old, battered trench coat he wore and gradually raised himself, in stages, off the floor using one of the large shop windows as a prop. As he eventually stood, he steadied himself for a few seconds to check for signs of pain. He brushed off the street detritus and continued his slow pace to his destination. The only thing he left behind was a small matchbox at the foot of the window he had used to prop himself up on. He continued and smiled slightly. Everything was in place.

Chapter 1: Present day.

Lucca. A beautiful, medieval walled town in the Tuscany region of Italy. It attracted the modern Italian as well as the many tourists who visited the town to marvel at the sites and the narrow pedestrian streets with old, tall buildings that once were inhabited but are now converted to shops.

The old man sat in one of the many chairs outside of the coffee shop at the end of Via Sant' Andrea with the junction of Via Fillungo. He was the picture of serenity sitting to one side of the seating arrangement with his back to the shop, wearing his trademark trench coat, black faded trousers, grandad collar blue shirt with his Blackthorn stick held in his left hand, wearing his usual half smile. His wide shoulders hid his average height and his thin frame was testament to a lifetime of physical fitness. He wore rounded, dark sunglasses hiding the movement of his eyes as they darted amongst all the other customers and passers-by. Nobody batted an eyelid at him, he just looked so peaceful and as more customers took their seats outside, he began to relax. He was particularly pleased to watch a young couple take their seats, as they did every Thursday at the same time and make their usual order to the waiter who very promptly attended them before they had even settled. He knew how long they were going to be there, so he took the time to watch them, study them and pray for them.

The young man, full of confidence, was dressed in a beautiful dark blue silk shirt, with tan coloured slacks and a pair of wonderful handmade black Italian leather shoes without a single scuff or piece of dirt on them. Around his neck, a thick heavy gold necklace testament to his love of high living and, to the old man, the proceeds of a very bad life. She was the perfect model. Dressed in a figure hugging white dress, her perfect make up and ruffled long black hair only augmented the scene. But it was obvious she was very fond of her partner as she lavished him with affection, touching him regularly and smiling her gorgeous smile at every opportunity. He seemed to shrug her affections, paying more attention to his mobile phone as she completed the charade for him. They were sitting facing the shop to the left-hand side of the old man and as he made a mental checklist of everything that was in place, he then moved on to whisper his prayer.

"Forgive me lord, yet again. I will be changing lives forever for what I am about to do. The innocents have no idea of the carnage I am about to create, but the fallen angel before me is a worthy sacrifice. Forgive the taking of life and have mercy for their soul. Please, I beg you, forgive me; for evil prospers when good men do nothing and I know nothing more than the act."

It was a prayer he had said, in some form, many times and his heart momentarily filled with grief and sadness as he slowly started to raise himself from his seat.

"What's your name?" said a little English voice to his right as an inquisitive little tourist girl suddenly appeared, quickly followed by her mother who was already trying to grab her arm and as she whispered her distaste at her little daughter for running off, again, the old man smiled at her and said, "Archer.......Adrian Archer," as he steadily raised himself to his feet, using the cane as a support to complete the manoeuvre. The mother of the little girl hurriedly apologised and dragged her daughter off, still chastising her for running off and talking to strangers. He straightened himself, paused for a few seconds to check for inquisitive glances and slowly moved towards the young couple.

The front of the shop was alive with sound. People talking, cutlery making its high-pitched clinking sound against plates, cups being lowered onto saucers and the general murmur of people talking and laughing.

Archer moved closer and closer, slowly but surely; with his left hand on his stick, he moved his right hand into the deep, wide pocket at hip height on his coat and sought out the familiar grip of the Ruger .22 silenced pistol. His eyes sought for people watching him, but as a seventy-seven-year-old man amongst a much younger crowd, he drew no attention. He counted down the distance, "Ten metres.........eight metres....now!" and at that he pressed the tiny transmitter switch at the top of his cane. The matchbox he had placed at the foot of the window earlier that morning, was still there when he sat with his coffee. Nobody saw it, but now it came to life as the small electronic receiver attached to a pencil detonator inside, made its electrical current thereby triggering a small explosion that shattered the window of the clothes shop he had placed it at!

At that very moment, as the young man whipped his head around to look in the direction of the explosion, Archer twisted his hand upwards inside his pocket and fired two very quick shots at the base of the young man's neck. An act he had practised hundreds of times. The commotion of people screaming, the man's partner already standing and screaming in shock at the explosion, the sound of crockery smashing on the old stoned floor was a perfect distraction for Archer. The pistol had done its job, yet again. He pretended to stumble and fell backwards to the ground, his cane still upright in his left hand. He brought his right hand out of his pocket and sat to look at his target. The young man was clearly dead but hadn't been noticed yet by his partner who was staring and looking at everybody else as the commotion of people running in all different directions distracted her. Archer saw the usual relaxing of the body as the soul departed it and looked closely as he then saw the blood starting to stream from the man's neck from the small bullet holes. A perfect time to make his escape and gingerly he stood, turned his back to the coffee shop and slowly walked away from the scene towards the apartment he had rented, months ago.

The scream from the young woman pierced the other sounds as she had realised what had happened to her partner. It was a scream that added to the grief of the old man as he made his way down the alleyway and he drooped his head in sadness for her.

He made his way along the narrow streets to his small apartment, the counter surveillance skills he had learnt over a lifetime of assassinations kicked in. Through his sorrow he listened and watched carefully for signs of being followed. He stopped regularly to pretend he was out of breath or adjusted his clothing all the while sensing for signs of hostile activity. He ducked into shop entrances, paused a few seconds then leaned out to look back where he had come from momentarily to see if he was being followed. Archer was aware of the surveillance culture and kept his head down as he walked the streets in order to disguise his features from any prying eye who may subsequently carry out a thorough investigation of his latest work from CCTV footage. He stopped to check the reflection from a shop window and immediately saw the little girl on the opposite side of the street, still being hurried along by her mother who was desperate to get away from the wreckage Archer had caused. He turned to smile at the little girl, his heart filled with grief, so he needed something, anything, to show he was still human. The little girl, with her scruffy blonde hair and wearing her little pink dress and small Wellington boots, caught his smile and waved back enthusiastically. Her mother was too busy to notice and before he knew it, the little girl was gone. They were soon replaced by the announcement of police and ambulance involvement in the form of wailing sirens echoing around the streets. Archer relaxed as he got closer to his apartment on Via Dell'Angelo and walking through the tall, steel entrance gate he paused one last time to find his door keys in his clothing to carry out one last check before he went inside. Nothing. He was in the clear and the adrenaline started to subside allowing his emotions to take over.

Sliding the key into the door lock, he quietly entered his little apartment, locked the door behind him and paused a few seconds more to listen for footsteps, but still there was nothing. It was then that the tears started to pour down his cheeks.

"Pull yourself together man!" he chastised himself, "How many times have you done this?!"

But as much as he tried to fight it, he knew he needed to settle himself down in the only battered brown leather chair he had and collect himself. Archer turned from the door and looked around his apartment. It was a simple affair with very few belongings. He had to keep possessions to a minimum, not only to easily spot danger, but also to leave very little behind for his impending return to England. To his left and around the corner of a wall was the kitchen, the living room in front and to his right were two closed doors next to each other; one the bedroom, the other the bathroom. He surveyed the apartment from the door and studied the polished old wooden flooring for subtle signs of different footprints to his own. He looked for signs of movement in pictures he had carefully placed on the wall shelves to the side of the full-length windows in the front wall. His memory was photographic and he knew how he had placed objects in all the rooms meticulously. He was so exacting that any sign of a foreign agent having been in the room would be noticed very quickly by him. Slowly he moved into the room and walked gingerly into the kitchen all the while scanning for any signs of activity. The small, chipped blue mug was still upside down on the draining board next to the sink. He had scattered small patches of sugar on the floor but saw none of the grains had been crushed by footfall and was satisfied that no one had been there. Quietly he moved across the apartment to the door to his bedroom and looked at the bottom of the door where he had taken two strips of sellotape and taped a hair between the door and the frame. Anyone opening the door would have broken this almost invisible seal, but it was still intact, as was the door to the bathroom. He made a quick check of both rooms anyway and satisfied that he had not been compromised, he relaxed and went to the kitchen. He grabbed the blue mug, reached into his white tin tea bag container and placed one in his mug, put water into his kettle and reached into his little fridge against the wall to his left to take the fresh pint of milk for his cup of tea and turned the kettle on. All the while his mind was starting to drift as he relived the kill. It was yet another security measure and he had to relive it in order to spot any mistakes which could lead to the finger being pointed at him. The only sound to break his concentration was the point the kettle had boiled and the switch clicked to show the water was ready for pouring. He mixed the water with the teabag and milk and walked over to his leather chair to reflect.

Slowly and with a bit of a grunt, he lowered himself into the comfort of the chair and allowed himself to mould into it.

Reaching into his trench coat pocket, he found the two empty bullet shells towards the muzzle of the pistol and felt relieved they hadn't fallen out of the two small bullet holes in the bottom of his pocket. He knew the chances of them falling out of those tiny holes was absolutely minimal, but he still felt relief knowing they were there and that he hadn't left any evidence at the scene. He left them and the pistol in his pocket and went over the details of the whole operation, sipping at his steaming cup of tea.

"Forgive me, forgive me....." he whispered, as he stared at the fireplace between the front windows and allowed his mind to drift. He went over his morning walk to place the matchbox at the foot of the window, the walk to the coffee shop to prepare for the assassination later that morning, the eyes of the waiter who took his order as he sat at his chosen seat, the other customers who were filling the seats and finally seeing his target as he entered the scene with his lover to take their usual seats.

His target didn't stand a chance. Archer had spent months studying the man, following him and working out any signs of a routine, his work augmented by local Italian teams who had some semblance of an intelligence file that Archer became privy to. He was, indeed, a very busy boy but the chink in his armour was his Thursday morning breakfast at the coffee shop with his girlfriend. The young man was one Antonio Ricci, his girlfriend changed...often. Ricci had a finger in every pie. He was a drug dealer, a pimp, a murderer and an extortionist. A few years ago, he had killed the elderly mother and father of one of his rivals. When the police found the bloodied bodies, even officers with decades of experience vomited. The victims had been bound to their kitchen chairs, had their feet skinned to the ankles, their wrists cut open as well as their necks and just to add insult, they had been scalped. But they couldn't get Ricci as he never left evidence and managed to evade arrest. The police and the Italian government grew increasingly frustrated.

Archer had received his instruction and intelligence file, as usual, at his post office box located in his home town of Retford in Nottinghamshire. It was his preferred method of communicating with his controller and the most secure. When he had completed a job, he sent a sympathy card with the words, "Sorry to hear about the loss of…." scribing the name of his most recent kill to his controller's post office box. It would be a couple of weeks before he would receive his payment via the box, but he had saved enough to live on from previous assassinations. His digital footprint was zero. No social media profiles, no mobile phone, no broadband internet, no bank account with an ATM card, in fact nothing electronic that can be attributed to life in the twenty first century. His passport was fake and was changed often so that his movements were incredibly difficult to trace, as was his trip to Italy a few months earlier. He had paid for the rent of the apartment up front, in cash, to the delightful landlady who looked to be the same age as him and wasn't going to question a seventy-seven-year-old man paying for things with cash! He found it ironic that with life in normal circles being mostly electronic and therefore cyber security was big business and absolutely paramount, the most secure way to live was his. Everything was paid for with cash and his needs were simple. He never bought high value items, instead opting for a simple life and yet despising material objects that were only designed to boost the ego. With his simple life, the money he received from his line of work went a long way, but his penance was loneliness which filled him with grief, sorrow and a yearning to go back in time and change his life to one that was more normal. Sipping at his cup of tea, he allowed himself to relax further and think about his past and how it had come to be.

He had learnt most of his trade from the only master of it; himself, and he tried to fight back the memories of how he had gotten himself into this mess, but the cries of the little boy he was, came back to haunt him.

Chapter 2: Retford, Nottinghamshire 1959.

"Archerrrr!"

The angry shout from across the classroom shook him from his daydream and he jumped in his seat from the shock. With a stunned look on his face, he looked past the sniggering faces of his fifteen-year-old peers to his geography teacher, Mr Turner or "The Bald Eagle" as the other pupils used to call him. He had attained that title because of his habit of peering out from the teacher's restroom, high up in the main Georgian school building on the third floor and shouting chastisements to pupils up to no good in the playground during breaks. He would command the victim to report to his office immediately and so the pupils joked that he was like an eagle on his perch, waiting to swoop down and take a victim back to his lair....never to be seen again! The "Bald" part of the title was obvious.

"Right young man, I've had enough of this. Get to the front here! NOW!"

Archer slowly and with trepidation, rose from his seat and shuffled up to Turner with his head bowed, knowing full well that trouble was coming his way. When he got close enough, Turner slapped the side of his head with the ends of his fingers, "Awake now are we?!"

Archer slowly nodded as he listened to the chorused sniggers from the pupils of the class at the sound of the slap and was immediately shamed.

"Right. Go and sit down and stay awake!"
Archer turned and with his head still bowed, he shuffled
back to his seat. The side of his head felt sore and hot
from the slap. Although he pretended to listen to the rest
of the geography class, his mind wasn't there: it was far
off. Far, far off. Constantly planning.
Geography was the last class on a Thursday and as he
packed his books away and made his way out of the
classroom, the mocking from his so-called classmates
started.
"Archer you dunce!"
"Thick as fuck Archer!"
"Bald Eagle fucking loves you Archer yu thicko!"
But they were just words to Archer. All through the
verbal vilifications, he was planning and took no notice.
To Archer, his classmates weren't even there and he felt
no emotion. He returned, through the abuse, to his main
classroom where registration was taken each morning
and placed his books inside his desk, only leaving his
homework in his satchel to take home. He knew the
books would be all over the floor the next morning, but
he didn't care. As he left the school building, to walk the
one mile back home, his heart filled with dread as he
resigned himself to the journey home. It was a slow
mile, but he needed to get back to support his mother.
His father, he didn't care about.
Daddy was not a nice man. Not a nice man at all to
either him or his mother, who only tried her best, but
nothing seemed to be good enough and she bore the
brunt of his anger. For as long as he had been alive, he
only knew misery, anger, drunkenness and violence

from his father. Sometimes the verbal abuse was as bad, if not worse, than the physical abuse he and his mother suffered.

He shouted his arrival when he entered the door of their terraced house on Whitehall Road. The street was quite small with only about twenty-five houses and formed its own little community. Everyone knew everyone on that street, but they also knew each other's business and despite his father's reputation, everybody treated Archer and his mother with kindness. More than likely due to sympathy, which was the only action they could take.

"In here love!" replied his mother from the kitchen as she prepared a simple meal of the usual meat and two veg. She tried her best to sound cheerful for him and also tried to maintain the facade of a normal family life.

Archer walked down the hallway towards the kitchen and as he passed the living room door on the left, he saw his father sleeping on his back on the sofa surrounded by empty cheap lager tins and an ashtray filled with dead cigarettes. His clothes, or lack of them, were unkempt and the smell of body odour was almost overpowering. Archer walked on and found his mother in the kitchen, happily emptying a pot of boiled potatoes from its water and placing it on the worktop. Without a word, he walked over to his mother, dropped his school satchel and wrapped his arms around her waist from behind. He placed the side of his head that had received the slap against her back and sighed deeply.

"Oh hello love! Are you alright? Your dad's sleeping, so best not to wake him up."

Keeping his head and arms where they were, he said, "I'm fine mum. School was good. I'm going to change out of my uniform."

Quickly he released his grip, grabbed his satchel and quietly ran past the living room on his tiptoes and made his way upstairs. He entered his bedroom, closed the door quietly and sat on his bed with another sigh.

It wasn't lost on Archer that his mother was always happiest when his father was asleep.

A few minutes passed as Archer changed into his blue jumper and battered trousers, when he heard the muffled conversation coming from the kitchen between his father and mother. He could tell his dad was asking questions of his mum and the conversation became clearer as he listened intently at his father's voice which started to get louder to a shout.

"What the fuck is this Claire?!"

The familiar demeaning questioning started from his father.

"I..I..it's potatoes, cabbage and pork chops," his mother sheepishly answered.

"Oh the same fucking shite we had yesterday! Are you too stupid to think of anything other than this crap?! No, don't answer that you thick bitch!" and Archer heard the smashing of plates, his mother yelping in fear and the sound of a pan being thrown across the tiled kitchen floor.

"No Tom, please. No, don't. Pleeeease..." she pleaded, yet again, but the sound of the slaps across the face and the dull thumps to the stomach resounded around the kitchen and hit the eardrums of Archer as the adrenaline rose in his body from dread. He was frozen to his bed. He knew he must go downstairs to stop his father, but he also knew his father was too powerful so he would have to pick up the pieces of his mother when daddy had left the house. He always did, after giving his mother a beating and he would find solace at the bottom of empty pint glasses in the local pub. He would return late at night, drunk and would fall asleep on the sofa. When the dreaded sounds of domestic violence had ceased and when Archer heard the front door slam, he made his way slowly out of his bedroom and down the stairs. As he descended, he looked over the handrail towards the kitchen and saw his mother's feet in the doorway, lying on their sides. It spurred him to rush down the remaining stairs, run down the hallway and into the kitchen to see the battered, dishevelled shape of his mother. Her face and left eye were swollen, her beautiful ruffled blonde hair was in clumps and blood dripped from her nose. She lay in the foetal position with her arms around her stomach and couldn't make eye contact with her son due to her shame. She had no words, she just sobbed as she tried to keep her breath. Archer grabbed a clean kitchen towel and wet it under the cold-water tap, he squeezed out the excess water and rushed over to his mum. Bending down to her he gently placed the towel on the left-hand side of her face, took her hand and placed it over the towel and slowly wrapped his arms around her to pick her up off the floor. "Oh God. Thank you Adrian," she sobbed as she propped herself up.

"I'm sorry son, your dad is unwell. Don't worry, everything will be fine," she said, dabbing the wet towel against her face, looking at the blood on it as she tried to regain her dignity.

Archer felt the tears roll down his cheeks, but he held back the desire to sob and make the shallow breathing associated with grief. He had to be strong for his mother, but also had to be subtle.

"I know mum. It will be fine, I promise you. Dad will get better."

"That's my boy. Come on, there's a few bits left for us to eat....."

His mother gathered herself and the two of them rustled up a meal together and sat at the table, in silence, eating their scraps of food.

Archer's plan was in place. He knew what he had to do. He went to school, as usual, the following day. Friday. Fridays were always good and there was a buzz among his peers because they all knew it was coming up to the weekend. As predicted, when he arrived at his desk, his books had been strewn across the floor and whilst the different cliques within the classroom stuck to themselves, everyone sneered as he picked them up quietly.

"Weirdo," he heard someone say, but he ignored it and as he picked up the last book and sat down to await registration, a slight smile grew across his face and he leaned back in his chair as his teacher entered the room.

Throughout the day, he was consistent in his usual trait of keeping himself firmly to himself, but nobody noticed

his smile. His last lesson on a Friday was Religious Education which, for some reason, he enjoyed. It wasn't because of the old lady teaching it, Mrs Fulton, it was because he enjoyed the human aspect of what religion was about and today, they had a talk about morality and forgiveness. He listened intently as the lesson unfolded.
"Who knows what Jesus said to God as he died on the cross?"
The question was met with the usual silence from pupils who didn't really care. Archer raised his hand.
"Yes. Adrian. Go ahead," as the rest of the class turned slowly in their chairs to look at him.
"Yes miss, it was "Forgive them father for they know not what they do"," he replied.
"Yes, well done! It was Jesus asking for forgiveness to those who had killed him and so the message was about forgiveness: a very Christian thing to do and ask for."
She beamed a lovely smile at Archer to show her appreciation that at least one of her pupils was taking an interest.
"But what about vengeance miss?" Archer asked.
"Revenge is the opposite of forgiveness Adrian and is best never sought."
"And so evil prospers when good men do nothing," he replied.
Mrs Fulton smiled back as did Archer. It was a knowing smile and as the final bell to signify the end of the day and the start of the weekend rang out, he exited the lesson quickly and ran out of the school to start his walk home, lest he be stopped for a fight with another pupil.

He announced his arrival, as usual, when he opened the front door to the family home which was acknowledged by his mother in the kitchen, "In here love," she replied and he could almost sense the smile on her face at his arrival.

Archer walked down the hallway and he peered into the living room and saw that his father was on the sofa as usual, surrounded by the obligatory empty lager tins and overflowing ashtray.

"Dad….." he started his preamble to his impending question.

"Dad…." he repeated.

"Fucks sake, what?!" his father gruffly replied with his back to him.

"I have to write about my weekend when I get back to school on Monday. Can we go swimming tomorrow?"

"I can't fucking swim you little prick!" he retorted.

"Sorry…..can we go fishing?"

His father leaned down and shook a lager tin to see if there were any contents left.

"Aye alright, but get me a couple of tins from the fridge," he demanded.

Archer, excited, skipped into the kitchen, smiled at his mother and gave her a hug. This time he smiled as he placed the side of his face on her back.

"Aw bless you dear! Now go on, get those tins for him before he gets mad," she whispered. On que, the demanding shout came from the living room, "Where's those fucking tinnies?!"

"Oh Jesus, quick Adrian," she whispered again.

Archer rushed to the fridge, grabbed two tins and walked quickly into the living room. His father turned slightly at the noise of Archer entering the room and held his right hand out, to which Archer filled with the tins. His father, sighed deeply, opened a tin, put the other on the floor and raised his legs up onto the sofa. He took a swig and without making eye contact he made another demand, "Tell your mother to fucking hurry up with tea."

To the relief of Archer and his mother, the evening meal passed inspection and she had a violence-free meal. It was eaten in complete silence of course, but this was far preferable to the alternative and as the empty plates were gathered up, Archer's father belched, slapped his belly and got up from the dining table in the kitchen. He shuffled down the hallway, grabbed his coat from the hanger at the door and exited, slamming the door behind him to start his saunter to the pub. Archer and his mother washed the dishes and pots as they talked about his day at school. Archer didn't like to lie about his school days, but he knew his mother had enough to contend with, so he kept the truth to himself.

Saturday morning and Archer woke after sleeping beautifully. He hadn't heard his father come home after midnight, but he peered out of his bedroom window to see his father loading the fishing gear into the boot of the car and the back seat with the usual slow, malevolent style he used to make himself look tough. Archer rushed into the bathroom and had a quick wash, dutifully cleaned his teeth and threw his clothes on back in the bedroom. He made his way downstairs and into the kitchen where he met his mother who had her cleaning uniform on in order to start her Saturday job as a cleaner at the local factory.

"Here love, I've made you and your dad a few sandwiches."

She presented him with a plastic box with the sandwiches wrapped in tin foil.

"Here's a flask of tea and for God's sake, behave. If he tells you to do something, just do it. Ok? Please son?" she almost pleaded.

"Yeah Ok. Don't worry, everything will be fine!" he cheerfully replied.

"Good. Well, there's a couple of rounds of toast on the worktop and a glass of milk. Get that inside you before you set off. Right, I'm off to work so I'll see you tonight. Please be careful."

She smiled at him, placed her hand on the side of his cheek and cracked a smile.

"Right, I'm off."

"Bye mum," he muffled as he chewed on the toast and he watched as his mother went out of the door, but left it open for Archer. As Archer looked through the doorway, he saw his mother look at the ground as she passed his dad and tried to hurry past. He grabbed her arm, said something with a cigarette hanging out of his mouth and threw her arm back as she paused and walked away, still with her head towards the ground. The anger grew in Archer, but even at his age of fifteen he had to suppress it. Finishing his toast and milk and at the shout from his father to, "Fucking hurry up!" he exited the house clutching the sandwich box and flask and sat in the stinking passenger seat of their battered car while his dad slammed the front door shut and got into the car. Dad never locked the front door; nobody dared to burgle that house.

"Right, let's go," his dad said as he started the car and drove off.

"Dad...have you got a good fishing spot?" Archer sheepishly asked.

"Yep. Got a couple of things to do first."

After a stop at the bookies and the local supermarket to buy a small bottle of vodka, they drove out of town for a few miles. The journey was made in complete silence and eventually the car was parked off a beaten track from the main road and left in a gateway to an overgrown field.

"This is MY spot lad. Nobody fucking comes here. It's mine."

Archer's father got out of the car and started to drag the fishing rod and tackle box out of the back of the car. Archer got out and, still clutching the sandwich box and flask, his father tried to hand him the fishing rod, but Archer fumbled and dropped it.

"Fucking hell! You're as useless as your mother!"

"Dad I'm sorry, I've got it now," as he bent down and picked up the rod after forcing his fingers through the handle of the flask leaving them free to pick up the light rod.

"Follow me then you idiot!" and they set off through the overgrowth to a doubly overgrown riverbank about two hundred yards from the car. Archer looked back and couldn't even see the horizon, let alone the parked car from their fishing spot. Perfect.

His father set up the fishing rod with its weights, float and hook from his wicker tackle box and laid out his float box, maggot box and different accessories by his side as he sat down on the tackle box, expertly hooked a couple of maggots and cast out his line to sit and await his first bite. Archer sat on the ground to his right, folded his arms around his knees at his chest and watched the float bobbing up and down in the river.

Despite the company, it was a lovely spring day and Archer enjoyed the surroundings. It was quite cloudy, but dry with the odd dapple of sunlight from breaks in the clouds. Crows and rooks were flitting around a nearby field and calling out to each other and blackbirds jumped around the branches of the hedgerow on the opposite side of the river chasing each other for territory or looking for a mate. He also enjoyed the lack of conversation, preferring the silence.

His father reached around to his back pocket of his trousers and fettled about for his bottle of vodka. Archer noticed the small, fixed blade knife he always kept on his belt in its leather sheaf whenever he was out of the house and his father started to take glugs of vodka as they waited for a fish to bite. The knife was always kept razor sharp and was probably the only thing his dad took pride in.

"Fucking good spot this," his father grumbled, drinking more slugs from the bottle.

Archer waited.

The time went by quite slowly. Too slowly for Archer as he listened to his father curse at every nibble from a fish on the line, but never got a catch. Archer continued to watch him drinking the bottle of vodka and noticed his father start to sway on his tackle box as the alcohol took effect. Eventually the bottle was drained and his father started to sway much more as his attention dropped from holding the fishing rod and the end of it started to droop into the water.

Archer stood to stretch his legs and get the blood pumping around his body. He twisted his upper body from side to side, all the while studying his father who was now trying to fight sleep taking over his body. Archer's father leaned over to the left from the next bout of impending sleep, Archer quickly and silently took the knife out of its sheath which had been exposed as his father swayed. He darted his eyes to him to see if he had noticed, but he hadn't.

Archer tiptoed sideways a couple of steps so he was behind his dad. Gripping the knife purposefully with his right hand, he reached forward and without hesitating he placed his left hand on the left side of his dad's head and sliced viciously, twice at the right side of his neck. The whole move was done with speed, precision and was perfectly timed. Archer stepped back and admired the initial spurt of blood as it shot out of the jugular vein from being sliced open. As his dad yelped, straightened up and started to raise his right hand to his neck, Archer kicked him in the back with all his strength, propelling him into the slow-moving river. His father rose to the surface after a couple of seconds as the crimson blood mixed with the murky water around him. The river was deep enough that Archer's dad either had to stem the blood with his hand and try to stay afloat at the same time. He spluttered his shock and panic at Archer between bobbing up and down at the river's surface. "You......little bastard!" he kept repeating. Archer stood on the riverbank, passively watching, almost enjoying the show knowing that his father couldn't swim.

"We're free now dad," he said to him, "We're finally free!" he smiled. His dad tried desperately to gain a purchase of the riverbed with his feet so he could try to walk to the bank, the blood gushing heavily between his fingers. It was a futile act.

After a few minutes of spluttering and desperately kicking to keep his head above the surface, his father's complexion went a yellowy grey. Archer watched the final act of his head staying below the surface and the arms went limp as the soul finally left its body. The flow of blood went thinner and thinner, until it stopped. The body was too heavy for the river's slow-moving current to take it away and Archer whispered.

"Forgive me lord. The fallen angel before me is a worthy sacrifice but forgive me for taking his life and have mercy on his soul. Evil prospers when good men do nothing."

He knew he had committed the ultimate sin, but he couldn't bring himself to feel compassion for his father. He waited about ten minutes, placed the knife on the ground and scrubbed it in the dried soil and cleaned it with the grass on the riverbank before sliding it into the back of the waist of his jeans. Then he entered the water and tried to move his father closer to the riverbank, but he couldn't shift the body which suited him perfectly.

His clothes sodden, he made his way back up the bank to the fishing spot and went back to the car. He was only a few miles from town, so he started to run back. He needed to appear soaking wet, exhausted and stinking of damp river water when he arrived at the police station to raise the alarm. When he had calculated he had run far enough towards the town, he stopped and listened. He could see he was very much on his own and couldn't hear voices, cars or the sound of wildlife having been disturbed by human activity. Fetching the knife out of the back of his jeans, he stood close to the hedge at the side of the road and stabbed it into the ground. He stamped hard on the hilt a few times, burying it into the ground; it would never be found there.

Archer was fit but it seemed like an eternity to arrive at the police station and he stumbled quickly into the front foyer where a young constable was busy with pen and paper at the front counter.

"Help! Please help!" Archer gasped as he fought for air, "My dad is in the river!"

"Alright son, calm down, calm down. What do you mean? Is he stuck in the mud?" asked the young constable, trying to understand and studying the young man in front of him who was soaking wet, dishevelled, muddy and fighting for air in his lungs.

"No....I don't know.....he's under the water. We were fishing and I went for a pee, but when I came back, he had fallen in! He can't swim.....I tried to help him out but I think he's drowned. He was too heavy!"

"Shit!" the constable hissed, "Stay there!" he instructed Archer and the constable was gone in a flash, shouting, "SARGE! SARGE!"

Archer sat on the bench opposite the counter, tired, filthy and exhausted and watched as seconds later, the police officer ran out of the building with his fat, ruddy faced and bushy moustached sergeant who looked at him, stopped and asked, "Are you alright son? Where were you fishing?" he panted.

"Up London Road, pass through Eaton and there's a gateway on the right. Dad parked just off it and walked the overgrown field to the river. Somewhere there."

Archer realised that even though he appeared distressed, he actually wasn't so he put his head in his hands and started to sob, forcing himself to cry.

"There, there. Ok son, we'll find him from here. Stay put ok? One of the other constables will look after you."

And at that, the sergeant disappeared and Archer was left in the safe haven of the police station.

The hours passed, the activity from the police station became frantic as other police officers were called to the scene and Archer witnessed all sorts of people, often in plain clothes, talking urgently to each other. He overheard two men in suits talking to each other just outside the foyer on the footpath, "He deserved it," said one of them, "Yeah, bad bastard that one."

Archer smiled inwardly.

The hours passed, followed by the days, followed by the weeks. The police had discovered the body, with his neck cut open and investigated the crime as a murder. But they also knew that Archer's father was very much hated, not only in public life but also criminal life and he had made enough enemies that his murder came as no surprise. They had quizzed Archer about his whereabouts, but his story was totally plausible, so he was treated kindly and without suspicion.....except for one man, who appeared in the foyer with the officers that day. He was middle aged, tall and thin with a straight back, wearing a well-tailored suit and didn't seem to interact with the uniformed officers much. He listened to the officers talking, then looked down at Archer and winked and smiled at him before purposefully walking out of the station and disappearing. As the months passed, his mother's demeanour changed. As much as she had been distraught about her husband's killing, she couldn't bring herself to cry at his cremation. When she was handed the vase of ashes, she went to the river with Adrian and scattered his ashes at "his" fishing spot. As Adrian held his mother's hand while they watched the ashes slowly spread on the water's surface and meander their way downstream, he felt the sense of relief not only through himself, but also through his mother. She sighed and it wasn't a sigh of sadness; Archer knew it was to signify the end of an old life and the start of a new one.

The bullying and the name calling at school ended for Archer when he returned a week after his first kill. He didn't receive sympathy, which he never wanted or asked for anyway, but was finally left alone by his peers. He continued to study, but never quite grasped the concept of school and despite his intelligence, his academic achievements would be of no importance to him.

One evening, as he was sitting at the kitchen table completing his maths homework, a gentle knock came from the front door. His mother, who was reading a book opposite Archer, rose from the table and answered the door. Archer watched with intrigue. She opened the door to a dark, rainy evening and saw a tall, thin shouldered middle-aged man standing there and smiling a warm smile at his mother. He wore a knee length light brown Wayfarer coat, grey suit, white shirt with a dark blue tie and black shoes, topped with a tweed flat cap. Archer very suddenly realised it was the same man from the foyer of the police station and he felt his heart pump suddenly.

Words were exchanged and he removed his cap as she invited him in. Gratefully he bowed slightly and walked into the hallway, smiling at Archer. As his mother closed the door, the man turned to her and said, "I wonder if I could talk to your son in private? I won't be long, I promise. I can see the young man is at his homework and I really don't want to intrude for too long in your evening missus Archer."

"Oh….call me Claire," she sounded a little surprised, "Yes, of course. Anything we can do to help."

She walked quickly up to Adrian, leaving the man in the hallway and whispered, "This man wants to talk to you ok? He's here about your father, that's all, so don't worry."

Archer nodded.

"Good boy. See you in a while. I'm just in the living room."

She walked down the hallway, nodded to the man and turned right into the living room.

The man reached into the doorway to the room and started to slowly close the door.

"Thank you ma'am, I won't be long."

When he shut the door, he walked slowly to Archer, trying not to seem threatening. Archer checked his feelings and realised he didn't feel threatened.

The man took one of the wooden kitchen chairs to the left of Archer and settled himself by undoing his coat buttons. He placed his cap on the table and looked at Archer.

"So young man....." he started in his well spoken accent, "Don't be alarmed, I work for the government. I'm not a police officer, ok?"

Archer nodded.

"I know what happened to your father....." his smile grew, "I mean I REALLY know what happened to your father and believe me when I tell you this, you are not in any trouble whatsoever."

Archer felt an instant rise of adrenaline coming from his chest. He'd been rumbled by this man. He had found out what really happened, but how? The man had an aura of intelligence about him and Archer knew he couldn't lie. He took a gigantic leap of faith.

"It was mum. Life is good now," he mumbled, staring at the man's eyes to see how he would react.

The man sat back in the chair, "I know lad, I know. Daddy was a bad man. We know that. You took the only course of action possible. We know that too. How is school going? You'll be finished soon, won't you?" he asked.

"Yes. It's not great. I don't like anyone there. I just want to leave," he answered, feeling a lot more comfortable with the stranger.

The man smiled more and nodded in agreement, "I hated it too. What do you want to do when you leave?"

"I don't know. Probably get a job in the coal mines. Something to look after mum."

"Well young man. I work for a particular government department. We're higher than the police, in fact higher than anybody else and we are particularly interested in young men who have a particular skill set and intelligence......such as you."

He paused to let that sink in with Archer.

"We will be keeping a close eye on you and very soon we will be making you a job offer and believe me, you won't be able to refuse it. Your mum will be looked after because of this offer, but you will never know who you work for. Your pay will be excellent, but we will be asking you to complete tasks that may very well put you in danger. There's just as much danger in working down the coal pit though, isn't there?" he chuckled quietly and held his smile at Archer.

The excitement grew in Archer. This sounded like a dream come true!

"I will be back again to make you this offer. There will be practically nothing in writing son. If you accept, we will take you away for several months of training and look after your mum for you. You'll inform her that you're going away on a mechanical apprenticeship and you will be paid as soon as you start. Everything will be catered for. Understand?"

Archer allowed himself to smile, "Yes. Sounds ok. Thank you!"

"Don't thank me yet son. If you accept, you'll have a lot of hard work in front of you, it won't be easy and you can't tell a soul about this conversation."

The stranger stood, placed his cap on his head and shaped it in. He looked down at Archer and held a stare at him, "But you'll hack that no problem," he winked and smiled again.

The man turned and walked down the hallway, he opened the door to the living room and leaned in still holding the door handle.

"Claire, ma'am, thank you for your time. I've finished with your son and no further action is needed. I'll bid you goodnight."

"Oh..ok. Thank you. You didn't have enough time for a cup of tea!"

"Quite alright." He said as he touched the edge of his cap to her, "I'll make my way out. Goodnight."

The man opened the front door, stepped through the doorway, turned to close the door and as he did so he looked down the hallway to Archer and also touched the edge of his cap in salute, closed the door and was gone.

The months passed by and Archer continued the charade that was school life. The bullying stopped as did the name calling, but Archer still couldn't bring himself round to getting close to any of his peers. He found that he excelled at physical fitness, in particular running but always refused to take it further by representing the school in races or joining a local club to pursue an athletic career. He also noticed on the odd occasion when he left the school to walk home, the strange man who talked to him in the kitchen stood watching him briefly from a distance, still wearing the same knowing smile.

When Archer turned seventeen and was leaving school with very good exam results in 1961, he closed the door on academia, content he had done enough to make his mother proud.

And so on his last day at school, when his peers were celebrating together, Archer walked away from the school aware that he was turning his back on a past he would rather forget.

He arrived home, called out his arrival which was returned by his mother in the kitchen and walked down the hallway without even glancing in the living room out of habit. Life was so much better. His mother whistled and sang a lot and managed to get by on the meagre wages she received from her cleaning jobs.

She received the obligatory hug whilst she peeled potatoes at the sink and he threw his schoolbag on the floor and sat at the kitchen table with a big, relieved sigh.

"All over then?" his mother asked, but it was more of a statement.

"Yep. Done. Have to think about what I'm going to do now mum."

"Try not to worry love. Have you any idea what you want to do?"

"Not sure yet. I thought about the mines or the rope factory."

"Well, you've done good at school son. I'm proud of you. Something will turn up."

"Yeah, I have a feeling you're right," and he rose from his chair to set the table out with the cutlery they would need for their impending dinner.

That very evening, a soft knock on the door sounded down the hallway. Archer was continuing to read his book at the kitchen table whilst his mother was out at her cleaning job in the local rope factory.

Archer made his way down the hallway and tentatively opened the door and almost gasped in surprise when he met the stare of the strange man from the government office.

"Hello lad!" he said with the familiar warm smile and as he took his cap off, he asked, "Can we have that chat?" and he proceeded to allow himself in.

Archer nodded and stood back with the door to allow him in.

"Let's move to the kitchen then, shall we?"

Archer closed the door and they both walked into the kitchen.

"Take a seat lad."

Archer realised that the man in front of him was ordering him to sit; had made his way into his home and was aware that this was the start of something big. He sat as did the man, placing his cap on the table and crossing his left leg over his right.

"The last time I was here, I told you I would make an offer of a job for you that you wouldn't be able to turn down. This isn't a job; this is a career. You and your mother will be looked after and you have my word on that. My job is simple. I will be your controller; you will know me as Mercury. You will know nobody else but me. Do you follow so far?"

Archer, aware of the enormity of it all and with his body filled with adrenaline, felt his mouth go dry. It was the first time he had ever felt that. Even as he carried out the act of killing his father, he never felt like this. He nodded.

"Good. Your job sounds simple, but in reality, it is not. You'll be eighteen soon and I'll send you away for training which will last several months for your particular trade and then you will be tasked for jobs as and when needed. Any questions so far?"

Archer felt sheepish for asking, "What will I be doing?"

Mercury paused and smiled, "You'll be terminating state targeted enemies. People who are a complete drain on the government and public either at home or for our allied foreign governments. Drug dealers, murderers, child abductors and spies to name but a few. The list is quite extensive, but you'll essentially be eradicating evil men. They sometimes lead criminal empires and let their foot soldiers do the work. You'll be cutting off the head of the snake so to speak. Prison is too good for them and in order to stop something, we have to stop it at the source," he paused to allow it all to sink in.

"Killing people?" Archer asked, but already knew the answer.

"Yes lad, yes. Problems?"

"No. None at all. But why me?"

"Because you have a rare skill at such an early age. I know you killed your father, but my department knows it would have taken very careful planning. Your plan was perfect and it fooled the police and their detectives, but not us. Our intelligence circles are far superior to the police and we knew your father would not be touched by any other criminal element due to the deals he was doing. That left only one suspect.....you. So, I traced your movements and followed your line of travel back to the station and found the knife when I found faint footsteps in the trodden grass leading to the hedgerow. I saw you at the police station when I was called up about the murder and I studied you. Your body language gave you away and so I attended the scene the next day. And so here we are."

Archer nodded, "Indeed."

"We'll iron all those minor things out, but we need you son. It won't be easy but believe me we'll look after you and your mum. So......are you ready for this?"

Archer thought for a few seconds.

"When do I start?"

Mercury sat back and allowed himself to be pleased, "A week today. Next Thursday, you'll go to the train station at 9am and wait outside the station. You'll be picked up from there. Bring whatever clothes you have and that's all. We'll look after the rest."

"Will it be you picking me up?" Archer realised he had become quite attached to the man.

"No. You'll be approached by a man wearing a blue boiler suit that will be covered in oil stains. He'll look like a mechanic. You'll tell your mother when I'm gone, that you have an apprenticeship at an engineering firm which could lead you into a career in ship building. From there on, you're ours."

Archer allowed himself to smile with excitement, "Good," he simply replied.

"One more thing...I need one signature from you," he reached into the inside pocket of his coat and pulled out a few folded pieces of paper.

"This is your contract with us to say you agree to your conditions of employment. That you are handing your life over to us. Be aware that the government will never be seen to sanction any of your activities and have complete deniability. Sign at the bottom and we're done."

He moved into his side coat pocket and brought out a silver fountain pen. Archer didn't hesitate. He took the pen from Mercury and swiftly signed the contract and handed back the pen. Mercury studied the signature, blew on it gently to dry the ink, then folded the paper and shuffled it back into his inside pocket.

"Ok son. It's done. Welcome to government service. You'll be hearing from me soon. Good luck!"

At that, Mercury stood up, adjusted himself and held out his hand to Archer. Archer stood, looked him in the eye and shook his hand with a firm grasp.

"Good lad."

Mercury walked down the hallway and as he approached the door, he donned his flat cap. Archer watched from the kitchen as he opened the front door, stepped into the night and turned to close it. As he did so, he touched his cap in salute once again and quietly closed the door.

A few hours passed, which gave Archer plenty of time to process what had just happened. Funnily enough, he didn't feel any apprehension or regret about his new career choice. He had always held the feeling that he would be alright after school and trod his path into adult life. He held his book in front of his nose but couldn't digest the words as he read them and as he thought about the road ahead, his mother came in the front door.

"Evening love, you alright? That was exhausting, I think I'll have a quick cup of tea. What did you get up to?"

"Not a lot mum. Just sat here reading my book."

He knew if he talked about his job offer, his mother would find it strange that he got the offer in the evening rather than through a working day, so he resolved to tell her tomorrow. He continued his book as best he could, trying to block out thoughts of the future and what he would be required to do, but it was useless.

"I'm off to bed mum. I'll see you tomorrow when you're home. I'll peel a pot of spuds for you."

"Aw bless you son, thank you! Alright, I'll see you when I get home from work."

He closed his book, left it at the kitchen table and with tired feet he made his way upstairs, peeking into the living room, which was in complete darkness and incredibly quiet, he allowed himself to feel proud.

Chapter 3: It begins.

The next day, Archer busied himself around the house all the while watching the clock as time passed by oh so slowly. He felt more nervous about telling his mother he was going to be sent away to start a new life, than the thought of his future.

As evening approached, Archer was sitting at the kitchen table with his book in front of him and a pan of potatoes awaiting his mother's attention when she came home. The front door opened and she called out, "Home! Phew, what a day…" and she continued as she walked down the hallway, "That was hard work. How are you son?" as she entered the kitchen, Archer was standing by his chair which stopped her for a second to look at him, "What's up?" she asked.

"Mum, I'm going away," he said nervously.

"Oh….what do you mean? For how long?" she asked inquisitively.

"Well…..for good. I've got a job," he smiled.

"Awwww brilliant!" and she stooped and walked towards him holding out her arms to hug him.

She held him tight, knowing that her little boy was on the brink of leaving home and her life would change forever. She held him for a short while, smiling and fighting back tears then stood back to collect herself.

"So, tell me all. Where are you going and who are you working for?"

"I've got a mechanical apprenticeship. I applied about a week ago and went for an interview today. I didn't tell you because I didn't think it would get anywhere but I'll be training away then I'll be sent to a shipyard somewhere. The money is really good mum and I'll be well looked after," he smiled an excited smile, but felt guilty at the same time for lying.

"I'll have enough to send home mum, so you can have a life too. A good life."

She allowed a tear to roll down her cheek, burning its way to her jaw line.

"Oh son, I'll be alright, I've got my own work to do and plenty of friends at the factory so I'll be fine. I'm so proud of you, well done! My boy is leaving home!"

They hugged again and Adrian allowed himself to shed a tear too.

"I'm sorry mum," he sobbed a little and wondered if she would ever know what he has done and what he is about to do. There were also tears of regret that he couldn't tell her exactly what his new career would entail.

She stroked his hair, stood back and held his shoulders, "Adrian it's fine. I'm so proud of you, so proud. We all leave our parents eventually, so I'm well prepared for this."

They hugged a little more and spent the evening eating their meal, reading and talking. Adrian was going to miss these moments.

The week went by faster than Archer realised and before he knew it, he was packing his suitcase ready to head for the train station the next day. In the morning, he gave his mother a huge hug at the front door. She repeated how proud of him she was and gave him several pieces of advice that only a mother could and as he walked off, he turned several times to wave to her before he was out of sight and on his own. She smiled fiercely and returned the wave from the doorstep as she watched her little boy start a life of his own and didn't even feel the necessity to fight back the tears.

He turned the corner and was gone. After a twenty minute walk, he arrived at the train station and waited at the large entrance.

He blended in with the hustle and bustle of people carrying out their lives and he studied them with a new inquisitiveness. As he looked around himself at all these other humans, a voice announced in his left ear, "Archer. Follow me young man."

As promised, a man in a blue boiler suit with oil stains had come to meet him. He was a rotund man with scruffy dark hair and an unkempt beard. The oil stains were mostly on the front of the boiler suit, especially over the tops of the legs, but Archer could easily tell the man was not a mechanic. The clothing and look was right, to him, but he studied the man's hands as he walked off to the awaiting car and saw no oil ingrained into the soft skin, or dirt under the fingernails that always seemed to be there with seasoned mechanics.

Archer dutifully followed anyway and as they entered the car, the man started it up and looked across at him. "Ready?" he asked, staring Archer straight in the eye. "Yes, definitely," he replied and turned to look out of the windscreen.

"Good....good," and the mechanic set off.

The next four hours of travelling in the car felt like an eternity for Archer but the following months of intense training flashed by.

He was trained in a small farm-like complex, well off the beaten track in the middle of nowhere. With the constant route change on the way there, he had absolutely no idea where he was in England. From the casual look of a passer-by, the complex really looked like a small farm; a concrete forecourt opening up at the end of the long gravel drive with a two-storey farmhouse on the left and three barns in front of the house, to the right of the forecourt. Archer was to be billeted in the farmhouse on the ground floor and his instructors came and went and spent the odd night in rooms upstairs. His room was a simple affair, with a solid wooden bed, a battered leather chair in the left corner and a large wooden wardrobe and dresser at the foot of the bed to the right of the room. The barns held secrets of their own. They were sound proofed and held all sorts of activities for him. He was trained in explosives, knife fighting, unarmed combat, sabotage techniques, deception techniques, surveillance and counter surveillance, map reading, operation planning, morse code and firearms training to name but a few as well as normal things like driving cars and motorcycles. His physical fitness training was also rigorous, but he impressed his instructors with his prowess and quickly became muscular and athletic. They also gave him basic mechanics training so that he could prove his ability should the need arise in order to consolidate his cover story. He had no idea when the training would end as he was constantly tested and was regularly subjected to sleep deprivation. To his instructors, he was almost unnatural. He coped with everything thrown at him at such an early age and excelled at pistol shooting.

He was also encouraged to write home to his mother and handed over his letters to an instructor, who not only vetted them, but also made sure they were sent from a coastal town with a shipyard. The return address was fake, but if his mother wrote, the letter would definitely make its way to him.

A month after he turned eighteen years of age, he was informed that he would be deployed on his first mission. What he didn't know was that it was going to be his final test which brought together all of his training.

One evening as he was sitting in his room, he was given his intelligence file about a man who lived in a suburban part of a town. He was a director for an industrial firm responsible for engineering parts for missile systems. What the other board members of the firm didn't know, but what the government did, was that he was a spy and had been creating havoc for a foreign agency. The government held its own secrets about the man and wanted his death to look like a burglary that had gone wrong.

Archer was duly deployed and putting his skills into practice, he had planned on doing exactly that. He was dropped off about a mile from the man's house, kept to the shadows and used every skill available to ensure he wasn't followed or watched. He broke into the house in the early hours of the morning and made his way to the man's bedroom. He had armed himself with a kitchen knife from the man's own set and crept into the room. His eyes had adjusted to the darkness and he could see the shape of him sleeping in his bed. As he crept ever closer, suddenly a light came on in the room. Archer's eyes quickly searched for the source of the light switch, ready to swing into action but he relaxed instantly when he saw Mercury, smiling like a Cheshire cat in the corner of the room with his hand still under the shade of a table lamp where the light switch was.

"Well done lad. Very well done!" he continued to smile, "You'll do nicely."

The man in the bed was one of his instructors and he sat up, with his back to the headboard, also grinning wildly.

Archer relaxed his shoulders, dropped his stoop and smiled back, "You buggers!"

"That was a smashing idea to use one of the knives from the kitchen. I'm bloody glad you didn't get any closer to me!" his instructor said.

Archer dropped it, point first, into the floor where it stuck and swayed gently.

"Well I knew if I was to bring something with me, it would look like a premeditated murder rather than a burglary that had gone hot. My plan was to wake this chap, take him to the kitchen at knife point, kill him and ransack the place. If I had killed him in his bed, it would look like murder again. The police would have seen him in the kitchen and come to the conclusion he had been disturbed by me and had come down to either investigate or take me on. Didn't expect to see you two idiots though," he grinned.

Mercury didn't hide how impressed he was.

"Excellent, just excellent. That's how we wanted it to look. Ok let's hit the road, you need some rest."

They gave him a week off at home and Archer decided he was not going to write home and give his mother advance notice of his impending return. He decided to surprise her and just turn up out of the blue.

As he was packing his suitcase back in his room at the training complex, Mercury entered the room.

"Ah there you are…"

Archer stopped packing and turned to look at him.

"Right. I don't need to tell you not to talk about any of your activities here to anyone….including your mother, do I?" he asked, already knowing the answer this brilliant and intelligent young man would give.

Archer half smiled and cocked his head to one side, raising his eyebrows to Mercury as if to question the very question itself.

Mercury smiled and gave a little chuckle, "Good. Well, here's some money for you with a little bonus and back pay for the time you've spent here so far. You've done well sir. We're all delighted with your progress."

Mercury handed over a thick brown envelope, stuffed with paper money.

Archer felt a deep sense of pride and belonging, he hadn't realised how well he was doing because nobody told him. He gingerly took the envelope but decided to check the contents later, lest he appear to be greedy, but he could already tell the pay was substantial.

"Well thank you governor. Are you telling me we're at the end and you're letting me step into the big bad world?"

"Ha! Have your time off and get back here. You will be picked up at the train station in the usual way at zero nine hundred hours, the same day next week."

Archer pretended to salute by touching the front of his head with two fingers and Mercury turned towards the door. As he walked towards it, he stopped, paused a second and turned his head to Archer.

"I'm proud of you lad. I should be, I'm the one who found you. Be very aware that we have plans for you. Don't slip up, don't drop your guard. Remember everything we have taught you and you'll be fine. As time goes on you may question what you are doing and why, but believe me, there is a bigger picture," he paused and looked towards his feet, "There always is."

At that, he left the room leaving Archer to ponder.

Archer continued to pack his suitcase without giving Mercury's words another thought. He rushed outside to his awaiting car to the railway station and started the journey home. He was made to lie on the back seat and wear a blindfold for the first part of his journey, only removing it when the driver said he could. His masters knew if he was captured and tortured, his enemies would want to know where he was being trained and so security was incredibly tight. Once the blindfold was removed, he was allowed to sit in the passenger seat for normality purposes and he enjoyed the feeling of excitement about returning home. It had felt like he had been away for a long time and he pondered at the changes he would see to the homestead.

When they arrived at the station, the driver passed Archer a train ticket and reminded him, "Nine o'clock in the morning this day next week, ok?"

Archer noticed he had dropped the official way of telling time by using the words "zero, hundred" and "hours" in case someone overheard and so the driver would seem more civilian. The driver had smoked cigarettes all the way and so his window was open to allow air flow through the car. Archer nodded, got out of the car and the driver selected first gear and drove off at a normal speed, instead of rushing off in haste.

Archer stood for a minute and studied his surroundings. He breathed in the smells of normal living. During his training, the prominent smells were mostly gun smoke and sweat and so this was a welcome distraction. He also scanned for danger and subtly studied people around him. The man leaning against the wall reading a newspaper beside the entrance doors to the ticket office and platforms. He checked to see if he raised his eyes momentarily to look at Archer. He checked people sitting in cars for anyone using cameras. Mothers tending to children, groups of teenagers, old men and women, anybody who could be used as the eyes for an enemy. All his training combined to keep him aware and safe, but he also added his own little touch to the training. He would pretend to notice his shoelaces needing to be tightened so when he stooped to tie them, he would look up quickly to catch the eyes of an enemy who would not expect that kind of behaviour. It was subtle, but very effective and on this occasion, Archer felt safe.

He made his way through the entrance to the station and sat on a bench on the platform to await his train to Retford. Although he felt safe and excited to be returning home, he continued to scan all of the people around him. He went over his cover story that he would tell his mother about his new job and noticed he was starting to feel comfortable about lying to her. He remembered Mercury's words as he was packing his suitcase about the bigger picture and realised that cover stories were just a small part of it. If it kept him and his mother safe, then so be it.

His train duly arrived and he boarded it, carefully watching who sat near him and especially anyone facing his direction. He would continue to be alert throughout the rocking motion of the train as it sped along the tracks to his destination, never allowing himself to doze off.

When he arrived at Retford, he alighted from the train and paused to look around him. Nothing had changed. As he went through the station building and started his twenty-minute walk home, he realised that the only thing that had gone through major change was himself. The buildings, the trees growing through the pavements, the grass and other people all seemed the same to him, but he knew he was now going home as a man, not the boy anymore.

His excitement grew as he rounded the corner to the row of terraced houses on Whitehall Road and he wondered if his mother would be home. This was going to be a complete surprise for her!

When he got to the front door, he paused. He decided to knock on the door rather than use his key, just to add to the surprise and he gave the door knock a few well timed raps. He stood back, smiling as he heard footsteps approaching the door. He knew it was his mother; he recognised her footfall as she dragged her slippers along the hall floor.

She opened the door and her face burst into surprise, "Adrian!! Oh my God son, you're back!"

Archer beamed, "Hi mum! Thought I'd give you a surprise."

"That you did, that you did! Look at you! Oh come 'ere!" and she grabbed him and gave him a huge hug at the doorstep. She could see and feel that Adrian had developed muscle and felt an enormous sense of pride, "Good grief son, you've been working hard haven't you? Come on in then for goodness sake. I'll put a pot of tea on and you can tell me all about it."

Archer stepped foot inside the hall. Nothing had changed. Nothing. His mother was still wittering away as they walked towards the kitchen and as they entered, Archer saw a beautiful young woman sitting at the kitchen table with a cup of tea already before her.

"Ah, Adrian, this is Sandra Walker from the factory. She's new to it and we've become quite good friends haven't we San?" using the nickname his mother had obviously adorned her.

Archer, still holding his suitcase, suddenly felt lost for words. She was slim, with blonde hair tied back in a ponytail, with green eyes and a slim neckline which flowed down to a slim body. She sat with her legs crossed, leaning on the table with her elbows and she blushed as she noticed him studying her. He couldn't help looking into her eyes with his own hazel-coloured eyes.

"Hello," she said softly, "Pleased to meet you," she continued and stood to hold out her hand.

Archer saw how her blue dress hugged her figure; the slim white belt on her waist pulling the dress in, contouring her petite frame.

He almost dropped his suitcase but managed to lower it to the kitchen floor as he stepped forwards and shook her hand gently.

"Pleasure is mine. I'm Adrian," he said sheepishly.

She smiled, "Yeah I know, dummy. Your mum introduced us."

Archer giggled, "Yeah, sorry!"

She sat back down and Archer pulled out a chair as his mother joined them.

"Here you go son. Here's a cup of tea. Now, tell us all about your adventure," and they all talked and talked for at least a couple of hours. Archer lied about his apprenticeship, talking in general terms about mechanical things and talking more about the characters he had met. He noticed Sandra smiling constantly and also noticed how he was smiling back uncontrollably. So did his mother, but she was discreet and said nothing about their connection. As Archer talked, he couldn't stop gazing into her gorgeous eyes and Sandra held his gaze.

"Oh goodness, is that the time?" Sandra said as she studied her watch, "I must be getting on. I have to make granny her tea then head off to the factory, I'm so sorry." Archer stood to show his respect, "Let me show you out."

"Oh, yes, thank you," she smiled with gratitude and she turned to his mother, "I'll see you at the factory then Claire."

Archer's mother smiled a knowing smile and looked from Sandra to her son, aware the two had connected so well.

As the two of them walked towards the front door, Archer turned to her, "Erm, I'm home for a week. Would you like to meet me tomorrow for a walk?" he asked, raising his eyebrows. She smiled and her eyes lit up, "Yes, that would be lovely. I finish work at two, is that alright?"

"Yes of course!"

"I can get changed at the factory, so we can walk from there if you like?" she looked up at him as he was several inches taller than her. He guessed she was about five foot two inches and as she looked up at him, he was captivated by her green eyes again.

"Sounds like a plan," he smiled and opened the front door to allow her out.

"Thank you. Ok then, I'll see you tomorrow," she beamed at him.

"Already looking forward to it," he replied as he watched her walk out of the house and turned left on the footpath to make her way to her grandmothers. He chuckled as he watched; he marvelled at how she seemed to trot down the path rather than walk. Before she disappeared from view, she turned to see if he was still there at the door. She was delighted to see he still was and waved back to him. Archer raised his hand and smiled at her. When she was out of view, he turned back into the house and closed the front door, smiling as he walked back into the kitchen.

His mother saw his smile, "She's lovely Adrian and also very single."

"Stop it mum," he blushed.

"Right. Get yourself upstairs and unpack your suitcase then son. Your room is the way you left it. So good to see you back."

He drained his cup of tea, grabbed his suitcase and almost skipped upstairs to his room which was just as his mother described and had been left as it was. He sat on the edge of the bed and brought out the envelope stuffed with money that Mercury had given him. His eyes widened when he counted out the money. If this was the shape of things to come, he would never have to worry about keeping his mother and himself in good shape.

The following day he met Sandra outside the factory and paced around the entrance because he had arrived early. He was excited to be meeting her and yet, for the first time, he felt nervous. His new career path never left him feeling like this so he had to give himself a talking to. It was as he was mumbling to himself that he was almost caught out by Sandra who suddenly appeared at the entrance gate. They walked and talked for what seemed like a short time, but in fact two hours elapsed

and Sandra told Archer she had to go to her
grandmother's in order to provide care.
"Yeah no problem, can I see you tomorrow?" he asked,
feeling the nerves rise in his stomach.
"Yes, that would be lovely! Same time again?"
"Brilliant," and they paused, looking at each other.
Archer noticed she was fixing his gaze with a beautiful
smile and as the adrenaline rose in his chest, he moved
his head towards hers. She responded likewise and as
she closed her eyes, they kissed. The kiss was only for
about a couple of seconds, but they both looked at each
other with a sparkle in their eyes. Neither of them could
stop smiling and as much as Archer didn't want to lose
the moment, Sandra had to leave for her grandmother.
"I really hoped I would meet someone like you," she said
softly, twisting her shoulders in excitement.
"Me too. I didn't see this happening before I came
home!" he laughed. She laughed with him and turned,
"Ok, I've really got to go. See you tomorrow then
Adrian," and she trotted away, looking over her shoulder
to him as she went and giving him a quick wave with a
smile.
Archer's legs felt weak and he was rooted to the spot as
he waved and smiled at her whilst she walked away.
Returning home, his mother asked how his day had
gone, but he didn't reveal the intimate details of his walk
with Sandra. He told her they were meeting the next day
and his mother smiled knowingly. They spent the rest of
the day and evening talking about work, her friends and
local gossip. Archer tried to listen and for the most part

he succeeded, but he couldn't get Sandra out of his head.

He met Sandra the next day and they grew closer and closer. He realised he could talk freely with Sandra, as she could with him and they were totally relaxed in each other's company. They kissed regularly and held hands as they walked, but before they knew it, Archer's time at home was coming to an end. But neither of them felt overly sad about his departure.

As they reached Sandra's grandmother's house, hand in hand, she turned to face him.

"When will you be back?"

"I think it'll be a couple of months. I'm not sure, the training is varied and one lesson lasts longer than others. It depends on what tools they want to train me on. Are you ok with that? I'll understand if you don't want to see me anymore."

"Oh no! I want to see you Adrian, of course I do. A couple of months or so is not long and you'll give me something to look forward to. I'll write to you in between, is that alright?"

Archer smiled and almost felt his face aching from how hard he was smiling.

"Thank God for that!"

"Right then silly Billy, I'll get your address from your mum."

She leaned in for a kiss and Archer didn't hesitate. They kissed for much longer than usual and Archer felt his heart heave with sadness and excitement at the same time. He didn't want this moment to end, but end it must and he inwardly vowed not to lose her. They parted without tears and Archer made his way home, tinged with sadness but knowing Sandra will be there for him when he returns. He also knew he needed to concentrate when he returned to training and remembered the advice from Mercury.

"Don't drop your guard lad."

Archer smiled to himself and made his way home.

That evening, his mother didn't ask him about Sandra as she knew the two of them had effectively become partners, but during a pause in their conversation she smiled with sympathy and said, "You'll miss each other when you go back tomorrow."

Archer raised his eyebrows and nodded, "Yep. Too right. But she's going to write to me in between so it's all good mum."

"Brilliant Adrian, brilliant. She's so nice."

She left it at that and Archer went to bed early.

The next morning, Archer left money on his bed for his mother, to fulfil his promise to himself to look after her. He went downstairs with his suitcase to find his mother in the kitchen wearing her work uniform and rushing around to tend to him.

"Right son, there's toast and a fresh pot of tea on. I have to go, I'm already late."

"Oh, no problem. Thanks mum!" and he rushed over after dropping his suitcase and hugged her back, placing the side of his cheek against her back.

"Aw! Bless you Adrian," she turned and held his face in her hands, "Now you go and look after yourself. Be careful around all those machines and tools, ok?" and a tear fell from her eye, rolling speedily down her cheek.

"It'll be fine mum, I'll be right."

She kissed his forehead, "Good. Right, I'll see you soon!" and she rushed down the hallway, paused to say something, but carried on after looking at her watch. She went out of the front door and Archer was left alone in the kitchen. The silence suddenly grabbed him as the usual sounds of his mother busying about and their conversations were gone. Everything was still.

He sat at the kitchen table, eating his toast and a sudden feeling of malevolence hit him. It was almost as though he sensed him as Archer quietly called out.

"See dad. I told you we were finally free."

Chapter 4: A new friend

Archer returned to his ramshack training complex and unpacked his suitcase in his room. As he was placing his clothes back into his wardrobe, Mercury appeared at the door wearing his customary smile.

"Welcome back lad. I've no need to ask you if you had a good week at home, we already know."

Archer slowly turned to him as it dawned on him they had been watching.

"You sneaky ba…."

"Ah ah! No need for bad language now," he smiled and laughed, "Now…..time to concentrate. We've been evaluating your scores. You've really excelled at firearms, especially pistols. So….we're now issuing you your own personal weapon. Report to the range as soon as you're finished and we'll go through it with you."

He turned to exit, but quickly looked over his shoulder as he moved, "Welcome back!"

Archer felt a different kind of excitement as he unpacked and trudged his way across the muddy farmyard to the large barn that held the underground range. Passing through the required doors, he entered the fifty metre pistol range which was a simple affair with a human shaped wooden target placed in front of a sloped sand bank with a couple of rows of sandbags in front of it. The combined smell of pinewood, gun oil and hessian permeated around the confines of the range. Archer approached Mercury and a rugged looking instructor he knew as "Stitch", both standing at a rudimentary pine table. He was a very military styled instructor with his instructions and way of talking. Stitch was very fit. His skin was tight around his face, his frame was muscular and he appeared to be about forty years old. Archer couldn't really tell because of the scars on his face, which had been the result of some kind of military action that he knew he shouldn't ask about but was also the source of his nickname. Stitch always had a few days of hair growth on his face to try and disguise the scars, but the hair didn't grow there and so he was left with a very seasoned soldier's look. The blue eyes were dead though and Archer had trouble looking into them as he went through his instructions.

Mercury welcomed Archer to the range, "Good lad, you're here. Right, this is yours. This is your new friend," and he stood to one side to reveal a pistol on the table: the barrel pointing towards the target down range. Stitch moved to one side too and allowed Archer to approach the table.

"Pick it up, it's safe," Stitch ordered.

Archer picked up the pistol and studied it, he made sure Stitch was true to his word by checking the pistol was unloaded and didn't have a magazine of bullets in the pistol grip. Stitch smiled. He would have chastised Archer viciously if he hadn't checked the safety of the pistol.

As Archer studied the black pistol, Stitch started his brief.

"You now have a Ruger mark one target pistol which we have modified to suit. We've cut an inch off the barrel, threaded it and added a silencer. It's a twenty-two calibre and is virtually silent. With the silencer on, it makes the pistol front heavy so you will hardly feel any recoil. Lad, with ammunition at just below subsonic velocity this is one deadly machine and I am going to take pleasure in training you up with it."

As Stitch revealed boxes of ammunition on the left-hand side of the table, he added, "Oh and we've scrubbed out the serial number. It'll never be traced."

Archer carefully placed the pistol back on the table and turned to Mercury who held up a hand and said, "I'll leave you two to it," and walked off quickly. Mercury always had the appearance that he needed to be somewhere.

Stitch loaded up a couple of magazines with the barely subsonic ammunition he had described and ordered Archer to pick up the pistol and point it towards the target. He handed him a magazine and started his instruction.

"Now, load that up and make the pistol ready. You know the drill."

Archer kept the pistol pointing towards the target and inserted the magazine through the bottom of the pistol grip, he then grabbed the slide at the top of the pistol, pulled it back and let it move forward under its own momentum which chambered a bullet.

"Ok, take a couple of shots from here. Even at fifty metres, it's pretty damn accurate."

Archer, feeling the balance and weight of the pistol, took careful aim and squeezed the trigger as he held the sights on the torso of the wooden target. He had handled many pistols of larger calibre than this one, so he was well prepared for the recoil...or the lack of it. The pistol barely jumped and as he looked down the sights, he could see that even after the first shot they had hardly moved. He took another shot and unloaded the pistol. He showed the pistol to Stitch, to demonstrate that it was safe. Stitch looked, nodded and Archer placed it back on the table. They both moved down to the target and looked closely at the mid torso. As Archer leaned in to find the bullet holes, he found two black rimmed holes staring back at him right where he had aimed.

"Bloody hell."

Stitch smiled, "Good shooting mate, good shooting. Now, let's move on to the advanced stuff. Patch those holes and go back for the pistol. Bring it to the ten-metre point and I'll load you up some more magazines. This is where it gets exciting!" he rubbed his hands in glee. Archer pasted glue over the holes and covered them with black, square pieces of paper made for the job. He returned to the table, grabbed the pistol and moved back to Stitch waiting for him at the ten-metre firing point.

"Ok, we're going to move into the covert concealment and firing of this little beast. I'm going to show you how to move with the pistol concealed on your body so that it doesn't betray you. You'll have it hidden in your waist belt, the small of your back and in the deep pockets of a coat. Especially a trench coat which is perfect for the vast majority of close quarter assassinations. Firing the pistol from such a pocket means the bullet doesn't deflect from the target but it also means you get to keep the bullet cases to dispose of later on. Get it?"

Archer smiled as the knowledge settled in, "Yeah, great, let's go."

Stitch smiled at Archer's enthusiasm, "Good man, right load up."

They spent the rest of the day firing the pistol from all sorts of body positions and without using the sights. As Archer became proficient with it, he soon realised that aiming instinctively was just as accurate as looking down the sights. Stitch taught him to fire two quick, successive shots which Archer very quickly got the hang of. The pistol's low recoil was perfect for such a firing style and Archer grew to excel with it.

"Brilliant mate, simply brilliant. When you're aiming for the head, aim for the soft spots."

Stitch continued, "If it's from the front, aim to hit an eye. If it's from the back, aim for the base of the neck where it meets the skull. There's a couple of soft spots on either side of the spine; hit those and it's lights out. Tomorrow, we'll really see what you're made of," and they continued to shoot. Archer eventually became so used to it that it felt like just an extension of his hand. Stitch told him the pistol was his when Archer went to hand it back at the end of the day.

"It's yours lad. It goes with you….everywhere."

Archer suppressed the feeling to say thank you and returned to his room to clean it before sliding into his bed, thoroughly tired out.

The following day, he returned to the range in the morning after breakfast as instructed. When he entered the range, the wooden target had been replaced by a tethered live lamb which was bleating its panic, looking for its mother.

Stitch and Mercury both greeted him and Mercury welcomed Archer again and moved off, leaving him at the mercy of Stitch.

"Ok lad. This is where we test your steel. Load up and move to the five-metre firing point."

Archer took the pistol from his waist belt and inserted the magazine that Stitch held out for him. They both moved, side by side, to the five-metre point as the lamb continued to call out.

When they got to the right spot Stitch looked at the lamb and said, "Right. Kill it."

No sooner had he got the words out, Archer fired the pistol twice at the lamb's head from his waist.

Stitch actually jumped with surprise. He was waiting for a pause from his instruction to Archer firing the pistol, thinking the lad would wrestle with his conscience. He looked at the lamb, which was now lying on its side and twitching from the nerve reaction of having its brain destroyed, blood flowing freely from two very close holes in its skull.

"Holy shit….holy shit. Never seen that before. You're a beast, a fucking beast," he smiled wildly and Archer noticed that his eyes seemed to have brightened.

"They were right about you. You're going to be great for this department. It's a real privilege to train you young man!"

Archer made the pistol safe and Stitch insisted on removing the lamb himself, muttering, "This is my tea tonight," as he removed the body then covered the blood with sand from behind the target area. If Archer thought he had finished, he was wrong and they continued to shoot until lunchtime. After that he was given the usual physical fitness program and returned to his room, thoroughly tired, in the evening. As he sat on the edge of his bed, cleaning his pistol, he whispered a prayer for the lamb, "Forgive me lord. The lamb slaughtered today was a sacrifice to my skills. Skills needed to fight evil which is the battle I must wage. Have mercy on my soul."

He finished cleaning his pistol, placed it on the bedside cabinet and as he swung his legs inside his bedding, he sighed heavily and thought about Sandra. It was during the silences that he missed her most.

Chapter 5: Grimes

Archer rose out of bed the following morning, washed, changed, grabbed his pistol and concealed it and returned to the barn complex after breakfast. When he entered the barn he was immediately greeted by a serious looking Mercury. Mercury took him by the elbow and ushered him in.

"Ok chief. You're finished; the training is finally over. We're all extremely pleased with you, so now we're taking it to the next level. Follow me….." and they walked side by side to an adjoining barn, much smaller in size to the training barn. Mercury fetched a large key from his pocket and they stepped through as he opened it. There was a small concrete area in front of them and a wall with a grey steel door, marked, "Do not enter without permission". Mercury took another large key from his pocket and opened the door. They entered and as Archer took in the sights before him, he realised he was entering a live operations room. It was a simple, yet highly effective set up. There were radios, chattering in the background. Morse code could be heard bleeping away as Archer soaked in all the activity that was going on around him.

The room itself was square with a large table smack bang in the middle of it. Stitch was standing over maps and papers and looked up to the two of them, then fixed his eyes on Archer.

"You're ready for this mate, don't you doubt it. Now, come over here and we'll explain all."

Mercury allowed Archer as he moved forward and as he approached the table, he saw several black and white photographs of a scruffy, mean looking man who was oblivious to having his photograph taken covertly. The man had collar length, wavy hair, his eyebrows were down sloping, adding to his demeanour and he had a deep scar running down the left-hand side of his face. The man was either overweight or kept himself keenly fit through weight training as his neck was thick and short. The photographs showed him in different clothes, but he mostly wore a long leather coat that stopped just above the knees.

Mercury started, "Ok, this is your first operation young man. The photographs you see before you are months of surveillance carried out by other teams. They are given instructions and collect all the intelligence we need to plan a hit. The teams are all kept separate and have no idea about each other. Secrecy is paramount in this game. Anyway, this is mister Jonathon Grimes of Fleetwood fame. Fleetwood is a large town near Blackpool and he runs the place. There's nothing going on there that he doesn't know about or is involved in. He peddles drugs to anyone, he runs protection rackets, smuggles any kind of contraband and his real passion.....get ready for this.....is providing children to men of stature for sexual activities."

Stitch wretched and spat out bile from his mouth, muttering, "Fucker," and continued to look at the table.

Mercury continued, "Now. This should be a simple job. He has a load of foot soldiers carrying out his dirty work, so we can't start taking them out one by one. Remember what I told you, we're cutting the head off the snake and this particular snake is one nasty, grubby little man. All of the covert information we've gained is like a jigsaw puzzle in that as much as the teams don't know what each other is doing, we see the completed puzzle and can work out his habits. He's pretty slippery this one, but he does like a good fish and chips on a Friday night and pretends to be quite the snob in that he prefers to be driven around the town by one of his cronies in his Jaguar."

Looking at the street maps, Mercury and Stitch concocted a plan that would allow Archer to appear from the shadows of the alleyway opposite the chip shop and time it perfectly that he would be within target range as Mr Grimes was just opening the door to the premises. Mercury went on to explain their plan, "He's normally there for about twenty-one hundred hours, give or take twenty minutes, so we'll get you in position well within those times. This being October, by that time the darkness will cover you. You'll appear to be waiting for a date, so you'll be dressed in neat clothing, carrying a bunch of flowers to confirm that appearance. Keep looking at your watch and pace about the entrance to the alley a bit, ok? If people notice you hanging around, it'll appear like you're being stood up. If he doesn't show up by twenty-two hundred hours, abort the mission and go find your driver."

Archer nodded without moving his gaze from all of the photographs and intelligence in front of him.

"Now, your exit route after the job will be straight down that alleyway. Turn left at the end of it and there will be a waiting car with a young woman driving it about fifty metres down. She'll be looking out for you, so don't worry about having to find her if there are other cars about. We have our own people inside the chip shop and dotted around the streets close to the alleyway. They'll come forward to the police to act as witnesses, but their descriptions of you will all differ in one subtle way or another. You'll never be traced and the police will write it off as a gangland killing."

Archer looked up in amazement at Mercury and smiled. Mercury smiled back, "Yes, we think of everything. Now Archer, make sure your pistol is cleaned thoroughly. You know the drill. We've put the necessary clothes on your bed whilst you are here getting this brief. It'll take an hour or so to get there, so we'll set off tomorrow after a nice evening meal in the canteen. Stitch and I will dine with you and go over the finalities."

Archer took a step back away from the table, nodded his acknowledgement of the plan and looked at Mercury and Stitch in turn, "Sounds good. Right, I'll go and get some rest and see you both tomorrow."

Stitch smiled sarcastically at him, "Now don't you go relaxing mate. Report here after breakfast and I'll show you how this intelligence is collected and just brush up on your counter surveillance techniques. The training never stops."

At that, he slapped Archer on the back as they all turned to exit the control room and go their separate ways outside of the barn.

Back at his room, Archer found his clothing for the operation on his bed. Along with the brown v-neck jumper, white shirt and blue tie, grey trousers and brown shoes, was the obligatory long length coat with deep pockets, akin to a trench coat. He tried it all on for size and half smiled as everything fitted perfectly. He recalled Mercury's words again, "Yes, we think of everything."

Archer moved the clothing into a space in his wardrobe and hung it all neatly, then collapsed on his bed and fell asleep very quickly.

The next day, Archer had slept well and grabbed a good breakfast. As he sat in the canteen, alone, he checked his emotions and as much as he went over the plan of the operation in his head over and over again, he didn't feel a nervous apprehension about it.

He went over to the operations room, as ordered and met Stitch as he rapped on the door.

"Good, you're here. Come on in then and I'll show you what's what."

Archer stepped through and approached the intelligence files on the table. He studied the photographs again and tried to work out how they had been taken. Some of them were fairly blurry and had signs of motion in them, some were taken from an elevation and others were at ground level and quite grainy which meant they had been taken from afar with a zoom lens on the camera. Stitch confirmed what he had already worked out; the photos were taken from nearby offices or flats, or taken from parked cars or cars that were moving. Stitch also told him that in order to take the photographs in the first place, other mobile teams were deployed to follow their target in order to establish a pattern or routine that their target liked to take.

"Grimes isn't too hot on being surveillance aware," Stitch continued as they went over all the information, "So a man like that, who thinks he is above the law because of the people he is associated with, will not change his routine much. Don't get me wrong Archer, we're a government department without a minister in charge, but other ministers would never get involved in what we do because of the political implications. We certainly won't get any kind of sanction and we never question where our orders come from. Neither should you mate. It's one of the golden rules with our bunch; never question, just get on with it."

Archer added, "There's always a bigger picture."

Stitch nodded in admiration, "You've heard it before."

"Yes, an old man who's always in a hurry told me that."

"Ha! Mercury!" Stitch laughed.

They spent the rest of the day going over the plan, practising counter surveillance and shooting the pistol. Archer tried to make an estimate of how many bullets he had fired through the thing, but it must have been in the thousands, so it was probably easier to count how many hours instead.

In the late afternoon, Stitch checked his watch when it came to a natural break in the shooting range.

"Ok Archer, time to get the ball rolling. Finish up, get back to your room, clean your pistol and check it. Get into the clothes we have sorted for you, check your pistol again and be in the canteen for seventeen hundred hours. Mercury and I will meet you there." Archer made sure his pistol was safe and made his way back to his room, where he duly changed and tended to his pistol. Again, he felt no emotion for what he was about to do. He had already killed his father in order to make a better life for his mother, so killing Grimes would save other children and innocents having their lives destroyed by the monster. He thought about Sandra in the quietness of his room as he slowly put the clothes on. He remembered their kisses, the way she looked at him, her smile and the perfume she wore. He could almost smell it now. There was a tinge of sadness as he was reminded that he could never tell her or his mother about his real line of work.

He shrugged the coat over his shoulders to make sure it felt comfortable and slipped the pistol in the right-hand waist height pocket. It felt good, the pistol was free to move and the contours and cut of the coat ensured the outline of it could not be seen by the observer. He practised moving the pistol upwards as he had done for many, many hours at the range and smiled at how natural it felt. Looking at his reflection in the full-length mirror on his wardrobe door, he mimicked the movement again and whispered, "Pop pop," allowing himself a little humour before the act.

He entered the canteen just before seventeen hundred hours and saw Stitch and Mercury already sitting at the one solitary circular table on the awful plastic chairs allotted to it. As he walked towards them, Mercury piped up, "Ooooh look at you! Quite the dapper man. You scrub up quite well, young man!" Stitch laughed a little and gave a little wolf whistle.

"I would swear at this point, but I feel like I'm above that with this gear on," he joked back.

"Do come and join us then and we'll see what chef has managed to scrape together," Mercury invited him in a posh accent, holding out a hand over a chair. Archer enjoyed the sarcasm, but if they thought it would relax him, they didn't know he already was.

As they waited for their meal, Mercury instructed Archer, "Before I forget, one more item to issue. Give me your left wrist."

Archer held it out and Mercury slapped a watch on it. It was a simple watch, nothing fancy, just the necessary hours and seconds hands and a brown leather strap. Mercury placed it on his wrist and fastened it. What Archer didn't realise was that as he did so, Mercury did it quite slowly and as he buckled the strap on, he was taking Archer's pulse.

"How are you feeling?" he asked.

"Grand. Yeah, it'll be interesting to see how it all goes," Archer nonchalantly replied.

"Fuck me," Stitch murmured, "I was a bag of shite on my first op."

Archer resisted the urge to ask him about that first operation, knowing that it might have been the cause of his scars and having upset amongst the team before this particular first operation, could give room for mistakes.

They sat and ate a steaming hot plate of roast beef, Yorkshire puddings, with boiled potatoes and cabbage along with a thick gravy that seemed to slip out of the gravy boat rather than pour out of it. The meal was wonderful, but without dessert. They didn't want Archer to have a sugar rush and feel the need for sleep as they drove to Fleetwood.

After a few minutes to allow the meal to settle, Mercury looked at Archer.

"Ok, ready?"

Archer nodded.

"Let's go. Stitch, we'll see you for debrief at midnight all being well. Archer, I'm driving you there. We'll get a bunch of flowers on the way then I'm going to drop you off about a mile from the chip shop. You know the rest, you're waiting for your date. You know the car, you've had all the intelligence we can get. It's down to you now son. Check your pistol again before we leave and if there's any problems or doubts, you pipe up now," Mercury fixed his gaze at Archer and waited for a response.

"Nope it's all good. Bless you Mercury, you'll look like a father dropping his son off for his first date."

Mercury smiled warmly, "Exactly."

Stitch coughed at the irony and also smiled at their connection.

"Good luck young man. I have full confidence in you."

"Thanks Stitch."

They all pulled back from the table and Stitch started to clear the plates.

Mercury and Archer exited the barn complex and walked to the forecourt where a Vauxhall Viva, with its engine running, awaited them. Without a word spoken, Mercury handed out a blindfold to Archer and without complaining he put it on and lay down on the back seat. Mercury set off and after ten minutes, he pulled into a quiet rural area, made sure there was nobody following and ordered Archer to take the blindfold off and join him in the front of the car. They drove the rest of the journey and made small talk about the scenery. It was a nice evening, weather wise, being dry but cold and they often sat in silence, collecting their thoughts.

As they entered the outskirts of Fleetwood, Archer had a realisation.

"What about the flowers? We didn't stop?"

Mercury didn't take his eyes off the road, but smiled and said, "They're in the boot. We thought ahead and got some before we set off, just in case we couldn't get any on the way here."

"Thinking of everything again Mercury," Archer chuckled.

A few minutes later, Archer was beginning to recognise parts of Fleetwood he had seen on the many maps and photographs and Mercury pulled into the side of the road but kept the engine running.

"Ok, here we are. This is it. The boot is open, grab the flowers and take your time walking to that alleyway. It's eight o'clock now son, you'll be there in plenty of time and I'll see you back at home when you're finished."

Archer smiled slightly, "Thanks dad," but Mercury didn't reciprocate.

Archer exited the car, took the flowers from the boot and walked on. As he was just past the car, he looked back and gave Mercury a quick wave. Mercury winked.

As Archer walked, he took in the sights before him. The many family run shops, the rundown buildings and the passers-by. A woman with her young daughters passed him and as they did so, the mother smiled knowingly at him as the daughters covered their mouths and giggled. The persona of a man on a date was working perfectly. As he got closer, the buildings all became much more familiar to him when he looked across to the other side of the street and saw the chip shop. A few more yards saw him standing at the entrance to the alleyway and he resisted another urge to go down it and see if his lift was waiting for him. He checked his watch; it was now just a question of time. The pages of history were waiting to write their next story, but he still didn't feel the burden on his shoulders.

A few cars passed and he quickly checked the contents of them as he checked his watch from time to time. Not only to give the impression he was waiting for his date, but in reality, he was counting down the time for when his target should eventually appear.

"Nine o'clock," he muttered to himself.

He started to pace around and turned to look down the alleyway. It was in darkness with high walled yards to both sides, but he could see the yellow street lighting at the end of it. As he wondered about the people who lived in areas like this, so totally different to his own home back in Retford, he almost didn't notice the sound of a car engine idling behind him. He turned to see the Jaguar parked outside the chip shop, the driver still in his seat with the engine running. The passenger was just about to exit the car and Archer paused to time his crossing perfectly. As the car door started to open and he saw the passenger bending his head to exit, the internal roof light came on and illuminated his face. Archer instantly recognised him as Grimes. He was wearing the same stupid leather coat that many of the photographs showed him in. Archer checked the road, saw that it was clear and started his crossing, placing the flowers in his left hand and sliding his right hand into his coat pocket, locating the pistol. Grimes straightened himself as he got out of the car and the driver was looking at him as he did so, his head turned away from the approaching assassin. Archer walked calmly behind the car and as Grimes walked towards the front door of the chip shop leaving the car door open, Archer raised his hand instinctively and fired off a shot. The bullet found its rightful place behind Grimes's left kneecap as Archer continued to walk towards him. Grimes screamed in agony and out of the periphery of his vision, Archer saw the driver turn his head towards the rear of the car with his mouth open in shock. Grimes collapsed to the floor, blood soaking the back of his trousers. The searing pain from his knee meant he couldn't get up again and put weight on it. Archer very calmly walked up to him and stood over him as Grimes looked up at him, his face contorted in terror, clutching at his knee.

Archer was aware of everything going on around him. The driver who was frozen in fear, the customers in the chip shop all staring at him, not knowing what was about to happen and the few cars that passed unwittingly or unwilling to help the man on the ground.

"I told you to stay off our turf!" Archer scowled as he leaned in to make sure Grimes heard him. He said it loud enough for the driver to hear too.

Archer straightened and fired the next two shots straight through the left eye of Grimes before he could say anything. The eye popped and collapsed instantly, with blood and plasma squirting out of the crater that once held the eye. His head thudded on to the concrete pavement as his face relaxed and went still. The lungs gave up the oxygen in them and as the air passed the vocal cords, Grimes uttered his last groan before his body started to twitch slightly.

Archer turned slowly to the driver and stared at him. The driver held up his hands in terror and started to utter the words, "No, no....."

Archer bowed to him, walked behind the car, across the street and entered the alleyway. As he entered the pitch darkness of it, he felt an overwhelming feeling of power, like he couldn't be touched and then felt the enormity of the pride he felt at having completed his first task. Mercury's voice entered his mind, "Don't let your guard down," and he checked his exit route to make sure he wasn't being followed. Seeing he was fifty yards from the street lighting to where his driver would be, he broke into a trot. Turning left as he entered the yellow lit street, he dropped into a walk again and checked his surroundings. Stopping to check his shoelaces, standing in the odd shop entrance and checking his rear on both sides of the street, looking into the reflection of windows to see who was on the opposite side and if they were watching him, all of his trade skills were in action. A few more metres and a young female voice called out to him, "Adrian!" and he saw a young woman of about his age, standing on the driver's side of another Vauxhall Viva waving at him.

"Yoohoo over here!" she called out excitedly.

Archer broke into a quicker walk as he smiled back and waved. As he got to the car, the passenger window was down and he looked in at the driver.

"Come on then, it's cold out there and the Mercury is dropping in the thermometer!"

Archer smiled as soon as she said "Mercury" and he knew she was on his team. As he got in the car, he got comfortable and looked across at her, "These are for you," and he slapped the flowers into her lap.

Archer looked across to her and realised she was quite pretty. She had straight, dark brown hair with a black headband and a rounded face and very little make-up. She had red lipstick on, a little bit of dark eye shadow and a hint of blusher. Not a patch on Sandra though.

"Aw thank you so much!" she replied and grabbed the flowers and placed them on the back seat.

"Don't mention it," Archer smiled at her, "Let's go, I'm starving," realising that his body must have filled with adrenaline, but he was too focused to notice.

She drove off and as they left Fleetwood, Archer started to reflect on his first operation. It had all gone very smoothly; whether or not luck played a part he didn't know or really care. The months of planning and preparation by the other teams all culminated to this point and it was to their credit that the operation went so well. Grimes was no longer on the scene and a message had been sent with him. As they drove in silence, he thought about Sandra again and he yearned to be with her at that very moment.

They drove for an hour before his driver pulled into a lay-by hidden from the main road and Archer recognised the other Vauxhall Viva as they pulled up behind it.

"Ok governor, your next lift awaits. Well done! I hope we'll be working together again some time."

She smiled and held out her hand, which Archer took and shook slowly but firmly, "Thank you for making your presence known to me, I did wonder how that part of the play was going to happen, but you made it easy for me. Well done to you too."

At that he got out of the car and walked over to the awaiting car without looking back to his driver. He opened the door and found Mercury, sitting with his hands on the wheel wearing a big smile that also showed a certain amount of relief.

"Well…..what can I say? Excellent job Archer, absolutely excellent. Have you still got the empty bullet cases?"

Archer felt a sudden rush of panic. It was the one thing he had forgotten about and he hurriedly shot his right hand into the coat pocket. He felt the pistol and delved his hand deeper into the pocket and managed to locate the three bullet cases, one of which was just sitting at one of the bullet holes in the pocket. He brought them out and showed them to Mercury.

"Phew. Good job you reminded me."

"Hmm. Don't worry, you may forget other things in other operations, so treat this as a lesson. Nevertheless, we don't have to worry about Grimes anymore. Sit back then, relax and let's get back for debrief. Stitch will have a large cup of tea waiting."

"How did you know it went well?" Archer quizzed.

"Your driver has a radio in her glove compartment. When she saw you coolly walking out of the alleyway, she radioed me. Simple as that. We'll find out the rest during the debrief."

They drove off at normal speed again, lest they gained unwanted attention from local police and Archer was sent to the back seat with the blindfold at a predetermined distance from the training complex. They arrived, exited the car and went straight to the operations room where, as expected, Stitch welcomed them from the operations table with three mugs of steaming tea and a plate of biscuits. Stitch thumped the table in total admiration of Archer.

"Fucking well done lad! That was textbook stuff! Mercury, this lad has nailed it for this department, he added a little extra to the job that will speed up the investigation by the police."

He smiled wildly at the knowledge he held. Mercury straightened up, "What do you mean?"

"He was overheard saying "Stay off our turf" or something like that before he shot Grimes. Bloody brilliant!"

Mercury smiled, looked down at Archer and slapped him on the back, "That's the ticket. My God it's not only us that thinks of everything."

Archer was not only proud of his first job, he was also a little confused, "Who heard me? How did you find out about that?" he quizzed Stitch.

"One of our witnesses was at the door to the chip shop. After the hit, he went to the phone box and gave me a call. He was delighted and has already approached the local coppers to submit a witness statement," Stitch was still beaming.

Mercury was equally delighted, "This is brilliant! But....down to earth now. Let's go over everything and see if we can find any holes. Right, Archer, go through the whole thing again from the moment I dropped you off. Describe what you saw, who you saw, the whole lot. Give us every detail then you can get back to your room."

It took them a couple of hours, but Mercury and Stitch wrote as Archer recalled the operation and emptied the plate of its biscuits. They would compare their notes later but allowed Archer to return to his room for well earned sleep.

Archer entered the quiet of his room and sat at the side of his bed and sighed. His elation of completing his first hit was starting to subside and he prayed.

"Forgive me lord. The man whose life I have taken is worthy of your judgement and I trust he is with you now. Have mercy on his soul and forgive me for committing the ultimate sin, but evil prospers when good men do nothing."

He took the pistol and empty bullet cases out of his coat pocket, placed them at the foot of his bed and hung his coat in the wardrobe. Sitting back down on the bed again, he pulled the pistol cleaning kit from under his bed and started to clean his pistol. Sadness started to wash over him as he thought of Sandra. Oh how he missed her more and more as he thought about her. He wondered if he was falling in love. As his mind drifted, he heard a couple of soft knocks on the bedroom door. Knowing it must have been one of the staff, he called out, "Yes, come in."

The door opened halfway and Mercury poked his head into the gap to look at Archer, "A quick word? I won't be long."

"Yeah, no problem Merc, take a seat."

Mercury nodded and entered the room and with a little groan he lowered himself into the leather armchair and settled himself.

"So, how are you feeling young man?"

"Fine. Absolutely fine. That went better than I thought."

Mercury scoffed a little, "They won't all be like that, believe me."

Archer turned the tables a little with the questions as curiosity got the better of him, "What about you Mercury? I don't know your real name? Have you got a wife and family?"

Mercury paused a few seconds, staring at Archer.

"Yes, you deserve to know by now. Names aren't important, but yes I do have a wife and two daughters. I'm fifty-two years old and they are in their twenties now and have well and truly left home. In fact, I'm a grandad.

My wife thinks I'm a travelling salesman and knows I can be gone for months at a time. This job pays well, so she doesn't question where the money is really coming from."

"How long have you been doing this?"

"Well, I started off a bit like you. Someone recruited me, I carried out operations and now here I am. I specialise in recruiting and keep an eye out for police reports that come through the operations room and now here you are," he chuckled.

"You found me very quickly," Archer exclaimed.

"Yes, well….our wheels turn very quickly and there are many cogs to them."

"What about Stitch? What's his story?"

"Ah Stitch. He has a wife but no children. He's only just forty years old, but he beats himself up a lot. He's very self-critical and everything has to be perfect, which is brilliant for training people like you. We need that. Don't ask about his scars, ok? He was involved in an operation that went a bit too hot. He lost a close comrade, but they completed most of the mission. I have the feeling Stitch blames himself for his friend, but it's part of the job. We all signed a contract, so we all know the risks. It's just part of the picture."

"I had the feeling I shouldn't ask, so I haven't."

"Yes, good. Ok, I'll leave you to it. You know what to do now and I'll take those bullet cases from you."

At that, Mercury half raised himself out of the chair, leaned forwards and took the brass cases. He straightened up with a stretch and turned to walk out of the door. As he got to the door, he paused, looked down at his hand and took one of the bullet cases.

"Here. That'll remind you of your first op in years to come. Keep it safe and bring that coat tomorrow morning, we need to replace the pocket," and he handed an empty case to Archer.

He took it from Mercury and clasped it in the palm of his hand, "Thanks. And thanks for the chat."

"You're welcome son. Sleep tight," and he closed the door softly behind him as he exited.

Chapter 6: Sandra

A few weeks later and as Archer was having his breakfast in the canteen inside one of the barns, Mercury approached him waving a couple of letters that had been sent to him.

"Here you go. One from mother and an extra one from I wonder who?"

Archer sat back and smiled, "Yeah yeah, all treated with privacy I trust?"

"But of course!" he smiled as he handed over the letters. Archer took them and waited for Mercury to turn back before he opened them.

"Get to the ops room when you're finished, ok?"

Archer grunted his acknowledgement.

He recognised the handwriting of his mother and knew that the other must have been from Sandra or at least he really hoped so. He pondered which one to open first and decided on his mothers, prolonging the excitement of opening the other.

His mothers' letter started off by chastising him for the amount of money he had left on his bed for her but said thank you anyway and was then filled with her latest gossip and what was happening in Retford and a little bit about Sandra. Then he opened Sandra's and his heart filled with joy. She had the most beautiful, flowing handwriting and her English was perfect. She wrote about her work, her grandmother and her memories of the week they spent together. She also wrote about how much she was missing him and couldn't wait to see him again. She hoped he was doing ok and he resolved to send them both a return letter. He had been hoping the letter would confirm that she was waiting for him rather than the opposite. Sitting for a short while to digest the letters and his breakfast, he got up from the table and practically skipped to his room to hide them in his wardrobe.

Trudging back to the operations room, he rapped on the door and was greeted by Stitch. Mercury was in the background talking to someone on the phone.

"Alright mate," he whispered, "Come on in, Mercury is just on the phone. He's been waiting for this call so give us a second."

Archer walked through and they both stood looking at Mercury from the table as he finished his call.

"Ok, that's excellent news. Yes, I will. Thank you," and he slowly placed the handset back on the receiver.

Turning to Stitch and Archer with a grin, he said, "Well that was our masters. The police have confirmed they are pursuing the investigation as a gangland killing, but also know it'll probably go nowhere because both sides will keep quiet. It may end up with a bit of a turf war, but that means they'll end up fighting each other. It worked, well done you two."

Stitch recoiled, "Nothing to do with me governor. It was all down to laddy here," as he slapped Archer on the shoulder.

Before Archer could say anything, Mercury instantly rebutted, "No Stitch, you trained him so you both get the credit. Absolutely brilliant op, well done."

On the table in front of him were two large envelopes that were full.

"Payday chaps," and Mercury threw one envelope onto the table in front of Stitch and the other in front of Archer. They landed heavily with a thud and didn't even bounce as they landed.

Stitch rather nonchalantly took his and said, "Thanks chief."

Archer, wide eyed, took his gingerly and uttered, "Thank you Merc."

Stitch scoffed at the nickname Archer had given Mercury.

"Our pleasure gents, our pleasure. Archer, the money you are paid is a fraction of the amount of money you save our masters, so don't be surprised when you open the envelope. We're giving you a few days at home and you'll be issued a rail ticket tomorrow morning. Usual routine, the driver will take you and you return in the usual manner. The driver will confirm the day and time, but it should be in three to four days."

Archer smiled with excitement, "Yes, great. Thank you."

"Again, don't thank me too soon son, we have more to do when you get back. Now, Stitch run him through the shooting range, report for physical training after that Archer then get a good night's sleep."

Mercury turned from them as Stitch and Archer turned to the door, clutching their envelopes and as they got to the door, Mercury shouted out, "Oh and Archer......don't drop your guard."

Archer didn't reply, he knew to keep his guard up as usual, but he was too excited to say anything anyway.

As he started to walk back to his room, Stitch slapped him on the back, "You're a special man you know. Mercury thinks very highly of you, as do I. Keep on top of things ok? I'll see you in ten minutes at the range." Archer nodded and pretended to salute a sloppy salute and turned to walk to his room. He was also excited for his mother and Sandra who would be expecting a letter but would instead be getting a personal visit for a few days.

Stitch drilled him hard at the shooting range, continuously ensuring Archer was well on top of his game. Physical training was no hardship whatsoever for him though and after a good couple of hours of exertion, sweat and vomit, he was feeling invincible. Spurred by the thought of going home for a week, he gave it everything and returned to his room in the evening, thoroughly tired but excited at the thought of seeing his mother and Sandra again.

He cleaned his pistol, made sure it still operated perfectly despite the thousands of bullets he had put through it and concealed it in his suitcase that he had packed with the clothes he needed for a few days at home. Sliding into his bed, he smiled to himself as he pictured Sandra's smile and drifted into a deep sleep. The following morning, his alarm clock woke him with plenty of time and he was taken to the train station and given his ticket with the usual instruction to be at Retford train station in a few days. The varying length of time they gave him at home was not only to ensure he had plenty of contact outside of his work, but it also avoided a routine of having a week off every time he was at home.

Archer boarded the train, carrying out the usual counter surveillance and again he resisted the urge to doze off with the slow rocking motion of the train as it sped along the tracks. As he travelled, he allowed himself the odd smile as the thoughts of Sandra crept into his mind. Arriving in Retford, he almost pinched himself at how soon he was back. He thought he would be away for months, but it hadn't been that long and as he walked the familiar route home, forever making sure he was devoid of enemy activity, his pace quickened through excitement. He realised he was getting used to how nothing had changed despite the length of time he had been away and the operation against Grimes felt like it had taken him out of society for years.

Arriving at his home, he knocked on the door hoping to surprise his mother, but there was no answer. He fetched his key out of his pocket and let himself in.

The house was silent and peaceful as he walked slowly through the rooms, looking for any changes of which there were none. Feeling tired he trudged upstairs to his room, placed his suitcase under his bed and flopped on top of it. He took the envelope Mercury had given him, out of his coat pocket and peered inside at the contents. It was bursting at the seams with paper money and he leafed through the notes, counting as he went.

"My goodness," he muttered to himself. It was a bitter sweet reward. Bitter because of the nature of his work, but sweet because the reward was twofold: he was ridding the community of evil and being paid handsomely for it. He lay back and before he knew it, he was dozing off.

The noise of a key entering the front door lock woke him with a startle and looking at his watch, he realised he had fallen asleep for two hours.

"Not a bad thing," he muttered to himself and rose out of bed.

"Mum, I'm up here," he called out.

"Adrian? Is that you?"

Archer ran to the top of the stairs to keep her sense of anxiety to as short a time as possible and saw his mother looking up from the hallway.

"Good God son, you're back again! Come on down then, I'll put a pot of tea on," she said excitedly.

Archer felt like he was twelve years old again as he quickly moved down the stairs and gave his mother a hug.

"I'm doing better than expected, so they've given me a few days off mum."

They moved into the kitchen and sat for a couple of hours talking about her work life, local gossip again and her social life.

"I've started going to bingo with a few of the girls at work. In fact, I should be going tonight, but now you're home I'll wait until next week."

"No!" Archer smiled, "You go tonight mum. I'm worn out and I'll have an early night, so I won't be much company for you anyway."

"Awww ok son, if you insist. Sandra should be round soon for a cuppa. She'll be excited to see you," she smiled at him, tucking her chin in a little.

"Oh good," Archer actually felt himself blushing as his heart raced a little.

They talked at the kitchen table for a few minutes when there came a few soft knocks on the front door.

"That'll be her now…" his mother confidently said and practically raced down the hallway to open the door.

Archer looked at the front door as his mother opened it and smiled insanely as he saw Sandra.

"Look who's home…" his mother said as she stood to one side to allow Sandra to look down the hallway.

"Adrian!" Sandra called out with a huge smile on her face.

"Well come on in then," his mother ordered.

Sandra looked up at her, then raced down the hallway and collided into a huge hug with Archer as he stood to greet her. Sandra couldn't hide her feelings from Archer's mother and neither could Archer. They held each other tight and Archer heard his mother say a little, "Awww!" as they twirled around, Sandra's legs raised behind her. Archer felt like a soldier returning home. To a certain extent, he was.

He wanted to kiss her passionately but had to resist the strong urge to do so and he could see in her eyes that she wanted to do the same. They held their dignity and respect to Archer's mother and held off but held hands under the kitchen table as they sat side by side and talked.

"San, I'm off to bingo this evening with some of the girls; you're welcome to join us if you want?"

Sandra felt an obligation but lied to her, "Oh, heck I'm sorry, I've got to look after grandma tonight. I'm going to have to set off in a few minutes actually."

She looked knowingly at Archer and held his attention, "Do you want to walk with me to granny's?"

"Yes, of course! You ok for a while mum?"

"Definitely. I'll put something on to eat for when you get back love, but you get yourself off....the two of you, go on."

They didn't refuse and they left the house and started the walk to Sandra's grandmother.

"It's crazy," Sandra started, "I've missed you so much. I didn't expect you back for another couple of months, this is such a lovely surprise."

"I know, I'm progressing really well at work and I'm ahead of the game so to speak so they just decided to give me some time off. I've missed you too.....very much so. I couldn't wait to get back to see you again Sandra."

They stopped at the same time and faced each other. They held each other's gaze for a few seconds, the smiles growing on their faces when they both leaned in and kissed passionately. She was wearing the same perfume she always wore, the subtle floral and feminine scent that was also very sexy. Archer couldn't suppress how the excitement and adrenaline flowed through his body and he gave in to the feelings. Wrapping his arms around her, enveloping her in his muscular body, he felt the desire to protect her and Sandra was willing to allow him.

"Your mum is off to bingo tonight," Sandra started to hint.

"Yes, good for her too."

"She'll be gone for a good few hours you know?" Sandra smiled, swaying her hips.

Archer suddenly realised what she was hinting at.

"You're at your grandma's?"

She bit her bottom lip, "No. Sorry, I lied to your mum. I'll be round at eight."

Archer laughed and held her hips, "You little devil! Brilliant, I'll see you then."

They parted and as Sandra almost skipped down the road, she kept looking back at Archer waving a little wave. He stood where he was and watched her, smiling and waving back and as she turned the corner and went out of view, he turned and walked back to his home. It was a few seconds of thought that almost took him out of his profession, but quickly he came to his senses and carried out a quick scan of his surroundings. Nothing to be aware of, he got back to his mother's.

As he entered the front door, he called out, "Home!"

"Good timing son, tea's out."

They sat at the kitchen table and talked while they ate.

"I knew you two would become boyfriend and girlfriend," she smiled at Adrian.

"Stop it mum," he chuckled. She didn't talk about it anymore but felt proud for her son.

They cleared the plates away and tidied the kitchen together and as Archer sat at the table again, his mother declared she would change her clothes and brush up before heading off to the bingo hall to meet her friends.

"Are you sure you'll be alright son?" she asked as she put her lipstick on in the kitchen after getting changed.

"Yep, I'm fine. I'll be turning in soon."

"Ok, well if you're sure, I'll head off. I'll be as quiet as I can when I get back."

He checked his watch, seeing it was seven thirty and felt the excitement rise in him at the thought of Sandra arriving soon.

"Grand mum. Don't worry I don't think anything will wake me tonight."

"Bless you. Right, I'm off. See you tomorrow," and she kissed his forehead, wiped it clean and headed out of the door into a drizzly night.

He was sitting alone in the kitchen, watching the minute and hour hands creep ever closer to eight o'clock on his watch; the excitement growing as they did so.

Five minutes before eight o'clock, he heard three soft knocks on the door. He rushed down the hallway and opened the door wide to see Sandra, dressed in a beautiful grey cotton dress, with a thin red belt over the waist under an open black coat she wore against the rain. She had put on a little extra make up and the blusher on her cheeks made her look innocent but sexy at the same time. She covered herself with her umbrella and she smiled widely as he stood in awe at her.

"Wow Sandra! Quick, come on in out of that rain," and he stood to one side to allow her to rush in.

"What a night! You like what you see then?" she asked, already knowing the answer.

"I'm a lucky man, you are gorgeous," he said, wide eyed and smiling from ear to ear.

She placed her umbrella by the door, took her coat off and placed it on the stairs and without saying words, they hugged and kissed deeply. They were both breathing heavily as they kissed when Sandra stopped, stepped back, took his hand and led him upstairs.

They made love for the first time and Archer was lost in his emotions. As they lay in bed, with her head on his chest, she uttered, "I love you."

He paused and smiled to himself, "I love you too, San. Very much so. Never felt like this before."

"Me neither," as she sighed with contentment.

Archer suddenly took stock of his situation and thought about his profession. The emotions he felt became mixed and he felt the tears start to build up in his eyes. But he held them there in case Sandra looked at him and suppressed the feeling of guilt. It was a guilt of knowing he had taken lives and couldn't tell anyone about it. It was also the feeling that he didn't deserve any of this happiness knowing he had committed the ultimate sin. He consoled himself with his prayers and how he ended them with, "Evil prospers when good men do nothing."

Archer reminded himself, or tried to tell himself that he was, indeed, a good man.

They lay a little longer, warm and content with each other, when Sandra looked at her watch.

"Oh! I'd better make tracks Adrian. Your mum will be here soon and I have to stop over at granny's."

He stroked her hair and sighed, "That's fine Sandra, this has been so special though."

"Definitely. Can we do something tomorrow?"

"Yes, I'd love that. What about a picnic in Clumber Park? We can get a bus together?"

"That would be lovely! Yes, ok. See you at eleven o'clock?"

"Great," he replied. They smiled at each other, savoured the moment for a couple of seconds more and Sandra got out of bed and put her clothes back on, as did Archer.

They both quickly moved down the stairs like children at Christmas and he held the door open for her.

"I'd walk with you a bit, but if mum is home soon, I don't want her asking questions as to why I'm still up when I told her I was having an early night. Sorry."

"Oh no, don't be daft. I really don't mind. I'll see you at the bus stop tomorrow, ok?" and as she went out of the door, she stopped, turned and rushed back for a kiss. They hugged and kissed and she ushered him back inside then turned again and made her way to her grandma's.

Archer closed the door and trudged his way back upstairs to his bedroom. This time, he was thoroughly tired and as he slumped into his bed, conscious of the wonderful smell of their sex, her perfume and their natural odours, he fell into a very deep sleep.

In the morning, Archer woke feeling a little groggy but equally very much alive and in love. He washed and got changed and whistled as he went downstairs to the kitchen where he could already hear his mother busying herself.

"Someone is in a good mood this morning," she called out.

He didn't reply straight away as he had reached the bottom of the stairs and made his way down the hallway to the kitchen, "Just nice to be home for a while mum," he replied.

"Yeah it's good to see you son. There's tea and toast for you," as she looked towards the steaming pot of tea with a couple of slices of toast on a plate, with the usual dish of butter and pot of marmalade on the table.

"Are you seeing Sandra today?" she asked without making eye contact, forever hopeful that he would be.

"Yep. We're taking a bus to Clumber Park for the day," he smiled to her.

"Oh smashing! Aw, she is lovely Adrian. We get on ever so well and the other girls love her at work."

"We're getting on well too mum," he took a sip from his cup of tea, holding the little secret about the two of them.

They continued to talk, mainly about the bingo games last night and how his mother had won a little bit of money.

Archer looked at his watch, "Right mum, have to go. I'm meeting Sandra at eleven this morning and we're catching the ten past to the park. We organised it as I walked her to her granny's yesterday."

"Brilliant. Well off you go then; leave your plate and cup and have a great day, ok?"

He got up from the table, gave her a hug and trotted down the hallway. Opening the front door, he peered out to view the weather which was overcast and threatened rain but wasn't windy. As he looked up at the clouds and then to his surroundings, his only sight was an old man walking by on the other side of the road with a blackthorn walking stick and quite a bad stoop.

"See you later mum," he called out as he grabbed his coat and walked out of the door, closing it behind him. Sandra was already at the bus stop and right on time, the ten past eleven bus arrived and took them to the entrance to Clumber Park. Sandra was well prepared and had brought along some sandwiches and a flask of tea in her little canvas rucksack. He almost gasped at how beautiful she looked in her white flowery Gypsy dress and the coat she usually wears when there is rain.

"You're well organised," Archer cheered.

Sandra curtsied, "I aim to please my lord," she looked up at him smiling a cheeky smile.

They walked from the entrance gate down the tree lined private road of the park and after a while, they stopped at the foot of a big old oak tree in front of a group of large rhododendron bushes. They laid out a picnic rug and talked, joked and laughed. She lay between his legs as Archer sat with his back to the tree and soaked in the moment. Sometimes they didn't say anything and both felt perfectly comfortable with the silence. With a sudden movement of realisation, Sandra announced, "Oh I brought a camera!" and she brought out a small Kodak camera which she pointed at him, focused quickly and took a picture. Archer giggled, took the camera, wound the film on and took one of her. Handing it back to her, they laughed and held each other tightly.

"This is wonderful," Sandra said after one of the silences.

"Certainly is," Archer added. A few seconds elapsed and Archer continued, "You make a mean cheese and pickle sandwich too!"

Sandra squirmed around and smiled wryly at the sarcasm and slapped his leg.

"Ow!" he joked aloud and started to tickle her. She squealed in excitement and squirmed between his legs, bringing her legs into the foetal position and bursting into laughter. She turned to look at him and as they held each other's eyes, they kissed passionately. Archer stood up, held out his hand and when Sandra took it, he lifted her up and they kissed more. This time Archer took her hand and led her to the rhododendron's where he found a gap and led her through. The ground under the bushes was covered in dead leaves which were soft and Sandra knew exactly what was going to happen and giggled with the excitement of having sex outdoors.

"Ooh my lord. You're so daring!" she half smiled.

"I aim to please my lady," Archer replied with a slight bow. He took her waist, drew her towards him and they kissed. Sandra leaned backwards and let her weight take them down to the floor as they were kissing and she opened her legs, willing Archer's body to press into her. Archer lifted himself onto his knees and gently ran his hands up the sides of her legs, lifting the dress to her waist. He smiled into her eyes as he saw the white knickers with a pink bow she was wearing. She didn't resist as he softly ran his fingers up the sides of her legs, caressing her perfect skin and into the sides of the knickers, slowly pulling them down her legs and over her feet. The adrenaline rushed through their bodies as

Archer exposed his erection, leaned in and penetrated her slowly. She gasped as he entered her and he kissed her deeply as they writhed together.

They made love, climaxed as quietly as they could make it in a public area and laughed together at their first experience of love making in the outdoors. The two of them gathered their clothes and steadied their breathing before exiting the bushes and having a quick look around for other people. But the park had been practically devoid of people when they entered and it was the same as they went back to the oak tree, hand in hand. Sandra was oblivious to Archer making observations of the few people they did see. They were mostly older couples walking dogs, who didn't make any eye contact with Archer at all, so he was satisfied with their security.

They continued to talk, play and laugh for hours and before long, Sandra sighed and told Archer they would have to get back so that she could tend to her grandmother.

"I'm sorry," she said jokingly with her bottom lip pushed out.

Archer couldn't help his laugh, "Ha! It's ok. Come on...." He helped her up, they tidied their picnic and walked back to the bus stop, again hand in hand; swinging their arms in unison as they walked.

They caught the bus back to Retford, savouring the warmth of it as the day had got colder and when they stepped off, thanking the driver, they hugged and kissed before Sandra set off for her granny's.

"I'll be round to your mum's tomorrow after work as usual my lord," she smiled and curtsied again.

"I shall look forward to the pleasure of seeing you my lady," he bowed, tucking his arm to his stomach.

She giggled loudly, "Oh God you're funny! See you tomorrow then."

She turned and started to skip away. She only got a few paces away as she looked over her shoulder, "Love you."

Again, Archer stood where he was to watch her, "Love you too," he almost shouted, cupping his hands over his mouth as a makeshift megaphone.

As he watched her disappear around the corner, he made his way back to his home where his mother greeted him.

Again, they talked at the kitchen table after eating an evening meal she had prepared. He had to skip over the more intimate details of their day trip, but he gathered by the way his mother was looking at him, she knew that the young couple would do what young couples do.

"You have the morning to yourself tomorrow. I'm at work with San, so we'll both probably see you in the afternoon Adrian."

"Yep. Sandra said she might pop round after work as usual, so I'll see you both then."

After a while, Archer excused himself and retired for the night, wishing his mother, "Sleep tight," and fell into his bed and subsequently into a deep contented sleep.

Chapter 7: The pain

Archer woke later than usual and was pleased to realise he had slept deeply; so much so that he hadn't heard his mother leave for work. He was vaguely aware of the sound of her key unlocking the door as she went but had hardly stirred at the noise.

He washed, changed and went downstairs to make his breakfast of the usual tea and toast. The house was in silence as he went downstairs and it was something he was growing to enjoy more and more as time went on. Gone was the usual dank smell from the living room and the tirade of vicious, verbal abuse that came from the occupant of it.

As he walked down the hallway and past the living room, he entered the kitchen and was suddenly aware of someone sitting at the kitchen table. His awareness instantly heightened as his heartbeat increased so suddenly at the awareness of this presence. It took him by surprise as he was so relaxed in his own home, but he was ready to burst into violence if the presence became threatening.

As he looked at the man, he immediately recognised him as Mercury. He was sitting there, his left leg crossed over his right, wearing his trademark flat cap and Wayfarer coat. His dark grey pinstripe three-piece suit was immaculate as usual and he smiled at the realisation from Archer that he recognised him.

"Hello lad."

"Mercury. What the hell are you doing here? How the hell did you get….."

"In?" he finished Archer's sentence, "Come come now. You know the score."

Archer remembered the sound of the key opening the door lock and realised it must have been him he heard. He relaxed as Mercury continued, "Have a seat then. I took the liberty of putting a pot of tea on for you, so grab yourself a cup. I need to have a word."

Archer dragged a chair out and poured himself a cup of tea, intrigued at what Mercury had to say.

"We have a situation Archer," he started, reaching into the deep inside pocket of his coat and bringing out a large brown envelope. He opened it and brought out a few black and white photographs.

"This man…" as he spread the photos on the table in front of Archer, "…is Chris Jakes of Birmingham fame. He is a notorious armed bank robber, burglar and general thief. He's incredibly crafty, often having alibis in place before carrying out a job and so, yet again, the usual authorities are having immense trouble in putting him away and it's costing an arm and a leg. He's taken to being very violent if he doesn't immediately get compliance from his victims; especially with burglaries and now he's gone too far. He has burgled Welham Hall recently, murdering the two elderly occupants in the process and looting them of some quality antiques. He's part of an international ring of thieves and our friends abroad are doing their part to disrupt their activities. We need to be seen to be doing our part."

Archer raised an eyebrow in recognition of the venue. Welham Hall was only a few miles out of Retford and so the connection with Jakes started to sink in.

"Jakes has a lock up garage in Worksop, off Canal Road and he has left an item, or items, there. Now, one of his buyers has turned snitch to the police after they got him for a separate burglary, so rather than face jail he has snitched on Jakes. They know he'll return to the lock up soon, but we know he'll be there tonight. This is where you come in."

"I get it. Break into the lock up, lie in wait and take him out when he's inside. Sounds good."

"Not so fast lad. Jakes is always tooled up; he always has a firearm so you're going to have to be certain it's him and be quick with it. That won't be a problem for you, I know that but second to the firearm, he also has a sidekick. His best mate, Burkett who is equally as nasty. He's the chap in that middle photograph just behind Jakes. I've never asked you to take on two guys, but we are confident you can take these two. Do you agree?"

Archer studied Mercury's face for a second, looking for signs of worry or doubt about his ability, but Mercury's face was still and showed no sign of emotion at all. Archer slowly nodded as he thought about the job, "Yeah…..yeah, I can do that. Do you know what time he'll be there?"

"No, so it could be a long wait."

"I'll handle that."

"Good. Do you remember that young lady who drove you from the Grimes job?"

Archer nodded, "She'll be waiting for you in the same car, tomorrow up the Hallcroft Road on the outskirts of the town at fourteen hundred hours. She'll drive you to Canal Road in Worksop. Here's a map of where the garage is and it's door number six."

He handed Archer a hand drawn, but accurate, map of the location.

"We know for certain he'll be there tomorrow sometime after sixteen hundred hours in order to grab his loot. The buyer is waiting for it, the day after and it has to be shifted quickly," Mercury explained.

"Sounds fine, the usual routine? Drop off some distance from the garages?" Archer asked.

"Yes, you know the score."

"Ok then," Archer ended the brief with his acknowledgement as he realised it had reached its conclusion.

Mercury uncrossed his legs and pushed his chair back slightly.

"Excellent. Well then, it just remains for me to wish you luck. You won't need it; this is your bread and butter now son."

Archer nodded in slow agreement and stood up, placing the photos and map inside the envelope.

"When it's done, come back here and carry on as normal. Be at the train station in two days at the usual time and we'll get you back for debrief, ok?"

"Yep, fine," Archer replied confidently.

Mercury smiled the familiar friendly smile that relaxed Archer.

"Ok lad, I'll see you soon."

Mercury breezed past Archer and made his way down the hallway in his usual slow but deliberate way. As he opened the door and stepped through, once again he turned and saluted as he closed it.

Archer smiled and whispered to himself when the door closed, "Bugger even knew when mum was at work." He took the envelope upstairs, studied the pictures again and hid them with his pistol at the bottom of his suitcase which was still filled with most of his clothes. Taking hold of the book he was reading from the bedside cabinet, he moved back downstairs to the kitchen, added more boiling water to the tea pot and sat for a read.

Archer's mind wasn't on the words he read, but more about his impending job. There was something about this one that gave his semi-consciousness a reason to feel like there was an unanswered question. He tried to shrug it off, aware that his skills and fitness meant he had the edge over his adversaries, but nevertheless there was something there.

The sound of a key trying to find its way into the front door lock brought him out of this feeling and he looked up from his book, through the hallway to see his mother enter the home.

"Phew. What a day!" she called out as she took her coat off and hung it over the coat hooks on the wall to the side of the doorway. He had noticed that his father's tattered coat had been missing since his death and felt proud of his mother for disposing of all traces of him.

"Pot of tea on here mum. Do you want one?"

Archer had been very astute. As soon as Mercury had left, he washed and dried the cup he used lest his mother twig on to Archer having company and asked questions.

"Love one. San will be round in a bit, so keep it warm," she said as she entered the kitchen and sat down at the table with a little groan. Archer got up, grabbed a cup from a kitchen unit and poured her a cup of hot, strong tea and added milk from the bottle he had left on the table.

"Oooh thank you son," she sat back, holding her cup and blowing gently over its surface, "Well what did you get up to today?"

They talked over their tea, when the usual soft knocks on the door sounded out. Archer's heart raced, but he hid it from his mother.

"That'll be San. Get the door will you love, I'll top up the teapot."

Archer tried to act cool as he walked down the hallway to the door, but he couldn't help how his excitement grew as he opened the door slowly and peered around it..

"Yeeesssss?" he joked as Sandra's beautiful, glowing and smiling face appeared.

"Can I help you?" he joked in a posh English accent. Sandra giggled and covered her mouth, "Hello my lord, I understand they serve good tea here?" speaking in an equally impressive posh accent, changing it from her usual northern one.

"Ah that we do. Please, do come in," as he stepped to one side and bowed, smiling towards the floor.

Sandra whispered, "Silly Billy," as she breezed past him and jabbed a finger in his stomach. He breathed in a whiff of her perfume as he closed the door and returned to the kitchen to hear the two women already deep in chat and took his place at the table.

Archer's heart thumped when during a lull in the conversation, Sandra took a sip from her cup and asked, "Did you hear about Welham Hall?"

He steadied himself by taking a sip from his own cup as his mother replied, "No?"

Archer continued, "What happened?"

"Got robbed the other day. The swines that did it cleared the place out apparently, but they killed the Chapman's in their beds."

"Oh no," his mother grimaced, "They were a lovely old couple. I used to see them around the town every now and then. Totally harmless. They walked hand in hand everywhere those two. Oh that's terrible!"

Archer couldn't say anything, he didn't know the couple but had intimate knowledge of the culprits and wanted to tell them both that they would get their comeuppance.

He shifted in his chair, supped at his tea and said, "Let's hope they catch them."

In unison, the two ladies said a reflective, "Hmmmm.." and they continued to talk.

Sandra looked at her watch, then looked at Archer,

"Yep, I know. Grandmother calls," he joked at her.

"Sorry. Have to cut loose here."

She slid her chair back and took her coat off the back of it.

"I'll walk you a bit," Archer said and looked at his mother who was smiling her approval, "Back in a few mum."

"No problem, I'll start tea."

Sandra and Archer made their way out of the house and started the walk to her grandmother's.

"Can I see you tomorrow?" Sandra smiled at him as they walked.

"I might be around in the evening, but I'm not sure yet, sorry."

"Oh…" she bowed her head a bit.

"I need a special tool for work and there's a bloke out Worksop way who might have one. I phoned him today and he asked me to call round to his house where he has his own workshop. I know what these fellas are like, once they get talking about engineering you can't stop them."

Sandra skipped a bit, "Oh I see. Well, I'll call round to your mum's after seeing to granny and if you're there, you're there. If you're not, you're in big trouble mister!" she laughed.

"Well, that's me told," he laughed and jabbed his elbow into her side softly.

"Ouch! Bully!" she giggled.

"What about the day after if you're not home then?" she asked.

"I'll be free for definite then. Are you at work? Do you want to come round in the morning and we'll head off somewhere?"

"Yeah, that sounds good," she smiled and hooked her arm into his. She looked up at him through the top of her eyes, "That was fantastic in Clumber Park."

He held her look, smiling mischievously, "It was VERY nice my lady," he winked at her and they laughed, skipped and walked, bumping into each other and fooling around.

They kissed passionately when they parted and Archer thought more about the next day's operation, feeling ever more content that what he was doing was the right thing. Not that there was ever any doubt but seeing how people react to heinous crimes such as Jake's had carried out, he was more determined to make sure Jakes paid with his life.

He went home to his evening meal, talked to his mother and read his book in bed but couldn't focus on the words again. He was in love with Sandra and the swell of sadness that he couldn't tell her what he had done and was about to do, almost overwhelmed him. Eventually he fell asleep and his book falling onto the floor didn't even stir him.

He woke in the morning, washed, changed into his clothes and returned to his bedroom where he took the envelope out from the bottom of the suitcase along with his pistol. He checked the pistol first. It had been drilled into him from day one of this training and he remembered Stitch's face as he instructed him, "Always check your kit Archer. When you're finished with it, clean it. When you're about to use it, check it. Check it once, then again and then again. Leave nothing to chance and always have confidence in your equipment."

He went downstairs and into the kitchen and smiled as he saw the plate of toast his mother had left him before heading off to work. He made a fresh pot of tea, ate his toast and thought about Sandra.

The silence of the house was mesmerising, but he didn't think about his father again. His focus was on the operation now and he checked his watch regularly.

As the time approached for him to leave the house, he made ham sandwiches and ate them until he felt he had sufficient food and protein to keep him going for the afternoon and into the evening if the operation went on longer.

He went back upstairs, took his pistol and concealed it in his belt at the small of his back, tucked the intelligence envelope into the bottom of his suitcase and made his way outside, taking his wool trench coat as he took his first steps out of the house, into a grey but dry day.

Walking through Retford, he was still checking for changes and carried out his usual counter surveillance tricks as he made his way to his rendezvous with his driver. His confidence grew, aware that he was just blending into the comings and goings of ordinary people. It was a Friday and he passed the thriving market stalls in the centre of Retford, bustling with people buying all sorts of items with the smell of earthy vegetables and fish wafting over to him as he walked by. The stall holders yelled out their unintelligible promises of bargains to those who walked by, hoping for new customers with an eye for a good price.

He made his way up Hallcroft Road and soon spotted his transport, reliably parked at the side of the road at the last group of houses on the edge of town. He made sure he was well visible to the driver and stopped on the passenger side of the car where the window was already half open.

"Hello again. I see the mercury hasn't risen much since we last met."

She smiled knowingly, "Come on then. Get in, I'll drive for a change," she said sarcastically.

Archer laughed quickly and sat in the passenger seat, noticing the car was lovely and warm against the cold of the winter's day.

"I'm Rachel by the way," she held her right hand across her body to him.

He shook it gently, "Nice to meet you," he said courteously, "Right, let's do this…."

She set off without speed as usual. It was a good technique to avoid attention and again, it worked.

They talked small talk about the weather for a while, but Archer was happy with any silences as he concentrated his mindset on what he was going to do.

"They all think you're brilliant, you know," Rachel suddenly said.

Archer turned to look at her, "They?" he asked.

"Mercury, Stitch, the people I know on my side of the team…...me," she added.

"Good to know."

"I'm told you have a girlfriend," she stated rather than asked.

"Yes," he said, uncomfortable that his private life was far from private.

She waited a couple of seconds, "Pity," but nothing more was said.

They drove for a further twenty minutes, when Rachel pulled over to a residential area with parked cars outside the houses on the Canal Road of Worksop.

"Be careful…." she said, "There's a lock picking kit in the glove compartment. When you're done, go to the phone box past the garages on the other side of the road, about two hundred yards from the entrance to them. Give this number a call and simply say, "Taxi," and I'll pick you up there after a few minutes, ok?"

She handed him a small piece of paper with the phone number scribbled in pencil.

Archer took it and the small, leather wallet from the glove compartment, which he checked and stuffed it into his coat pocket. He looked across at Rachel and noticed the furrow lines in her forehead as she genuinely looked worried for him.

"Relax. I'll be fine. See you soon," he reassured her.

He got out of the car, turned round and stooped to look into the car. He gave a little wave and watched as Rachel selected first gear, checked her mirrors and drove off gently.

He checked his surroundings quickly and saw the only human activity was the back of a man in a miner's coat walking away from him on the other side of the road, about eighty yards away.

He walked normally to the garages and turned into the entrance of the two rows of lock ups that stretched away from him for about a hundred yards. He waited for a few minutes in the shadows to see if anyone followed him into the entrance, then made his way down the garages until he was outside number six. Quietly he took the lock picking kit and slid the tools into the "T" shaped door handle with an internal lock and worked them until he could turn the handle and unlock the mechanism. As quiet as he could, he turned the handle gently and in stages until it was fully unlocked and he could swing the garage door open. To his relief, Jakes had kept it well maintained and oiled so that it didn't squeak as it opened. Archer wasn't the only person who wanted a quiet door that didn't attract attention as it opened.

He looked back at the entrance again then looked inside so that he could see a suitable place to hide and wait, illuminated by the fading daylight that was spilling inside the garage with the door open and with the poor light from the thick grey cloud just managing to highlight the interior. As he observed, he stuffed the lock picking kit into his inside pocket.

He saw a gap in the furniture, lamp shades and boxes in the right-hand corner and made a mental note of where it was as he turned and closed the garage door slowly and quietly. When the door was shut, he worked the lock mechanism and checked that the door was locked so that it would appear as so from the outside.

Allowing his eyes to adjust to the dark, he gingerly worked his way over to the chosen lair and prepared himself to wait. The cold concrete floor was uncomfortable as he sat, so he tucked the bottom of his coat under his bottom to make it more bearable. When he shifted his weight around, he selected his most comfortable position and mentally prepared for a long wait.

The time went by as he watched the daylight around the edges of the garage door turn to darkness. He thought about Sandra and tried to keep those thoughts out of his head as the cold started to creep its way in.

He brought his knees in closer to his body and thought about Jakes.

"Forgive me for what I am about to do lord. They must face your judgement and plead for your mercy and so I beg your forgiveness when I return their souls to you. Evil prospers when good men do nothing," he muttered. As he waited, he looked around and pondered at what exactly was hidden there that was of so much value. He resisted the urge to feel around and open boxes to his immediate left and concentrated on staying alert. As the darkness fell, Archer was intrigued to hear the comings and goings of animals as they carried out their business of survival in the darkness. He heard light scuffing sounds of claws against concrete and the noise of something sniffing his scent at the bottom of the garage door. Cats are near silent as they meander around, so he deduced the noise was from a fox.

As the time passed, his backside was becoming numb so when he felt that feeling he shifted his weight around which allowed the blood to flow around the affected area. It wasn't perfect, but it helped.

After what he thought was a few hours of waiting, the light from car headlights swept across the bottom of the garage and he heard the sound of its engine idling closer. His body came to life. Slowly and with extreme caution he slid his hand into the right-hand waist pocket of his coat and took hold of the all too familiar grip of the pistol in preparation. Silently he lifted himself slightly with his left hand on the floor and pulled the coat from under him by raising his right, all the while pointing the pistol in the direction of the door.

The car seemed to idle outside of the door for ages, but really it was a matter of minutes before the main headlight went out and the driver put his sidelights on and kept the engine running. He heard the sound of a car door opening, followed by soft footsteps that approached the very garage he was waiting in. Instinctively raising the pistol ready to pull the trigger, he watched and listened as the key went into the lock. The mechanism to open the door worked slowly and deliberately and Archer watched as the door started to open, slowly. Jakes was obviously making sure he didn't make a noise. As it opened he saw his feet, followed by his ankles and the door rose to show his legs. Soon it was followed by his waist, then his chest and finally his whole body was on show. The soft street lighting was strong enough for Archer to recognise Jakes and he knew he had to wait until Jakes had stepped inside the garage by a couple of feet. He didn't want to shoot him at the entrance to the garage because the blood would be on the public side of it and he wanted to contain it within.

Jakes stood with his arm raised, holding the door and when he was satisfied that the door was held by its runners, he stepped inside and started to make his way over to the left side of the garage.

Archer didn't hesitate. Already his hand was raised at the right angle he instinctively knew and he fired his two shots at Jakes' head. The knees gave in instantly and Jakes dropped heavily to the ground without making any other sound except the clattering of boxes as his body fell against them. Archer raised himself and keeping the pistol trained on the body, he staggered a little not realising the cramped conditions had taken a small toll on his ligaments and blood flow. As he stretched after standing, he heard the body relax as Jakes exhaled his last remaining oxygen in his lungs. As usual, the body twitched slightly. Archer moved over to examine the shot placement, when his senses alarmed him to another presence at the garage door.

"You fucking bastard."

He heard a hissed, malevolent voice. Archer went to turn to look at the new presence.

"Don't you fucking move. Drop that pistol," the voice hissed.

Archer's heart was beating heavily now. He knew he had made a huge mistake and he was now trapped in a situation he didn't know how to get out of. If he made a move, the presence he now knew was Burkett, would fire. He remembered Mercury telling him that they would be carrying firearms and Archer tried to think quickly as to what he should do. He had to oblige, so he dropped the pistol, hoping it would buy him some time and show his assailant that he was totally vulnerable. Archer slowly turned his head towards Burkett and stood to face him. If this was the end of his life, then so be it. He mentally prepared himself for what was to come next and immediately thought of Sandra and his mum. Very quickly, in his mind, he said sorry to them both and bid them farewell.

"Just make it quick and be on your way my friend," he told Burkett.

"Nothing would give me greater pleasure you bastard!" Archer straightened and puffed his chest out. He closed his eyes and waited, holding back the real urge to urinate.

Burkett suddenly gurgled and was trying to say something, but the words wouldn't come out. Archer heard the metallic sound of a firearm hitting the concrete floor and he opened his eyes to see another man behind Burkett. The man was in black clothing and had Burkett's head pulled back with his left hand and his right hand was slicing vigorously and extremely violently with a knife that glinted in the streetlight as it moved horizontally. His knees collapsed and as Burkett fell, the man was still cutting away at his neck. It all happened very quickly and as Burkett looked up in terror from the garage floor in his last moments, Archer heard a familiar voice and suddenly felt a mixture of bewilderment but more importantly a sense of relief.

"Got you at last, Burkett! Remember me you fucker? Remember what you did to my friend? Die you bastard!" Archer looked on as the familiar sight and sound of Stitch filled the garage and filled his heart with joy. Like a bystander, he watched as Burkett died in terror. His face contorted with recognition of Stitch as he stood over him.

Stitch spat in his face as the body relaxed and the soul departed. He looked over to Archer, "Good job lad, but always remember; where there's one, there could be two."

Archer relaxed his shoulders and breathed out a huge sigh of relief, "I only heard one car door opening and just the one set of footsteps. Where the hell did you come from?"

"I was on the roof mate. Laddo here stopped the car to take a piss at the entrance," Stitch smiled his toothy smile and Archer could have sworn a star of light gleamed off his teeth.

"Did you pray earlier on?"

Archer didn't answer; that was his private moment.

"Come on, we'd better get these two inside," he replied as he went over to Burkett's body.

"You grab that leg and I'll take this one."

The two of them dragged Burkett deep into the garage and laid his body next to Jakes'.

They stood side by side at the garage entrance and looked around the floor at the blood.

"I think we'll be alright Archer," stated Stitch as he looked around him.

"Lucky enough Stitch," he replied and they both slowly peered out of the garage towards the road entrance. Stitch stepped forward out of the garage, followed by Archer who took hold of the bottom of the door and slowly lowered it to shut it and lock it. Stitch stood guard as Archer locked the door and he stood, quickly checked his pocket and found the two bullet cases.

"Well done, you remembered this time!" Stitch smiled at him.

"Yeah yeah, alright. Are you getting a lift with us?"

"Nope. Rachel will take you back to Retford, I'm heading off back to base in my own car."

Archer held out his hand and Stitch took it firmly. They both felt the bond of two men who had carried out a successful operation and had rid the world of two more thoroughly evil men. They had also exacted revenge for the Chapman's of Welham Hall. The police would find the bodies after the smell of them was reported a week or two later and would also find the proceeds of a life of crime. They would be able to link the valuable antiques within the garage to the Welham Hall burglary and murder, then come to the conclusion that Jakes and Burkett had upset the wrong buyer; probably for asking too high a price and selling to a competitor.

Archer and Stitch strolled over to the entrance of the garages, looking like two men who were just minding their own business. Archer turned left as Stitch turned right muttering, "Well done lad," as he split off.

Archer walked further down the road and saw the phone box in the location described by Rachel, as he counted down the distance, he was totally aware of his surroundings. The living rooms of the houses on either side of the road were mostly lit, with curtains closed and the occupants keeping warm as the smell of smoke from their fires filled the atmosphere. There was no sign of human activity as Archer tuned in to his counter surveillance skills. Even though he had again committed the ultimate sin, there was a warmth he felt from his bond with Stitch and he immediately thought about Sandra again. He had come as close to death as he had ever been and had come away unscathed; in fact, he had come away as the victor and then the sadness hit him quite suddenly. It rose up from the pit of his stomach and he felt it in his throat as he suppressed the urge to cry. This barrage of emotions almost let him walk past the phone box, but he collected himself and opened the heavy metalled red door to the phone box. The usual putrid smell of urine permeated from the floor of it. Fishing the piece of paper with the telephone number on it from his pocket, he dialled the number and after a few rings a male voice just said, "Yes?"

"Taxi," Archer replied and the voice instructed him, "Two minutes, wait there."

He hung up abruptly and Archer replaced the handset. Stepping out of the phone box, he scuffed his feet at the floor, pretending to kick something away and meandered around slowly. To the casual observer it would look like he was waiting for a phone call. He checked his watch and saw it was just after eight o'clock and was a bit taken aback by the length of time the whole operation had panned out.

After a couple of minutes of pacing around the door of the phone box, he heard the now familiar sound of the Vauxhall Viva as it approached. When it got to within fifty metres of him, he could see the silhouette of Rachel and she quickly flashed the headlights at him to confirm the rendezvous. He crossed the road in front of her so that he was ready to quickly enter the passenger side and as the brakes squealed a little when she stopped, he opened the door and immediately felt the warmth of the car's interior which welcomed him in. He also smelt her perfume and noticed how Rachel had added a bit

119

more blusher to her cheeks and thickened her eye lashes with mascara when he looked at her to thank her for being prompt.

"This car is properly warm. Thank you so much Rachel."

She turned and smiled, "You're welcome. Everything ok?"

Archer paused, realising he was very tired, "Yeah, went well. What can I say? Stitch was there too, the bugger. Did you know that?"

She smiled and looked through the windscreen as she selected first gear and drove off gradually, "Yes. Stitch had a personal reason for being there and Mercury sanctioned it. I don't know the full ins and outs, but I was glad you had some back up."

Archer shifted in his seat, aware that Rachel had an interest in him, "Well, it's done now. I'm so tired."

"Leave your coat on the back seat before you get out won't you. It'll be repaired as usual when you get back to base and you can put the lock picking kit back in the glove compartment."

Archer nodded and grunted his acknowledgement and closed his eyes as the warmth enveloped his body and he felt his face glow.

Twenty minutes later, Rachel stopped the car slowly which still woke Archer up.

"Ok, we're only a few hundred yards from your mother's. We haven't been followed, I've done all the precautions and we're safe to stop here."

As Archer sat himself upright, he croaked, "Thank you Rachel. You've been brilliant. You take care of yourself, no doubt we'll meet again," he smiled and held out his hand.

Rachel took it and they shook hands gently, "I enjoy working with you Archer. Glad you're safe, take care yourself," she half smiled with the realisation that Archer was totally loyal to Sandra and he could see there was a hint of sadness in her eyes.

Archer took the lock picking kit out of his inside pocket and placed it inside the glove compartment, then shuffled the coat off in the car and placed it on the back seat.

"Instead of repairing the coat pocket, you could ask Mercury to just get me a new coat!" he scoffed.

"Ha! You could buy your own you tight git," she retorted. He smiled at her and exited the car then tapped on the roof when he closed the passenger door and Rachel drove off quietly. He felt the two empty bullet cases deep in his front pocket, knowing full well that unless he was searched, they wouldn't be found. Then he ensured the pistol was well and truly secure in the small of his back, trapped by his belt.

He made his way down the street and approached the front door. Before he put his key in the lock, he pressed his ear on to the door and heard the recognisable voices of his mother and Sandra, gossiping away.

The excitement and relief grew in his body when he put the key in the lock and opened the door to hear his mother say, "Oh he's here now," and Sandra squealing with excitement. The door was half open when he looked towards the kitchen and saw Sandra already running down the hallway with her arms out to welcome him. He had no sooner stepped through the doorway when she collided into him, wrapping her arms around his neck and saying, "Hello honey! I missed you loads!" Archer, trying to close the door with his left hand and holding Sandra with his right, managed to get a reply out as he multi-tasked with the door and her.

"Good grief Sandra. I've missed you too, my lady. What a night I've had."

She released him eventually and they walked down the hallway towards his waiting mother in the kitchen.

"Bad night was it?" his mother called out, smiling at the young couple as they came into the kitchen.

He sat down with a grunt, with Sandra sitting next to him, "Yeah. I've come away empty handed. The fella I met didn't have the right tool, but boy could he talk about engineering. I told him I had a bus to catch, but he talked on and on and then, bless him, he insisted on driving me back."

"San's been here a couple of hours waiting for you, but we had a good laugh, didn't we?" his mother laughed, smiling at Sandra.

"Yeah, we had a right laugh. Did you find his house alright then?"

"That wasn't a problem," Archer replied, then realising the pistol was starting to dig into his spine, he shuffled a bit and tried to shift it with the body movement. It didn't work and only made it worse, so he made his excuses.

"Look, I'll be back down in a minute, I'm desperate to use the toilet."

"Oh of course, go ahead son," his mother replied, pouring them all a cup of tea.

Archer slowly got up from the table and turned, sucking in his stomach a little more hoping that a bulge would not be seen sticking out from the small of his back. He knew he had escaped their attention when he got past the kitchen doorway and into the hall. He took his normal time to go upstairs and didn't rush. When he got to the top, he tiptoed into his bedroom and quickly removed the pistol from his belt and stuffed it into his suitcase under his bed. He tiptoed into the bathroom, urinated as loudly as he could into the bowl of the toilet, flushed, washed his hands with a whistle and returned to the kitchen with another wave of relief that he had managed to extricate himself from another potentially sticky moment.

He sat with another sigh, relieved that he was totally in the clear when Sandra asked, "I bet he had a lovely fire on, you smell of smoke."

It suddenly dawned on Archer that the gun smoke from the pistol firing its deadly missiles from his coat pocket, must have settled on his thick wool jumper but he wasn't aware of it.

"Ah yes, but his chimney must be a bit blocked because the smoke came back into the room the odd time."

Sandra and his mother both smiled and they all sat, sipping their tea and chatting for another hour but Archer was rapidly becoming very tired as the relief of a successful operation and post operation activity started to creep into his body and mind.

In a brief lull in the conversation, Sandra looked at him and with sympathy said, "Aw look at your eyes Adrian. They're all bloodshot, you must be shattered?"

Archer managed to slur a reply, "It's been a long day Sandra, I'm sorry, my eyes are burning out of my head." They all laughed and Sandra stood up from the table, "Well come on then. You can walk me to the door and I'll make my way home, ok?" she looked sideways at Archer's mother.

"See you the day after tomorrow at work then."

"Yep, ok. Good on you San, I think sonny boy here will be in his bed as soon as you're out of the door."

Archer and Sandra stood and walked down the hallway, as they got to the door Sandra turned and looked at him. She whispered, "Your mum is at work tomorrow, but I've got the day off. Can we go somewhere if I'm here at eleven?"

Archer couldn't resist those lovely big eyes as they almost pleaded with him, "Of course, definitely, I go back to work the day after so we could get a bus to Doncaster and go somewhere for lunch?"

Sandra smiled widely and jumped up and down on her tiptoes with excitement, "Great!" and she leaned in to kiss him. Archer responded and they kissed deeply again. Sandra skipped out of the doorway and turned towards home. As she walked off, she was beaming her beautiful smile and quickly waved to him as she quickened her pace to get home. Archer waved back, smiling and yet the sadness was starting to build inside him again.

"Please forgive me," he whispered, half in prayer, half in pleading to Sandra and his mother.

He closed the door and turned his head to the kitchen.

"Mum. Sorry. I'm hitting the sack."

"Ok love, see you tomorrow."

Archer's feet felt like blocks of lead as he trudged his way upstairs to his bedroom. Each footfall felt like it was a struggle and when he got to his bed, he dumped his clothes on the floor and slid inside it, quickly falling into a deep sleep.

In the morning, he woke and stretched his body in bed. This time he hadn't heard a key in the door and felt confident he was alone in the house. He lay for a short time, listening to the noises inside and outside the house. He had woken to a bright and sunny winter's day as the beams of sunlight burst around the side of his curtains and he could hear the birds calling to each other, almost fooled into thinking it was spring. He got out of bed and carried out a quick physical fitness routine that would keep his upper body muscles primed. Completing fifty press ups, fifty sit ups and using the side of his bed to do fifty tricep dips he had done enough to keep his strength topped up. He shuffled into the bathroom and as he was about to open the bath taps to push water through the rubber shower attachment and wash his body, he heard the familiar soft knocks on the door from Sandra. His heart skipped and he rushed into his bedroom with a towel wrapped around his waist to peer at his watch.

"She's early," he hissed as he saw the time was half past ten.

He rushed downstairs and opened the door, standing to one side of it with one hand keeping the knot in his towel held together.

He peered around and saw Sandra's mischievous smile, "I couldn't wait!" she said.

"You little devil, get in here," he smiled, letting her in. She stepped in, wearing a beautiful beige wool coat that ended just past her knees. She had a lovely polka dot, navy blue and white dress, small white socks and wonderful navy blue court shoes. She realised he was naked, bar the towel and smiled at him, "Ooooooh!" she said approvingly, her eyes moving up and down his muscular body.

Archer quickly closed the door and still holding the towel he said, "Behave lady. Grab a cup of tea in the kitchen, I'll only be ten minutes then we'll head out."

She held a smile and reached forwards, weaving her hand through the gap in the towel and took him in her hand and massaged him.

"I'll be seeing this later on then will I?" she looked up at him.

"Oh yes," he replied with a knowing smile and winked at her.

She let go of him and turned to the kitchen with a smile still etched on her face.

Archer rushed upstairs and into the bathroom. He turned the taps on and mixed the water until it was the right temperature. Dropping the towel he stepped into the bath and sat to move the shower head around his body, soaking it in gloriously hot water that brought his body back into life. He manoeuvred soap over his body and hair and whistled as he spurted out hot water that had managed to get into his mouth now and then. When he finished, he grabbed the towel and ruffled his hair. He dried the rest of his body, wrapped the towel around his waist and moved across the landing to his bedroom.

It was as he stood at the doorway to his bedroom, that the sight before him made the blood rush to his head. His heart violently thumped as adrenaline instantly pumped around his body from the shock. He stood, stock still, staring at Sandra who was sat on the edge of his bed with a look of sheer terror. The suitcase that was under his bed, was now out from its hiding place with the lid open. Clothes he had in it were half spilled out. He saw the photographs of Jakes and Burkett on the floor to the side of the suitcase and his throat dried up as he saw Sandra, holding the pistol in the palms of her hands, her eyes wide and her mouth half open.

"Sandra....."

"I...I...can't believe....what the hell is this?" she looked up at him. Her smile had gone and was replaced with a grimace. Her eyes were filled to the brink with tears and her hands started to tremor with the pistol in them as she displayed it to him.

"Who the hell are those two? What is going on?!" her voice raised at the last question.

Archer was lost for words. He resigned himself to his fate as he started to explain.

"Sandra, before I tell you, I know I've lied to you and I've lied to mum. But please believe me, I never lied when I told you I love you."

"You love me?" she asked incredulously.

"You love me, but you've been lying to me for as long as I've known you!" she raised her voice, getting closer to shouting at him.

"Sandra, please! I'll explain…"

"You fucking better," she hissed.

"I got involved with people who carry out dirty work for other people, removing bad men from society. Those two are the ones who did Welham Hall. Remember you talked about it the other day? It was those two who did it," he pointed at the photographs, pleading to her.

"And so now they're dead. Is that what you're telling me?"

He paused, "Yes."

"You did it?" she hissed at him again, the fear from her eyes had disappeared and now the look of hatred stabbed at Archer.

"Yes," he said, dropping his head to the floor.

Sandra looked at the photographs, back to the pistol and then up at Archer.

"Who makes you God?" she asked.

"Who makes you judge, jury and executioner?"

"I can't tell you Sandra, but we're getting rid of really nasty people! If those two…" he pointed his finger to the photographs on the floor again, "….continued their life of crime, who knows who the next victim or victims would be? Don't you think they need to be stopped?" he pleaded.

"Yes. But that's why we have the police and courts!"

Sandra stood up and looked around her, the tears now flowing down her cheeks, the pistol dropping to the floor with a thud. She looked down at the pistol and held out her hands to see them trembling wildly.

"Oh my God…..you're a killer. Oh my God."

"Sandra, please."

Archer could feel his own tears and allowed his body to sob. His breathing now very heavy as he watched the love disappearing from Sandra. The pain was unbearable and he wanted to vomit, he wanted to hold her and tell her that, despite what she thinks, he is a good man. He yearned to feel her body comforted by his, yearned to smell her perfume and restore the bond of love between them, but he knew it was all falling apart as he watched her emotions of disbelief, betrayal and hatred consume her.

"No!" she suddenly looked at him, "It's too much. I can't be with a common killer," and she faced the floor, avoiding his eyes as she moved to get past him. He side stepped into her path, "Sandra I'm begging you, I love you, please don't leave me!"

"Why? Why have you done this?" she hissed again at him, pointing her finger into his face, her own face contorted with a mixture of fear and hate.

"I can't tell you, but I signed a contract with some very serious people. They look after me and mum, although she doesn't know it. It's something I believe in Sandra, but it doesn't change me."

"It changes everything!" she replied as she barged her way past him and got to the top of the stairs.

They were both sobbing loudly now, they both knew they loved each other but Archer also knew that he had to let Sandra go.

"Sandra....please.....you can't tell anyone. I don't know what they will do. Please just give me one last promise...."

The pain he felt was like someone tearing his heart out, he leaned forward and propped his upper body up by putting his hands on his knees.

Sandra paused at the top of the stairs and turned her face to his direction without turning her body, "Yes. That's my last promise."

And at that, she practically ran down the stairs howling as she went. She composed herself at the front door and tried so hard to control the sobbing and when she had managed some form of self composure, she opened the door, stepped through and closed it gently as she left.

Archer knew she had gone forever. He had to let her go, he had already committed the ultimate sin in the eyes of many and Sandra couldn't live with that even if he had decided to stop. He shuffled into his bedroom and sat on the side of his bed, crying and sobbing wildly as he slowly tidied the clothes back into the suitcase. He struggled to regulate his breathing and with a heavy heart he picked up the pistol. He held it in his hands and tried to focus on it through the tears.

"So this is my life, is it Lord? I'm tied to this one piece of metal. Tied to this life of assassinations, ridding this world of evil and forever being alone?"

He thought for a minute and suddenly felt his sorrow turn to rage. Gripping the pistol purposefully in his right hand and turning it in the light cascading through the bedroom window, he resolved, "Then so be it. I'll never love anyone again, the way I did with Sandra."

The tears were still burning his cheeks as he packed slowly. His last act was to tidy the photographs into the brown envelope and tuck them away, with the pistol, safely into the suitcase. He raised his legs onto the bed and lay there with one forearm over his head as he thought about Sandra. Tiredness and grief swept over him as the rage gave way to those overwhelming emotions. He knew Sandra couldn't live with the knowledge of his work and as he thought about it more and more, he burst into tears again.

He spent the whole day in his bedroom, going over everything in his mind and hoping to hear the soft knocks on the front door. But they never came.

His mother returned from work late that afternoon and called out to see if he was home.

"I'm up here mum."

"Ok, I'm going to stick dinner on. Do you want a cup of tea?" she shouted from the hallway as she took her coat off.

"I'll put a pot on mum, be down in a minute."

He listened to her usual footsteps as they trotted to the kitchen. Archer composed himself, sighed very heavily, accepting the fate of his first ever love and slowly clumped his way downstairs.

As he entered the kitchen, his mother was already peeling potatoes and when she heard him entering, she turned to look at him. Instantly she noted his red face, bloodshot eyes and tracks of tears that had left a tell-tale sign of a salt track.

"Adrian! What's wrong?" she placed the knife down and took off her rubber gloves.

Archer felt the tears well up again, "Oh mum. Sandra and I have parted. She's gone." he whimpered.

131

"Sit down, sit down love. What's happened?"

She pulled out a chair from the kitchen table for him and also one for her. Archer sat and staring into the middle of the table, he replied, "We've had a big argument mum. I said stuff which is unforgivable. So unforgivable.....I'm so sorry."

This time the grief was too much and he broke into uncontrollable tears and breathed in heavily between bouts of crying and wailing.

Archer's mother got up and rushed over to him, wrapping her arms around his shoulders and tried to console him.

"Oh son, don't worry. She'll be alright, she'll come round, don't worry. I'm sure that whatever was said, the two of you will work it out."

"No mum. You don't understand. She's gone for good."

She couldn't say anything and held him, stroking his hair and doing her best to comfort him. She allowed him to cry it out.

"There there. It'll be alright. You're young, there will be others. I know it feels hard now, it always does, but you'll get over it. Both of you will. Don't worry."

"I won't fall in love again mum, it's not worth this pain."

As the evening wore on, Archer and his mother sat in the kitchen and tried to make small talk about her work and local gossip. Try as she might, she couldn't shake Archer out of his grief and she allowed him to get it out of his system by not intervening whenever he broke into tears.

He eventually bid his mother a goodnight and slowly made his way upstairs to get ready for his return to base the following day. She bid him a restful sleep and, "It'll all look better in the morning."

But he ignored the advice and made his way to his bedroom. The emotional turmoil he had gone through, ensured he was fast asleep in no time at all.

In the morning, he sat on the edge of his bed, thinking. He realised that nothing was going to bring her back and he had better get used to it. He washed, changed and left his mother a substantial amount of money on the bed as usual. He knew that if he presented it to her, she would refuse out of politeness especially after the grief he had just suffered. So he grabbed his suitcase, let out a big sigh and headed downstairs.

His mother, as usual, was busying about the kitchen and was ready to head out to work in her working clothes.

"Morning love. How are you feeling?" she asked tentatively.

Archer saw she had already left a pot of tea on the table and a plate filled with toast.

"I'm fine mum. I will be fine."

"That's my boy. I'll be seeing Sandra at work, obviously, but don't worry I'm not going to bring up what's happened between you two."

"Yes. Please mum, don't let what has happened between us ruin the friendship you two have. I don't know when I'll be back, so at least Sandra doesn't have to worry about running into me."

She cocked her head to one side and looked sympathetically at him, "Oh love. You'll both be alright, I promise."

She looked at her watch, then shot into motion.

"Oh heck, I'd better go. You take care of yourself Adrian and keep writing, ok? Let me know how you're getting on. I'm so proud of you!"

As she rushed, she kissed him on the forehead, held his face in her hands and gave him a sympathetic smile. She was out of the door as Archer took a piece of toast and lathered it in butter and marmalade. He managed to eat a few of the half slices, checked his watch and went upstairs to get his suitcase.

As he walked to the train station, Archer carried out his usual counter surveillance techniques. He made a quick prayer as he arrived at the platform, "Please God, I hope she's ok. I understand now."

As he boarded the train, he pretended to step up into the carriage, lose his balance and take a step back again. Looking left and right along the carriages with a smile at his fake stumble, he didn't notice anyone stepping back to make sure he was boarding, so he got on and selected an appropriate seat and tried his best to keep Sandra out of his thoughts until he was back at the base. He replayed the assassination of Jakes and Burkett and Stitch's advice. Cursing his stupidity of almost allowing Burkett to take his life when he should have known that Burkett would be nearby. With the pain of losing Sandra, he almost wished Burkett had finished him off; but he didn't know then, what he knew now and he gave himself a shake as the thoughts of Sandra's face contorted in fear and loathing crept into his mind. He made contact with his transport back to base in the usual way, combined with the usual donning of a blindfold and lying on the backseat until he arrived.

Archer clambered out of the car, throwing the blindfold on the backseat and thanking the driver and looked towards the barns to see Mercury standing outside one of them. He was half smiling at Archer and as he stood there with his flat cap, rounded glasses and his hands in the pockets of his trademark Wayfarer coat, he gave Archer a salute by tapping the peak of his cap then turned to enter the barn.

Archer trudged off back to his room and unpacked his suitcase, slowly placing the clothes back in the wardrobe. Finishing that task, he realised he hadn't cleaned his pistol since his last operation because he hadn't had the time, so sitting on the edge of his bed he took it onto his lap and started to disassemble it.

Reaching into his bedside cabinet, he grabbed the pistol cleaning kit and started to scrub it clean of carbon. Half way through he heard a few knocks on the door of his room which he answered, "Come in."

Mercury peered around the door and joked, "Ah good, you're decent," referring to Archer's state of being fully dressed.

"Hello chief," Archer replied, with a glum look on his face.

"We'll have a debrief in the morning about Jakes and Burkett ok? You look as though something is troubling you young man, what's up?"

Archer stopped cleaning his pistol, sighed heavily and looked to one side at the floor in thought.

"You said you have a wife. How do you manage to maintain a relationship in this line of work?"

"I told you. She thinks I'm a travelling salesman."

"And she's never questioned you or found out what you've been doing?"

Mercury fully entered the room and sat in the battered armchair, "Yes she has questions which are easily answered, but no, she's never found out what I really do. Are you trying to tell me something?"

Archer thought about how he was going to explain how Sandra found out, but realised honesty was the best answer.

"My girlfriend, sorry my ex-girlfriend, found the pistol and photographs of those two," Archer nodded toward the brown envelope on his bed.

Mercury paused and breathed in deeply.

"Does she know about the department? Will she stay quiet?"

"No, she doesn't know about the department. I told her I got involved with people who take care of things, that's all. Her last words to me were that she promised to stay quiet. Right before she walked out of the door."

"Hmm…we'll keep an eye on that."

Archer sat up and looked into Mercury's eyes, "Promise me you won't touch her. Promise me she'll be ok."

"We're not monsters, son. She'll be fine. You have my word on that."

Archer relaxed and returned to his slumped posture with his elbows on his knees.

"Is this it for me? You've recruited me into a job I'm good at and I believe in what we're doing. But how am I going to find a life that is almost normal?" he looked at Mercury, tears welling up in his eyes.

Mercury leaned forwards, "Son, I told you this wasn't going to be easy. I wasn't just referring to the jobs we send you on. We all live a life of lies. Me, Stitch, Rachel, the other staff, we're all living a lie. It's part of the job and a big part of the contract that you signed. We've all signed the same contract and believe me when I say this….as much as you have your family at home, this is another family where we have the same belief systems and a bond that surpasses the usual bond you find in most other families."

Archer thought about how Stitch had saved his life by killing Burkett and he nodded his acknowledgement and understanding.

Mercury continued, "I understand Sandra has left you in these circumstances, but that doesn't mean you won't find someone else. When you do, you'll just be a lot more careful."

At that, Mercury leaned forward and ruffled Archer's hair with his right hand then stood up. Archer smiled a little at that, but continued to stare at the floor.

"Now, get a good nights' sleep and report to the ops room at zero eight hundred, ok?"

Archer nodded.

"Good. See you in the morning then."

Mercury turned to the door, stepped through and turned to Archer as he held the door handle in preparation to close it, "By the way…..you're more than just good at this job," he winked, smiled then closed the door gently, shutting Archer into the silence of the room and the thoughts in his head.

With the images of Sandra's face, Archer realised he was never going to love anyone else the way he did with her. He remembered her beautiful smile, the genuine look of love in her eyes when she looked at him, her clothes, her perfume and their love making. The pain. He made a firm promise to himself, never to fall in love again in order to avoid any more heartbreak and also out of respect to the love he felt for her. He finished cleaning the pistol, placed the cleaning kit back in its rightful place, set his alarm clock and fell asleep.

Chapter 8: Return to base

Archer woke to a rainy day. It didn't matter much, most of his work was indoors within the barns and he had completed the outdoor camouflage and concealment part of his training with flying colours, as usual.

He had his breakfast and took another cup of tea over to the operations room and rapped on the door. The door creaked open and Archer was met by Stitch who had a beaming smile; the laughter lines really showing through at the corners of his eyes.

"Come on in brother."

He held out his hand in comradeship which Archer took with a good grip and shook it with a telling shake.

"So good to see you Stitch," he smiled back, "And thank you."

"Don't mention it. That's a ghost laid to rest. Right, get yourself to the table, there's things we have to discuss."

Mercury was already standing on the other side of the table facing them and was reading from a brown cardboard folder that held different papers. He allowed the two of them to approach the table and played the power game by continuing to read, whilst they waited for him to speak. After a short while, he closed the folder and slapped it with his left hand.

"It's all there lads. A bloody good job. Bloody being the operative word."

Stitch and Archer looked at each other then back at Mercury.

"They haven't found the bodies yet, but already there's rumblings in the underworld about the disappearance of those two hoodlums. If the underworld are making noises, the police will not have a hard time sussing out why these two chaps bit the dust. Well done."

They both relaxed and shuffled on their feet a little. Almost in unison, they both said, "Thank you."

Mercury looked at Stitch, "Well? Have the demons been put to rest?"

Stitch, looking humble, said, "Yes boss. Well and truly. Thank you for that."

Mercury turned his attention to Archer, "Don't go thinking that we didn't trust you to take those two on by yourself. Stitch here had a personal reason as to why he wanted to join you and I sanctioned it. Turns out, it was a good job he installed himself on the roof of the garage well before you got there. We didn't want you to be overconfident in how the hit went, so we needed you to stay sharp. The only way to do that was not to tell you Stitch was already there."

Archer smiled but couldn't say anything. He felt a humility in having his life saved by Stitch and the feeling of failure to Mercury.

Mercury grabbed Archer's attention aggressively as he slapped the folder onto the table with force.

"Now didn't we tell you? Where there's one, there may well be two?"

Archer jumped a bit in surprise, spilling his tea over his foot, "Yes! Yes boss, I'm sorry! Stitch explained what happened and I won't let it happen again. Sorry."

Mercury relaxed and breathed in deeply, but kept his voice stern, "We've invested a lot of time and money in you lad, so we don't want any mess ups. Understand?" Archer nodded quickly a few times.

"Good. Now Stitch, drill him on the range, push him hard in the physical training, brush up his morse skills and I'll see you both later."

"Later boss?" Stitch asked as he turned to exit.

"Yes. We'll have evening tea together for a change....and that doesn't mean there's an operation on, ok? See you both at nineteen hundred hours."

Stitch turned on his heel to exit, but Archer looked at Mercury and studied him. Mercury held the pose that he was expecting Archer to leave any second, but Archer half smiled at him and pretended to touch the edge of a cap on his head. Mercury smiled and waved him away.

As Stitch and Archer left the operations room, Stitch turned to Archer.

"Go and get your pistol then and I'll see you in there."

"Right chief."

Stitch took his elbow as Archer started to walk off, "He's never done that before mate. I've never seen him lose his temper, never. You've really made an impression."

Archer turned and headed back to his room. He realised that his split with Sandra had Mercury thinking that he needed the comradeship of the team to counteract his loneliness and that Archer needed to feel like a part of this family as well as his one at home. Suddenly he felt incredibly relieved and resolved himself to make the most of his work.

Stitch put Archer through his paces, not only at the shooting range where he was practised over and over again in different shooting positions but also in the gym. In the afternoon, he attended the top floor of the farmhouse where he practised his morse code transmitting and receiving skills with another instructor. This man was a different kettle of fish altogether for Archer. He guessed his age at about sixty, he was short in stature, never smiled, spoke softly, but was vicious with a ruler if he noticed any mistakes. He would prowl around Archer as he tapped out a morse code message and strike like a Cobra rapping the back of his hand with the ruler at any mistake; no matter how small. Archer knew him as Edgar and the man was very proud of his work in Beau Manor Hall as a Radio Operator, intercepting German transmissions during the second world war. The transmissions being conveyed to the Codebreakers of Bletchley Park and Edgar didn't hide those facts.

All of this hectic activity served not only to keep his skills at top level, but also to keep his mind off his recent heartbreak.

That evening, a few minutes before the instructed time to meet Mercury and Stitch for an evening meal, he entered the canteen to see the two characters already sitting waiting for him, both wearing big smiles and arms folded.

Mercury stood, leaned over the table and pulled out a chair for Archer.

"Good evening squire, please have a seat."

Archer smiled at the sarcasm and duly sat, pulling the chair closer to the table.

"Good evening gentlemen and I do mean that description lightly."

Stitch smiled then looked past Mercury, "Ah here comes the chef to go through the menu with us."

They looked towards the kitchen area and Archer reeled a little in surprise as the man who had picked him up from the train station on his first trip to the base approached them. His beard was still as unruly but this time he was wearing a chef's outfit as opposed to a dirty, oiled boiler suit.

With his thick arms folded, he addressed them.

"Good evening sires. Your menu tonight is fuck all starters and a choice of beef, mash potatoes, carrots and gravy or beef, carrots, gravy and mash."

Mercury looked up at him with a smile, "Sounds splendid. I think I'll have the beef then please."

Stitch joined in, "Yes. I think I'll have that too."

The chef nodded and looked over at Archer with his eyebrows raised in question.

"Oh. Erm…..yes I think I'll join my comrades and go for the beef."

Mercury leaned back to bring the chef more into view, "And what's on the extensive menu for dessert?"

The chef looked down his nose and told him, "Fuck all."

Mercury recoiled a little, "Just as well. I'm trying to lose weight. Is there a wine list? I understand this establishment holds a wonderful wine cellar. The 1950 La Mission Haut Brion would complement the beef superbly if you have it?"

143

The chef slowly turned his head to address Mercury, "I do apologise sir. We do have a very good bottle of L'eau of this current year which I strongly recommend."

Archer leaned forwards and whispered loudly to Mercury, "What's that?"

"Water," Mercury smiled then looked at the chef.

"Well that all sounds scrumptious. Run along then, we'll await your culinary delights in excited anticipation."

The chef turned and grumbled, "Bloody better do. Some of us have homes to go to."

When the chef disappeared through the door to the kitchen, Mercury turned to Archer and Stitch. Reaching sideways into the pockets of his coat, draped over the back of his chair, he pulled out two thick brown envelopes and gently slapped them on the table in front of the pair.

"Before we talk, it's payday."

They both murmured their thanks and placed the envelopes on their laps, covering them with napkins. They figured the chef knew what their activity was, but there was no point in rubbing his nose in it or showing off.

"Right, before our substantial meal comes out, I need a word."

Stitch and Archer pulled their chairs in a little and leaned forward to listen.

"Archer, I'm sure you've learned your lesson after that last operation, yes?"

"Indeed Merc."

"I told you this morning we would be having this dinner, but not as a precursor to an impending operation. But something has come up this afternoon and in a month or two, we'll be heading off on an abroad operation."

Stitch raised his eyebrows, "Can you say where?"

"Looking like France."

Archer didn't panic or look worried by the announcement, but added, "I only know very basic French from my school days though."

Mercury wasn't perturbed, "It doesn't matter. We will have all the support and, more importantly, intelligence in place before we agree to do it. This is going to take some negotiation between our country and theirs."

Archer quizzed him, "So why us? Why can't their own people do it if they have all the right teams in place?"

Stitch seemed to know the answer but looked at the centre of the table to allow Mercury to tell Archer everything he already knew.

"Because the French have complete deniability then and nothing can be traced to any illegal activity by a French team, no matter how secret that team is. A brief history lesson Archer. You've heard of the French Resistance during World War Two?"

"Yes, of course."

"After the war, the Resistance didn't just disappear. The skills they developed working alongside our own Special Operations Executive and the network of operators they built, was too valuable to lose. They still exist to this day. They consolidated, got better, grew in numbers and installed highly influential people. They couldn't afford another invasion by a foreign government and made a promise not only to the French population, but also to the volunteers of the movement who had paid with their lives. Their intelligence network is impeccable and highly advanced. Not as good as ours, but we have a shared concern and so we often work together."

Archer nodded in understanding and looked sideways at Stitch who said, "You're getting an education tonight lad."

Mercury chuckled a little, "Well it's early stages yet, so like I say it could take a month or two. But at least you're forewarned. Now, I do believe that with the clattering and swearing ceasing from the kitchen, our delightful meals are on their way."

As if on cue, the chef burst through the kitchen door with three plates balanced on his hands and arms. He held out his arms and nodded to the first plate for Mercury, which he took by his fingertips expecting the plate to be hot, which it wasn't. The chef then waddled around to Archer placing the plate down in front of him at an angle and allowing it to drop to the surface. Then he moved over to Stitch and slopped the plate down, gravy spilling over the edge and on to the table.

Mercury leaned forwards and smelled the aroma of the meal, breathing in through his nose deeply and loudly, "Ah smells disgusting chef. Thank you so much, you are relieved."

Stitch rubbed his hands together in anticipation and also made comment.

"Bloody marvellous chef. Your talents know no bounds." as he grabbed his knife and fork and prepared to eat.

Archer tried hard to hold in a laugh, but it didn't work. The chef, looking down his nose in turn at the three of them, returned their compliments, "Fuck you very much gents, don't fucking choke," and he waddled back through the kitchen door. The three of them ate, smiling and chuckling at various degrees of chewing at the well-cooked meat. The chef reappeared briefly to slap three plastic beakers filled with water in front of each of his customers, turned and left.

After the meal, they all pretended to dab the sides of their mouths, laughed and went their separate ways. When Archer returned to his room, he checked the contents of his envelope and still gasped at how much he had been paid. He cleaned his pistol, settled himself in his bed and thought of Sandra.

Chapter 9: The French job

The weeks of continuous training passed by. At one point, Archer had to fill in for a surveillance team member and did a small job as part of the jigsaw in the movements of a target's life. One that he would not be responsible for taking this time and so he filled the gap, gaining vital intelligence for the right assassin. His brief was simple and he was surprised to find that the intelligence file he received for this man, was not given to him as an assassination file. The surveillance team merely didn't know where this particular man spent his Tuesday afternoon and Archer was able to confirm the sighting of him at a squash court. His one single snippet of information was enough to complete the picture of the life of the target and he never heard from the team again.

He continued to write to his mother and never failed to enquire about Sandra. He still felt the heartbreak when he thought about her and more so when his mother wrote to tell him they were both fine, after chastising him again for the large amount of money he had left her on his bed. He could tell from the letters that Sandra was not asking about him, because her reply was brief when the subject of Sandra was being addressed.

One particularly sunny, dry winters' morning in February as he was crossing from the farmhouse to the barn, Stitch intercepted him with a big, wicked grin on his face.

"Stop where you are, come with me. You don't need anything, just come this way."

He turned and waved him towards a waiting car, "Get in, do the usual and I'll be there in a jiffy," he ordered.

Archer obliged and as he entered the rear passenger seat, he found the blindfold waiting for him which he placed over his eyes and lay down.

After a minute, he heard the driver's side door open, the car rocked as Stitch got in.

"So are you going to tell me why you've got that grin on your face?" Archer asked.

Feeling Stitch turn round in his seat, Stitch replied in an excited tone, "Ooooh I'm going to show you the art of deception with a very loud noisy thing."

"Can't wait then," Archer replied sarcastically.

"Well if you don't like this, I certainly will. Right, let's go." Stitch set off at the usual normal speed and Archer was given permission to take the blind fold off after a certain amount of time. Stitch didn't stop the car, he just allowed Archer to climb between the gaps in the seats and park himself in the passenger seat. It wasn't lost on Archer that he was instructed to remove his blindfold at the edge of a village so that he would not see the sign with the village name on it as they entered it. There was a small, black canvas bag with a shoulder strap and lid, fastened by two brass buckles in the footwell in front of Archer and he leaned forwards to examine it.

"Ah ah!" Stitch stopped him, "Don't look in there yet, all will be revealed when we get into this village centre." Stitch drove slowly and found a suitable place to park the car, pointing towards the opposite end of the village to where they entered. He turned the engine off after applying the handbrake with a wrench of his left arm and leaned towards Archer, grabbing the canvas bag and lifting it gently.

"Right. Out you pop then and come hither with me," he smiled, "You'll like this."

They got out of the car and slowly made their way to a destination only Stitch knew, looking like two men out for a walk.

Archer didn't have a clue where he was, but he made note of his surroundings the way he was trained to. They arrived at the centre and Archer noted the road split in three directions, with a war memorial in the centre. They sat on a public wooden bench behind the memorial, where one of the roads stretched past them and up the hill on their right-hand side. Stitch placed the canvas bag at his feet. There was a row of shops and businesses opposite them, with a chip shop, a restaurant, a newsagents, a greengrocer and a butcher a few doors down, to name but a few. People were busying about these premises and the village seemed to thrive with shoppers, bustling about and stopping to chat to each other.

They watched this activity for a few minutes, then Stitch grabbed the bag and placed it on his lap. Unbuckling the two buckles that kept the lid over the bag, he opened it and moved it sideways closer to Archer.

"Have a peek inside. What do you see?" he asked him.

Archer leaned across and looked in. He could see what looked like a crumpled cigarette packet, with a small black box that would fit in his palm and an old square biscuit tin.

"Didn't know you smoked?" he flippantly said to Stitch. Without bringing the contents out, Stitch went into detail about the items, "The cigarette packet has one of the latest lines of detonators in it. Now, it's attached to a small receiver and battery set up and the black box you see is a tiny radio transmitter, both tuned to the same frequency. The biscuit tin to one side is my sandwiches. Now, I want you to pop across to the newsagents and do you see the bin outside it?"

Archer saw the metal public litter bin, with vertical wooden slats on the outside running up it, "Yep."

"Go and put that packet in it. I'll show you how you switch it on."

Stitch showed him how to power the unit up with his hands inside the bag. Archer looked up to view his surroundings and gingerly grabbed the packet and placed it in his coat pocket. He stood and crossed the road in front of them to the memorial, then crossed the road again when there was a sufficient gap in the traffic. Stitch watched on as Archer blended into the surroundings, nodding and smiling to people who made eye contact, gaining ground on getting closer to the bin. When Archer arrived, he simply rummaged around in his pocket to make it look like he was using the opportunity of being at the bin to get rid of rubbish and dropped the cigarette packet into the half full bin. He walked forwards to peer into one of the shop windows and saw Stitch make a subtle thumb up with his right hand, knowing full well that Archer was observing his reflection. Archer turned and crossed the road to re-join Stitch at the bench.

"Now Archer. You could put that packet at the bottom of a large shop window or under a car or anywhere you want really. The fact it looks like a crumpled cigarette packet means it won't hold much curiosity for anyone who smokes. But it's enough to hide the detonator unit. When you're planning a hit in public areas like this, it can be a really good idea to plan a distraction to create confusion and focus people's attention elsewhere and away from you. At the right time and when you're close enough to your target, push the transmitter, blow the detonator, do your job and then blend in with the chaos. But also, be quick in extracting yourself because this kind of distraction will definitely bring the area to the attention of the police. You know full well that I've parked the car so that I'm leaving on a different route to where I came into the village. Never use the same route in and out, ok?"

Archer nodded as he fixed his gaze on the transmitter inside the bag.

Stitch reached in and prepared to press the little button. They both looked at the bin and Stitch whispered, "Don't want any elderly people near that..." as they studied the passers-by.

There came a sufficient gap in the movement of people when Stitch jabbed at the button with his thumb. They both looked at the bin and grinned like two mischievous schoolboys as the contents of the bin instantly jumped out of it with a loud bang. Archer enjoyed the show, but as much as he almost laughed at the bin contents floating around, he noticed the chaos it had created. Some stood still covering their mouths with their hands, some held each other in shock, some ran away in opposite directions and a few took cover on the ground. Archer smiled; it was perfect.

"My God," he said, "Technology is amazing."

Stitch, still grinning, said, "The detonator is only a small one, but it's powerful enough to create quite a scene, eh?"

"Darned right Stitch."

"Right, quick, we'd better get over there and help out with a few people ok?"

Stitch grabbed the bag and slung it over his shoulder. They both got up and hurriedly ran across the road, splitting up to help with a young lady who had dropped her shopping and a middle-aged man who had dropped to the ground to take cover.

Archer ran to the lady and started picking up the oranges that had run out of her shopping bag, whilst she looked on, thanking him. Stitch helped the man onto his feet as Archer heard him stating to Stitch, "I were in't army you know. I was right back there in't war, it was like a gunshot whatever that was!"

Stitch, crouching behind the man, held his right elbow with his right hand and hooked his left hand under the armpit of the man, "Must have been kids letting off a banger firework," Stitch suggested as he raised him off his knees.

"Aye. Little bastards," the man agreed, brushing the front of his coat.

When they finished helping out, Stitch looked at Archer and motioned his head to the car. Archer understood straight away and they walked slowly back to the car and got inside.

Stitch slotted the key into the ignition but before starting the engine he turned to Archer, "In a live operation, don't bother to help out. Nobody will notice if you melt off into the background back to your vehicle or accommodation. Always remember to drive normally, walk normally, never run or drive away at high speed otherwise you'll compromise yourself. And always use a different route out to…"

"The one I used in, yes I get it," Archer finished his sentence, nodding.

Stitch smiled, started the engine and drove off. As Stitch drove off through the village, a local police constable had arrived at the scene and Archer noticed the middle-aged man pointing at the bin and waving his arms in an animated way to describe the bin contents exiting the vessel.

"What a laugh," Stitch laughed and carried on with his drive.

They left the village and Archer knew Stitch had been there before, probably many times. Stitch didn't ask Archer to wear his blindfold on leaving the village and he worked out it was because there wasn't a village name sign at the opposite end. It was only when they were about ten minutes away from the base that Stitch sighed and asked Archer to get onto the rear seat and put his blindfold on.

"I don't want to ask you to do that lad, but it's not worth the grief if Mercury sees us driving back without you wearing it."

"It's ok. Means I don't have to keep looking at your ugly mug anyway," Archer laughed.

"Fucking cheek," Stitch adjusted himself in his seat, feigning being offended.

When they arrived back at the base forecourt, Archer took the blindfold off and sat up. They both noticed Mercury lunging towards the main barn from the farmhouse, when he stopped after noticing the two of them. He waited until they were out of the car and shouted across, "Ops room now gents, before you do anything else."

"Right boss." Stitch replied and they jogged over to the barn and into the operations room, where Mercury, wearing casual clothing of a brown jumper, shirt, tie and grey slacks, as opposed to his usual suit, was spreading out papers from a brown cardboard file onto the operations desk.

"Gather round chaps," he instructed as Stitch and Archer entered.

When he finished spreading out the papers and photographs, Mercury stood back a little and addressed them.

"Ok, the French job is on. Before you are the photographs of one Sergei Brusilov. He is a forty eight year old Russian living in East Germany with strong links to the Russian Mafia. Now, the French became aware of him when he was arrested for smuggling a huge consignment of cigarettes through West Germany and into his distribution network in France. He bribed his way through, but the French are having none of it. They've dug deeper and found he is highly likely to be responsible for the murder of a French diplomat's daughter when he tried to disrupt Sergei's dealings. He's also known for espionage at a fairly low level, passing on French industrial secrets to the Russians for which he is highly paid for. He is now a primary target. The French want complete deniability for this job chaps, as I've already told you a couple of months ago. Europe is becoming closer and closer economically and the French don't want to upset the Germans and likewise the Russians, which will close certain doors for them. Despite that, he's a particularly nasty, murderous individual and our superiors have had no hesitation in accepting the French invitation in removing him. This will also increase our cooperative alliance with French intelligence. Have a look at what's in front of you chaps. Read it, study it, soak it all in as much as you want. We'll be leaving for Rouen in three days. Any questions?"

Stitch was the first to ask, "Who's going? The three of us?"

"Yes. We're heading to Dungeness fishing harbour where a boat will take us to Fort D'Ambleteuse on the French coast. We'll be greeted by the locals who will have two cars ready for us to drive on to Rouen. You two will be allotted a safe house by the French." Mercury then smiled widely at them, "I've been booked into a nearby hotel. Five star of course."

Stitch rolled his eyes, then Archer piped up, "Any associates? Do we have an idea where the job will take place?"

Stitch nodded his approval at the question, as did Mercury, "He will be in Rouen for the week that we'll be there. The French have discovered he has what he thinks is a safe house there which he uses before travelling on to Calais where he can monitor his shipments. He mainly travels alone, because he can move faster, so it should be quite easy. But he is surveillance aware and if he so much as sniffs the odour of an enemy agent, he'll be gone! The safe house you two are in is very close to his safe house. You'll have radio contact with me in the hotel and I'll have contact with the French, so I'll be guiding you."

Archer studied the photographs of Brusilov. He was an overweight, stout and scruffy looking man. His hair seemed to stick up in clumps, he didn't keep his beard well which grew longer in parts of his face than others, but he looked strong and brutal. The lack of a neck suggested to Archer that his frame would be muscular but fat.

"Could be a challenge," he murmured aloud.

"Hmm, could be," Stitch agreed.

"Nothing there that won't stop a bullet or two chaps," Mercury added.

The three of them stood over the intelligence file and photos. They leafed through all the information that was extensive and very detailed.

"They've really done their homework those Resistance guys," Stitch said as he turned pages in the brown cardboard file.

"They're not called the Resistance anymore though," Mercury added quietly.

Archer quizzed him, "What are they called now?"

Mercury paused and looked at Archer, "Names aren't important."

Archer smiled and studied the file again.

They all studied the intelligence for a few hours and when they were saturated with everything they read, they bid each other a goodnight and went their separate ways.

Stitch and Archer trained hard for the three days leading up to the operation in France. Mercury, forever busy, was seen bustling around the complex, looking in on them at the range and making sure they stayed sharp. The evening before they set off for France, they dined together as was customary now before an operation took place. They laughed, joked and swapped sarcastic insults with their usual chef and when it came to leaving the kitchen area to get some sleep and pack their final things, Mercury sat back and smiled like a father to his two boys.

"First job abroad Archer. Stitch has been overseas before, so keep close and learn from him. There's very little difference to the meat and bones of the operation, but there will be subtle differences. When we pick up the cars, I'll be in front and will guide you through Rouen to your meeting point with the French. Keep your radio on, you'll have a few batteries which will see you through."

The two of them, with serious looks on their faces, nodded their understanding.

"Oh and Stitch…."

"Yes boss?"

"Remember they drive on the right."

"Yes boss," he groaned.

"Leave a few cars or a good gap between me and you as you follow me and make sure you relax! Do all that and it'll be dandy. Right, off you go then and I'll see you in the morning."

When they got outside, to the darkness of the evening, Stitch turned to Archer and placed his right hand on his left shoulder to comfort him.

"It can add a certain pressure knowing you're going abroad to do an operation, mate. After this, I think life is going to change for you."

"In what way Stitch?"

Stitch pursed his lips together and nodded, "You'll see. Catch you in the morning."

He got in his car and drove off as Archer turned to the farmhouse and into his bedroom. On his bed, one of the staff had laid him out some different clothes that were decidedly French, giving Archer every chance to blend in with his new location. For once, Archer felt nervous and he felt a twinge of homesickness. After washing and climbing into bed, he thought hard about his mother and Sandra. Knowing that if the operation went horribly wrong and he died on foreign soil, the government would do nothing to return him and the chances are his mother would never know what had happened to him. He yearned to feel the warmth of Sandra's body next to him right then, comforting him and he felt the tears reappear as the pain returned from the pit of his stomach.

"Pull yourself together Adrian," he told himself, "It won't take long. You're strong, sharp and well trained."

But still he couldn't shake the image of Sandra in his mind's eye and for once, he cried himself to sleep.

Archer was up out of bed, had completed his strength exercises and eaten a good breakfast before returning to his bedroom when he heard the squeal of car brakes outside in the forecourt. He grabbed his suitcase, with the pistol inside and exited the farmhouse to see Mercury and Stitch standing beside a dilapidated bread van and looking very proud of themselves.

"Good morning gents," he called out as he approached them, "I do hope you've both slept incredibly well."

"Oh absolutely marvellous," Stitch mocked in a posh English accent. Archer approached them at the van and peered inside. To his surprise, Rachel was in the driving seat with a bright smile at seeing him again.

"Rachel!" he raised his voice in surprise, "Good grief, you get everywhere."

"At your service sirs," she beamed at them all, "Archer, Stitch, you two get in the back. Mercury you sit in the front so it looks like I'm driving my dad around."

Stitch coughed and looked at his feet, trying hard not to smile but Mercury caught him.

"I saw that. Now get in the back like a couple of peasants please. I shall enjoy the luxury of being driven in comfort by a beautiful young lady. That'll teach you!"

Stitch and Archer obliged and after opening the rear doors with a creak and throwing their suitcases in, they sat on a couple of sandbags provided for them, facing each other on opposite sides of the van interior.

"Well isn't this just splendid Archer my young man," Stitch said with the accent again.

"Positively opulent Stitch my good man," Archer replied with his nose in the air.

At that, Rachel gunned the engine and let the clutch bite first gear with a jolt, throwing Archer and Stitch towards the rear of the van. She giggled as they cursed and tried to maintain their balance.

It took a few hours of driving to get to the harbour and Archer was pleasantly surprised to not have to wear a blindfold when they set off. His vision was curtailed at the onset of the journey being sat in the back of a van with no rear windows, but he had the feeling the rules were being relaxed as time went by. As he looked through the windscreen from the rear, he could see the sea come into view and before long it stopped with a squeal of the brakes. Stitch and Archer looked out of the windscreen to see a small harbour with a few fishing boats. Hardly a bustling, working harbour but appeared more to be a private harbour used for locals to go fishing from.

Mercury ordered them, "Wait here, I'll go and make contact."

As he exited, Stitch leaned back against the side of the van and closed his eyes with a sigh as Archer looked on at Mercury walking away from them to meet a scruffy looking white haired elderly man with a torn woolly blue jumper and rubber waders who was walking to meet him. They shook hands as Mercury confirmed their contract and that he had met the right man, then turned to walk back to the van. He opened the door and looked inside without getting in.

"Right fellas, let's move. Rachel, thank you so much yet again. Back to base, get the van fuelled and oiled and get yourself away. We'll see you in a week….or less," he glinted a smile at her. Rachel smiled back and looked over her shoulder as Stitch and Archer took their suitcases and slid out of the back of the van. She looked back at Mercury and with a concerned smile said, "Look after him won't you. Please?"

Mercury smiled back at her, "He doesn't need it that one. He's something else."

The three of them stood and watched Rachel drive off, but before they went to their contact Mercury rummaged around in his coat pocket and brought out two British passports.

"Here you go chaps. Stitch this one is yours and Archer…." he checked the photographs inside them, "...this one is yours."

Stitch was curious as to what his cover name was and opened his passport, "Giles Bartholomew?" he called out.

Archer checked his, "Percy Harrison?"

They both looked pleadingly at Mercury who shrugged his shoulders, "Not my choosing gents. Remember your names now. Good boys, follow me."

They grimaced to each other at the names they had received in their passports and trudged behind Mercury as he walked along the concrete pier to their chosen transport across the English Channel. The old fisherman greeted them with a grunt as he held out his hand to help each of them on board his wooden fishing boat. Archer observed it as he stepped on to the deck. It was a bit ram shack and needed a lick of paint, but it seemed totally solid and he could tell the fisherman only dry docked it and catered for it when he absolutely necessarily had to. But then, would he pay for its repairs and upkeep, or would the department somehow look after him? Archer shook his head and kept those small details to the back of his mind.

In a broad Southern English accent the fisherman addressed them all as they stood in front of him in a loose semi circle, "Right gents, I know where I'm going and I'm not going to ask any questions so you can relax. The forecast is pretty good, but we might get a few chops in the water as we get out into the currents. Nothing to worry about. You can sit outside if you want, or get down below via this hatch I'm stood on."

Mercury added, "Don't worry about the French authorities gents, their normal search pattern for smugglers has been rigged such that we'll just slip through. Our rendezvous at the other side is going to plan, so this should be plain sailing."

He grinned and paused at the pun, looking for a reaction. Stitch and Archer looked at each other, straight faced, then looked in unison at Mercury still straight faced at his attempt at a joke. Stitch pointed to a bench seat outside the wheelhouse and said, "Thanks for that. We'll just be sitting over here then."

The old fisherman tried to hide a chuckle with a cough and turned to start the boat engine, "Get comfortable then lads, this will be an hour or two that's all."

Mercury, still smiling, brought out a steel hip flask, shook it in front of the two of them, unscrewed the lid and took a quick swig before closing it up and returning it to his pocket.

"Ah! That's the spirit. Hope you have sea legs."

Then he turned and joined the fisherman in the wheelhouse as he started the engine and turned the boat out to sea.

Stitch and Archer sat mostly in silence for the trip across the channel. So much as the weather was overcast and the sea was not too choppy, Archer was lost in his thoughts and knew that Stitch was too. There was no need to break the silence with conversation.

Mercury appeared out of the wheelhouse and announced their imminent arrival.

"Right lads, look sharp. We have a rowing boat coming out to meet us and take us to our transport. If questions are asked, ignore them, ok?"

They both nodded, stood and stretched their aching limbs and tried to balance themselves as they walked a few steps to take hold of their luggage. The boat's engine was just idling and chugging slowly as they approached the old Fort D'Ambleteuse and saw two men in a large rowing boat coming out to meet them. When the fishing boat was close enough, the old fisherman cut the engine as the two Frenchmen drew up alongside the boat. Archer observed them. They both looked to be in their early thirties. The one at the oars was stout, with thick black curly hair, an unshaven fat face and wore a dark brown leather jacket with black trousers. The other, sitting at the back, was clean shaven, very athletic with a thin face and chiselled chin, wearing a black polo neck jumper and grey trousers. It was him who cupped a hand to the side of his mouth and called out, "We are fishing for Mercury?"

Mercury smiled at him and gave him a thumbs up, "Tres bien! C'est moi," to which the Frenchman smiled and waved them on board. Archer and Stitch handed down their suitcases, then accepted the balancing hand from the man who had shouted while the other one sat at the oars. When the three of them had been transferred to the rowing boat, the old fisherman leaned out of the wheelhouse and shouted, "Good luck fellas," tapping his head in salute then starting the engine to begin the trip back to England. Luckily for the three of them, the only question from the Frenchmen was from the man rowing. "Sea was good for you, yes?" to which all three of them nodded. The two Frenchmen said something to each other and laughed as they continued their trip back to the shore.

They arrived on a pebbled beach, just in front of the old fort and all three jumped off the front before being handed their luggage. When they had their belongings, the athletic one said to them all, "Go round ze back of ze fort. Our friend is there."

Mercury replied with a "Merci," as did Stitch and Archer. The Frenchmen laughed to each other and rowed off back down the shoreline.

They gingerly walked around the back of the fort to find a man smoking a cigarette, leaning against the bonnet of a beautiful Jaguar car, behind which was a battered Renault 4. Archer smiled inwardly as this man too was very athletic in build but seemed to be in his early twenties. He wore a navy-blue wool jumper, with a grey shirt, the collar of which hadn't seen an iron for a long time. His grey trousers looked equally unironed but it was obvious the man didn't care for his appearance. When the three of them were a few metres away, the man flicked his cigarette away and gently tossed a set of keys to Mercury, then another set to Stitch. Without saying a word, he turned and walked off.

Mercury tried the key in the door of the Jaguar and was not surprised to see the door open, signifying that he had been given the more luxurious style of travel. Stitch groaned and shifted his balance, "Fucks sake. You can see which one is ours can't you?" he rhetorically asked Archer.

Mercury opened the boot of the Jaguar and placed his small suitcase inside. He brought out a brown canvas bag of the type Stitch used to carry the explosive cigarette during his deception exercise back in the village.

"Here you go. Radios, batteries and a street map of Rouen. Fire one of them up and follow me. Give me a quick transmission on the radio when we set off to check them. Ok? All good?"

Stitch was the one to reply, "Yeah, yeah. We'll just get into our wonderful car and hope the engine isn't so loud we can't hear your dulcet voice!"

"Excellent," Mercury said, "Let's drive...."

The cars all started up first time and they set off for Rouen to make their next rendezvous with the French at a location only Mercury knew. As instructed, Archer gave Mercury a quick check on the radio when enough distance had been placed between them.

"Check, check," he said and Mercury simply replied, "Ok." as did Archer to close the conversation. Their senses were on high alert, but they also managed to relax where they could and Archer managed to close his eyes in the comfort of Stitch's driving.

In just over two hours, they saw the usual signs of entering a city as they travelled the suburbs and saw affluent areas, run down areas and people bustling about their business. They crossed over the River Seine on one of the many bridges, always keeping distance from Mercury and allowing a car or two to enter their direction of travel from junctions. Stitch never lost sight of Mercury though and as they navigated around the streets, they eventually entered the residential area of Rue Guilbaud. The street was about four hundred metres long and had somewhat bland looking semi-detached houses on either side, with the odd detached house breaking the lines. Ahead of them by about a hundred yards, Mercury pulled in at the side of the road. Archer immediately noted two men, exiting the front gate to a detached house and walking down the pavement away from Mercury. He guessed that was the prompt to show Mercury which house was their safe house.

"See that gents?" Mercury piped up on the radio.

Archer, keeping the radio on his lap so that it wouldn't be seen, replied, "Yep. Got it marked."

"That's yours. I'm at the end of this street in another house."

Stitch grabbed the radio and also held it in his lap, "Thought you were getting a five star?"

"Ha! Get your stuff in there and I'll call you on this in half an hour. Over and out."

They drove forwards when Mercury had pulled out and drove down the road and stopped outside their new, albeit temporary, new home. They laughed a little, looking like they were relaxed in their surroundings, as they took their suitcases and Stitch carried the canvas bag slung over his shoulder. When they approached the door, Archer saw that the key had been left in the lock and he turned it, opened the door and stepped in after removing the key and putting it in his trouser pocket. Archer took in the interior of the house, noting it had been left with only the bare essentials. There was a small living room to the right, with the staircase on the left. Ahead was the kitchen and diner, with a simple table and two chairs. There was storage space under the kitchen sink, but it was simply covered with what looked like curtain material on a wire runner. The flooring was simply wooden slats which creaked with practically every step.

They took their suitcases upstairs and found two bedrooms and a bathroom. One bedroom was at the front and one at the back, with the bathroom to the right in between them. The bedrooms had only one bed and a wooden chair in each and nothing else.

Archer reeled at the simplicity, "Wow. No luxury here."
Stitch seemed unsurprised, "You don't need anything
else mate. Keeping things simple means you won't need
to feel the need to unpack everything and hide it away.
Live out of your suitcase as much as you can. Right...."
he said, looking into the front bedroom, "We'll set this up
as our observation room. We'll sort out shifts so that
there is a constant watch on whatever house we're
looking at. We'll share that bed," he nodded to the other
room.

"Now, get yourself in there and get your pistol out and
check it, ok?"

Archer tapped the side of his head with two fingers in
salute and took his suitcase into the rear bedroom.
Sitting on the edge of the bed and bouncing on the
mattress, he knew it would be hard to sleep on such an
unforgiving surface. He raised an eyebrow and
shrugged to himself, "Not quite home, but it'll do."
Rummaging for his pistol in the suitcase, he located it,
brought it out and disassembled it for the umpteenth
time to make sure it was fully operational.

When he had finished his checks, he passed the new
observation room and went downstairs to check the
contents of the kitchen. He had felt a sudden hunger
pang as he cleaned his pistol and realised he hadn't
eaten anything since that morning. The kitchen was like
the rest of the house; very simple. There was a pantry to
the left with a tall white door in the wall, a cupboard on
the wall to the left of the window in front of him as he
stood at the entrance, two cupboards on the wall to the
right of the window, a bread bin under them on the

worktop and a cooker to the right against the wall. Towards the left-hand corner, there was the half glass, half wood door to the rear of the house with a single piece of curtain on a wire. He peeled back the curtain arrangement under the kitchen sink and worktop to reveal pots and pans in sectioned off cupboards. There was olive oil in a tin and a drawer at the top that held a couple of knives and forks, a can opener, a corkscrew and spoons of different sizes. He noticed it was all very clean though and peering through the net curtain of the kitchen window to the back garden, he saw it was also well kept. It stretched about thirty metres away from the back of the house, with a well-groomed lawn and tall bushes dotted down each side. Wooden fencing at his head height separated the division between each house and it just all seemed normal. Moving over to the pantry, he opened the white door to reveal shelves stacked with tinned food and a large lump of butter on a plate with its glass cover and he selected a large tin of baked beans. Checking the bread bin revealed a fresh loaf of white bread and he set to making two plates of beans on toast. He smiled at his culinary prowess as he took the plates, almost overflowing with beans, up to the front room where Stitch was sitting on the room's chair at the window, the radio and map on the floor along with a pair of binoculars he had stashed in his suitcase. Archer handed him a plate of steaming beans on toast.

"Oh! Thank you, I could get used to this," Stitch smiled in gratitude.

Archer fetched a couple of knives and forks out of his back pocket as he placed his plate down on the bed and handed a set to Stitch. Placing the plate on his lap, he was just about to start eating when the radio burst into life. He sniggered at the sight of Stitch just raising a heaped fork of beans to an open mouth, which he let slip, spilling the beans back onto the plate when he heard Mercury.

"Check, check."

"Ok."

"No sightings yet. I'm in touch with our friends, I'll keep you posted. See the house opposite and three down with blue shutters and a yellow door?"

"Yes," Stitch quickly replied.

"That's the one. Out."

Stitch placed the radio back on the floor.

"Now if you don't mind boss, we are about to dine," he mumbled, slipping the fork into the mass of beans. They ate, without talking, smiling to each other as they settled into their surroundings.

"Right then mate," Stitch spoke up after they finished eating, "We'll do a rota of four hours on and four hours off, ok?"

"Yeah sure."

"Ok, it's sixteen hundred hours now. I'll do the first stint until twenty hundred, then you do twenty hundred to midnight and so on. This is the hard part young 'un, we need a lot of patience. Keep the radio on, don't move the net curtain, keep the photograph of Brusilov near and sit back a bit from the window in the shadows. You know the drill, this was all part of your training."

"Indeed Stitch, indeed."

Archer took the plates back to the kitchen, washed them up, placed all they had used back in its rightful place and went back upstairs to the rear bedroom. He lay on the mattress and closed his eyes, drifting in and out of sleep, thinking about Sandra and fighting back the emotion of loss.

Archer completed his couple of stints at the window, observing the street and paying particular attention to their target house resisting the urge to sleep in the early hours of the morning. He handed over to Stitch at eight in the morning and taking the map, he told Stitch, "I'm going for a quick walk to stretch my legs, old boy."

"Cheeky shit. Ok I'll keep a watch on you," he yawned as he slumped on to the chair and took the binoculars to his lap.

Archer went downstairs and out of the door. He stretched as he opened the door and stood on the doorstep, breathing in the air and savouring the sun in his face. There were a few fluffy clouds and a gentle breeze as he felt the endorphins rise in his body, accepting the beauty of the morning. He unfurled the map and walked down the front path studying it. Without looking from the map, he opened the small metal gate with his left hand, stepped through and slowly started to walk to his right, down the road in the opposite direction to where Mercury had installed himself.

Archer was trying to orientate the map so he could work out escape routes in case they were separated from Mercury after the operation, when he suddenly became aware of footsteps approaching his rear. At that very moment he felt a couple of fingers tapping him on his shoulder and a gravelly voice called to him, "Excusez moi, avez-vous une lumière?"

Archer relaxed the map in his grip and turned. His heart absolutely jumped in his chest as he instantly recognised the man as Sergei Brusilov. The beard was gone, replaced with a few days of stubble, but the hair growing in clumps and the lack of a neck, combined with his stout posture gave him away. Archer hid his surprise.

"Oh I'm sorry, I don't understand," Archer said politely with a smile.

"Ah English," Brusilov replied in his heavily accented voice.

Archer studied his eyes to look for signs of recognition as to who Archer really was, but he noted how little the eyebrows moved. The eyes were grey and seemed to look right through Archer and showed little sign of any kind of emotion.

"Yes, that's right. Do you speak English?" Archer enquired.

"Yes, yes. I asked if you have a light for my cigarette?" Brusilov pointed to the cigarette dangling from his lips.

"Sorry, no, I don't smoke."

Brusilov nodded, "That's good. A young man, such as you, should look after himself."

He looked down at the map Archer was clutching, "You are looking for something?"

Archer thought quickly and brought the map up to study it, "Yes actually, I'm trying to find my way to the Saint Sever Cemetery."

"You are tourist?" Brusilov asked in innocence.

"Sort of. I am tracing my family tree and have found I have a relative buried in the cemetery who fought in World War One. I'm over for a while to try and find him."

"Ah yes. I am from Poland," Sergei lied, "My family is thankful to the British. My uncle was pilot in your Royal Air Force in second world war."

"Ah Poland! The very reason we went to war," Archer smiled at him.

Brusilov smiled back, the crinkles of his face making him look very friendly and wisened. Archer almost felt a warmth from such a smile.

"Are you doing the tourist thing too?" Archer asked.

"No. I have business here. My house is just over there. I stay from time to time….when business calls, you know?"

Archer raised his eyebrows to pretend he was impressed, "Very good. Well it's a lovely city to be staying in."

Brusilov nodded in agreement, "Yes, it is. Listen, there is a bar I know near here. Join me for a drink tonight so that I can toast your dead relative."

"Oh, I don't know…."

"Please. I insist. We are comrades and it would be my duty to the British."

Archer couldn't work out if he had been compromised by Brusilov, the Russian somehow working out who he really was. He felt like he had been backed into a corner that he couldn't get away from. He studied his face for a second; there was no flicker of recognition.

"Yes, ok then."

Brusilov shifted his weight, "Good. I will meet you at ten o'clock outside your house, ok?"

"Ten o'clock it is then," Archer smiled and held out his hand.

Brusilov took it and held it firm as he shook Archer's hand. Archer felt the thickness and size of his hands and as much as the hand felt incredibly friendly as they shook, he was also aware it had more than likely killed many people who simply got in his way.

"I'm Adrian by the way."

"Yes, I am Sergei."

He coughed a raspy cough, which Archer thought he used as an excuse to break the handshake and cover his mouth with the side of his fist.

Archer instantly wondered why he hadn't lied about his name, but it could have been a test to see if he questioned it.

"Well, it's a pleasure to meet you. I'll see you tonight."

"Yes, good, I will see you tonight Adrian and we will toast your ancestors."

"Yours too, Sergei."

At that, they broke off; Sergei returning in the direction of his house, Archer knew he had to make the trip to the cemetery in case Brusilov had colleagues tasked to follow him even though he was confident he didn't. He stood still for a few seconds, studying the map then made his way through the streets to the cemetery. He dropped his counter surveillance skills, knowing that if he displayed them he would be compromised by anyone following. If Sergei had observers, they would be instantly familiar with the techniques and this would confirm Archer as an enemy operative. He remembered the intelligence brief and felt confident there would be nobody else anyway.

Archer found the cemetery and, more importantly, found the hundreds of graves of the soldiers who fought in World War One. They were all lined up at the back of the cemetery, looking immaculate and well kept. Archer couldn't help but think it was like they were welcoming him and he drew comparisons between him and them. So much as he was alive, they all had a common goal. They fought for freedom, for democracy and to maintain the very nature of life as they knew it at the time. In order to do that, they had to kill the enemy who was trying to change it. Ridding the world of bad people. Archer felt a comfort from the gravestones as he walked through them all, reading their names, seeing how old they were when they died and the regimental cap badges they fought under. He was impressed by how neat the gravestones were; all in line, all prominent reminders. A purpose in life as well as death.

He returned to the house, feeling somewhat humble at the sights he had seen in the cemetery. Archer climbed upstairs and poked his nose into the observation room where Stitch was sitting, arms folded, already looking at the bedroom doorway where he expected Archer to appear. As Archer looked in, Stitch unfolded his arms and held them palms up, shrugging his shoulders.

"What the fuck was that?!" he asked, eyes widened and eyebrows raised in incredulity.

"Relax Stitch, it's all in hand," Archer smiled at him.

"You.....but....I mean....seriously? I saw him exit his house and make his way straight over to you. I couldn't even rush out to warn you or anything and the next thing I knew, as I was almost screaming down the radio to Mercury, you and Brusilov were shaking hands and you both moved off! Mercury was in stitches! The French obviously got it wrong and he told me not to panic and just let you go! Fucking hell lad, you know how to get my heart racing!"

Archer felt very composed, "You can stand down now Stitch. It'll be done tonight. We're meeting for a drink tonight and I have a plan."

Stitch looked away and raised a hand to him, "I don't want to know. Just...don't...fucking tell me."

He looked out of the window, folding his arms again, "And I can't stand down can I? He might have comrades for all we know."

Archer remembered the brief, "He travels alone."

Stitch nodded slowly as he looked out of the window then looked at his watch, "It's your watch in half an hour you bugger."

"Right you are. I'll grab a quick bath and a bite to eat and I'll come and relieve you old boy."

Stitch grumbled and continued to look out of the window.

Archer bathed, went to the pantry and opened a tin of peaches in syrup and took it upstairs where he relieved Stitch who got up from the chair, stretched, groaned and walked off patting Archer on the shoulder as he went to the rear bedroom to sleep. Archer sat and looked down the road to Brusilov's house, planning.

The evening darkness came very quickly to Archer and there had been no sign of movement from Brusilov. When Stitch walked into the room, Archer stood and stretched.

"Where's the lock picking kit?" he asked Stitch.

"Oh, good evening Stitch, how are you Stitch? I'm fine Archer thank you. Shook hands with the enemy lately have we?" he mocked Archer, "It's in my suitcase, I'll get it for you."

Stitch went to his suitcase against the right-hand wall and opened it. He didn't have to search about, his suitcase was meticulously packed and he took the kit and handed it to Archer.

"Great. Thanks Stitch. I'll be leaving it by the front door, with my pistol, ok?"

Stitch dragged his feet across the floor in tiredness and sat on the little chair with a slump.

"Yes, yes. I hope your plan works lad."

Archer saw the worry in Stitch's eyes and felt quite touched, "It'll all be fine. Trust me."

Stitch laughed a little and looked through the net curtains towards Brusilov's house.

"Ok, I've got a couple of minutes. I'll get things set up."

Archer took the lock picking kit in its leather wallet, went into the rear bedroom and took his pistol from his suitcase. He moved downstairs and checked his pistol was functioning as usual. Placing both items down on the floor by the front door, he grabbed his trench coat, took one deep breath and opened the front door. He slowed his movements down and went into looking like a clumsy tourist who was a little naive about being street wise and unaware of any local danger. He closed the door and started to walk down the front path to the metal gate and as he opened it, Brusilov was already crossing the road to meet him.

"Good evening my friend," Brusilov called out. He had his hand in the waist pockets of the black miner's coat as he stepped towards Archer with purpose. As he got across the road and onto the pavement within feet of Archer, he pulled out his right hand. Archer felt the jolt in his stomach as he looked closely at the right hand. If he had been compromised and the hand held a pistol, he was doomed. He had a quick flashback of the Jakes and Burkett operation, where Burkett had the drop on him. Brusilov extended his right hand as it came out of his pocket and offered it to Archer for a handshake.

"Ah good evening Sergei," he smiled as warmly as he could.

"Good to see you. I am looking forward to our toast."

"Me too. Shall we?"

"Yes, I'll show you the way to the bar."

They walked off and Archer smiled to himself as he imagined Stitch pressing his eyes to the binoculars with big, wide eyes and screaming down the radio to Mercury.

Brusilov coughed his trademark raspy cough as they walked, "You found your relative, yes?"

"I did indeed Sergei. He is buried amongst hundreds of other soldiers from loads of other regiments."

"That is good."

They took a few more steps and Brusilov asked, "Which regiment was he in?"

Archer remembered one of the cap badges and the regiment name from one of the gravestones, "He was in the King's Own Yorkshire Light Infantry. Died in August of 1917, but I don't know why so I'll have to find out when I get back to England."

"Oh. That is sad. War is so futile don't you think?"

Archer thought about his reply for a second, "Depends on the cause I suppose Sergei."

Brusilov laughed quickly, coughed and slapped Archer on the small of the back, "That is good Adrian, I like that!"

Archer was fully aware that Brusilov had slapped him on the area of his back that a covert operative would keep a pistol and smiled. For the moment, he had outfoxed him.

Brusilov pulled out a packet of cigarettes as they approached the bar and offered one to Archer, who confirmed, "I don't smoke Sergei, but thank you."

"Ah yes. I forget, I'm sorry. Please, after you."

He waved Archer into the front door of the bar.

They both entered the bar which was a simple affair. Seating was just dark stained wood tables and chairs to the right, the straight bar facing the seats to the left and burgundy leather topped bar stools. There was a young couple talking, sitting opposite each other over drinks at the first table, an elderly couple ignoring each other, but sitting side by side looking nowhere in particular at the next table and a group of four middle aged men around another table, further down the area who paid no attention to them entering and carried on laughing with each other. Behind the bar, the barman stood leaning at the shelving which held the spirits, reading a newspaper and didn't even acknowledge them as they stepped into the establishment. As Brusilov and Archer approached the bar, Brusilov coughed a few times, covering his mouth with the side of his fist again. The barman went forward to them, leaving his newspaper open.

"Bonjour."

Sergei cleared his throat, "Parlez vous anglais?" he squinted at him, the smoke from his cigarette stinging his eyes.

"Oui, yes, a little," replied the barman.

"Good. I will have double vodka and my friend will have….?"

"Whiskey on the rocks please."

"Certainly gentlemen. Take a seat and I will bring them over."

"Bon. Merci," Brusilov answered. He looked at the small table and two chairs at the rear of the room and motioned to Archer, "Shall we?" to which Archer nodded and the two took the seats sitting opposite each other. Archer knew Brusilov would want the seat facing the entrance so that he could see who was coming in and out, so he held back and let him take it.

Brusilov sat, letting out a small groan and relaxed. As Archer sat, Brusilov took his cigarette out of his mouth and placed it in the ashtray, still burning.

"So, my friend. Here we are."

"Here we are Sergei. Did you have any other relatives who fought in either of the wars apart from your uncle?"

"Yes, but I do not know of them. My family talked about grandfather this or grandfather that, but I know nothing else. I did not meet them."

"Oh, that's quite sad Sergei."

The barman walked up to them and lowered their drinks in front of them, "Gentlemen, your vodka and your whiskey."

"Thank you," Archer said and waited for the barman to walk back.

Sergei took his vodka, looked at Archer and raised his glass to head height.

"To our soldiers, our ancestors, our warriors. May they rest in peace."

"God rest them," Archer said, raising his glass and he took a good swig as he looked over at Brusilov who cocked his head back and downed his vodka in one mouthful.

"Ahhh, that's good."

Brusilov looked over to the barman who was watching their toast with a smile and raised his finger to signify he wanted another. The barman nodded and turned to prepare another vodka. Archer paced himself so that the ice would melt into the rest of his whiskey and dilute it. He needed to stay mostly sober. Brusilov looked at Archer's glass, noting it was still quite full, "You are not used to drinking Adrian?"

"No, very rarely do I drink. I like occasions like this, but even then, I can't drink much because I have an aversion to it."

"Oh. I see. You must look after yourself Adrian, don't end up like me. You don't mind if I drink more?"

"Not at all Sergei, let's enjoy the night and thank you for honouring our ancestors."

"Ha!" Brusilov laughed out, "It was my pleasure. I am enjoying the company of my new friend," he said as the barman walked over and left another vodka for him. Brusilov coughed a few times, rasping and wheezing between bouts of coughing, all the time using the side of his fist to cover his mouth. Archer feigned concern, "Are you alright Sergei, that's quite a cough you have?"

"Yes. I'm fine Adrian. I must stop smoking!" he smiled and laughed. Archer couldn't help feeling the warmth from such a manly, comforting smile.

They continued to talk whilst Brusilov drank more vodkas and smoked more cigarettes and after a couple of hours, he yawned openly. They were the only customers left in the bar and Archer studied his eyes and saw they had that glazed look when someone who was drunk was trying to focus on his subject.

"Sergei, I think we'll call it a night my friend."

"Da comrade. I think you're right, let's go."

He stood up slowly, balanced himself by keeping his hands on the table and when he had gained his composure he walked slowly to the door. Archer hooked his right hand under his left elbow to steady him and chuckled as they exited.

"Goodnight," the barman called out as they approached the door. Brusilov raised his right hand and let it flop back down by his side again. Archer looked over his right shoulder and smiled.

As they walked back, Archer kept his hand under the elbow, keeping Brusilov on a straight line back to his house. The weather had turned for the worse a little as a breeze had enough strength to ruffle Archer's hair and there was a light drizzle which was too light to soak them through.

Brusilov started to sing some kind of Russian national song, or what sounded like it to Archer, interspersed with his wheezing and guttural coughing, waving his right hand like he was conducting an orchestra when they finally got to his house.

Archer escorted him to his front door and stood back as Brusilov fumbled in his pockets, swaying and trying to find his key. He pretended to laugh a little at Brusilov as he searched and when he found the key, Brusilov displayed it in triumph then tried to focus on the lock as he guided the key towards it. He eventually found the lock, turned the key and the door opened. He turned to Archer, still swaying and said, "Adrian my friend, I have enjoyed your company tonight. Perhaps we can meet again while you are still here?"

"Yes Sergei, that would be good. Sleep well my friend and I will see you soon."

Sergei smiled and swayed into the house as Archer turned, walked down the pathway to the gate and closed it, turning to check on Brusilov who was closing the door.

Archer crossed the road, walked to his safehouse and checked his senses. He was sober.

"Sober enough," he said to himself as he opened the door and quickly stepped in. He rushed up the stairs and stood in the doorway to the observation room to see

Stitch sitting on the chair, looking out of the window and shaking his head slowly.

"Fuck me. I've never seen this before. I mean.....words fail me. Words fucking fail me."

"Back in a few ticks comrade," Archer replied in a mock Russian accent and as he turned and headed back downstairs, he could just hear Stitch mumbling something incredulous. As he got to the front door, he bent down and took the lock picking kit and his pistol, pulling back the slide and letting it go forwards under its own steam which chambered a bullet then placing it in the usual right waist pocket. He opened the door slowly and peered out towards Brusilov's house which was in darkness. Stepping out into the night again, he went into professional mode and walked quietly to the house. Aware of his senses and surroundings as usual, he made sure nobody watched him walk down the side of the house to the rear of it which wasn't being illuminated by the street lighting. He skipped over the waist height wire fence of Brusilov's rear garden and slowly stalked to the kitchen door, bending down in front of it so that he could see what kind of lock held the door shut. He opened the kit and took a small dropper bottle of a high viscosity oil and dabbed the oil onto the hinges, waiting a couple of minutes for the oil to soak in. Looking at the lock he knew which instruments he needed but tried the door handle just in case. To his utter surprise, the door hadn't been locked and he gingerly opened it, the oil had done its work and it opened in silence. Archer stepped in, testing the surface of the kitchen floor with his feet which, unlike his own safehouse, was solid concrete. The soft lino floor covering ensured a silent stalk into the kitchen as he closed the door gently but didn't close if fully and left it slightly ajar. He listened to the house, listened for movement all the while stalking and feeling the ground with his feet. As he moved down the tiled hallway, the yellow street lighting spilled inside from the half glazed front door, softly illuminating the hall halfway down. There was a door to his left with the stairs reaching up on his right and as he got to the doorway, he almost froze in fear as a voice gently called out to him.

"In here my friend."

It was Brusilov. Archer slowly peered into the room and saw Brusilov sitting in a leather armchair in front of a fireplace close to the right wall, facing towards the front window. Opposite him, facing him was another leather armchair. Archer looked at the back of Brusilov's head and he turned to face him.

"Come on in, please, take a seat," he coughed and raised his hand, beckoning Archer to sit, Archer noticing that neither hand held a weapon. Archer had outfoxed him earlier in the evening and worried that the tables had been turned now, so he felt relieved to see empty hands.

Archer didn't say a word and slowly, ominously walked to the chair and lowered himself into it, placing his hand in his right coat pocket and locating the pistol.

Brusilov smiled at him, his face partly illuminated by the street lighting streaming in through the gap in the middle of the curtains.

"So, my friend, you have come to take my life?"

Archer settled himself for a few seconds and quietly replied, "Yes, Sergei."

"Then so be it, I no longer have the strength to fight. I am dead man anyway."

Archer was confused, "What do you mean?"

"Lung cancer. I do not have long."

Archer wondered why this hadn't shown up in the intelligence file but couldn't find words for a fitting reply. Archer settled into the armchair but didn't take the focus off his grip of the pistol.

"What happened with your family Sergei? I know about your uncle, but you have said little else about them tonight."

Brusilov thought for a few seconds, realising there was no point in lying.

"Yes, my family. As a child I was beaten by my parents, for the smallest mistake and then I was beaten at school."

Brusilov bowed his head a little, either in shame or from the freedom of relieving himself of guilt.

"Go on…" Archer allowed him to continue.

"When I was old enough, I became friends with the wrong people after stealing a car. I wanted money, what can I say? I stole the wrong car and instead of them killing me, they killed the man who bought it then took me in. I learnt many bad things Adrian, many bad things. I am not unlike you, no?"

Archer took a deep breath to think about his reply.

"We are alike Sergei, yes. But I use my skills for good, not bad."

Brusilov laughed a bronchial, rasping laugh, "Oh you think so Adrian?"

Brusilov continued, "So we are comrades here, yes? So, I will die tonight at the hands of a fellow warrior. This is a death of my choosing. A quick death rather than die like a poisoned rat with this wretched cancer."

He coughed and wheezed again, only this time it took his breath away and he panted afterwards like he had done a full workout at the gym.

"How long have you known about me Sergei?" Archer asked quietly.

"From the moment I saw you and your colleague enter that house my friend. I knew you were not tourists."

Archer was not surprised by his adversary's prowess, "Hmmmm. Very good."

Archer cocked his hand upwards in his pocket, raising the front of the pistol; instinct taking over.

Brusilov saw the movement and smiled a big smile, "So, I am ready Adrian. Please."

Archer paused, "Did you kill the girl?" asking about the diplomat's daughter he read about in the intelligence file.

"I will answer for my sins when I see God.........as will you! Now, let me show you how a Russian dies!"

Brusilov braced his arms, his hands clutching at the front of the arm rests, but he kept his breathing steady. Archer fired twice. The requisite two shots. Brusilov's head snapped backwards as the bullets tore through his left eye, lodging themselves deep into his brain. The hands let go of the arm rests, the head lolled forwards and as the muscles relaxed, it seemed to perch on his chest as the body slid slightly in the chair. In the semi-darkness of the night, the blood that was streaming out of every orifice in Brusilov's head appeared black. The body passed its last breath as the lungs relaxed and even in death, it sounded raspy as it exited.

Archer sat and looked at him for a minute. Sadness swept over him as he studied the man before him. As much as he was happy that the operation was over and he had rid the world of another thoroughly evil man, he felt compassion for this Russian. Perhaps he didn't have a good start in life with his family, not knowing who his grandparents were. Perhaps he just went through school as an odd child who knew nothing academically but was still highly intelligent and he had mixed with the wrong crowd.

Archer stood, located the two empty bullet shells in his pocket and stepped forward to Brusilov. Placing his left hand on the top of his head, he looked down at him. "Rest easy Sergei. No pain now my friend."

Without care, he walked to the rear kitchen door and stepped out. Pausing he looked up to the night sky, squinting at the light drizzle hitting his eyes, "Dear Lord, forgive me for taking this man's life tonight. This fallen angel returns to you for your judgement. Have mercy on him as well as me for I know nothing more than this act. Evil will prosper when good men do nothing."

He moved out of the doorway and quietly closed the door. Retracing his steps, he made his way back to the safehouse, sadness still sweeping over him. When he got inside, Stitch had made his way downstairs to meet him, eyes wide open in question with his hands out to his sides.

"Well?" he asked.

"Done." Archer simply replied.

Stitch let out a sigh of relief and dropped his shoulders, "Phew! Oh, thank fuck. Thaaaaank fuck."

He paused, studying Archer, "You are some piece of work lad. Right, we'd better get the ball rolling to get home again."

He moved forwards and slapped the side of Archer's left arm.

"Come on, one more job to do." and he rushed upstairs with Archer following.

Stitch entered the now defunct observation room and grabbed the radio he had left on the chair with the binoculars.

"Check, check."

The radio crackled and Archer heard Mercury's familiar voice, "Go ahead."

"All done."

"Pack up. Five minutes."

Stitch, moving with purpose went over to the suitcase and brought out a small transmitting device with a tiny morse code key and beckoned Archer over to him as he crouched over it.

"It's on the right frequency. Tap out the word "VODKA" three times then go and get your suitcase. Meet me at the front door as I pack up. We've got five minutes to get out of here and follow Mercury back to the fort. Everything will be in place from there, ok?"

Archer nodded quickly and crouched next to Stitch and tapped out his morse message perfectly. Stitch smiled at him, "Good lad. Right, go!"

Archer calmly returned to the bedroom and very quickly placed the pistol in the suitcase, closed it up and made his way downstairs. He laughed quietly to himself as he heard Stitch stumbling about, letting out the odd expletive as he made sure he was fully packed up within the five minutes Mercury had allocated them. Eventually he joined Archer at the front door.

"Got everything lad?" he quickly asked Archer.

"Yep."

"Ok, to the car. Mercury should be waiting for us. When we see him pull out of his parking space, we'll follow. Keep your eyes open!"

Quietly and with purpose they exited the house, locked the door and posted the key through the letterbox. They placed their suitcases and the canvas bag in the boot of the Renault and as quietly as they could, shut the doors and Stitch started the engine. Looking ahead a couple of hundred yards away, he saw the rear lights of Mercury's Jaguar pull out from the side of the road and away from them. Stitch followed, keeping the revs of the engine as low as possible to avoid disturbance.

They returned to Fort D'Ambleteuse where Mercury's headlights exposed the same young man who had tossed them the keys to the cars when they arrived. Mercury stopped his Jaguar, got out and took his suitcase out of the boot and looked behind him to see Stitch and Archer doing the same.

"Keys gents. Leave the bag with the radios and batteries in the boot."

Stitch walked over and handed him the keys and Mercury looked over at the young Frenchman and

whistled his attention. When he looked over, Mercury
carried out the same under armed toss of both sets of
keys towards him. The Frenchman panicked as he tried
to juggle the catch of the keys and Mercury smiled at
him.

"Merci. Au revoir!"

The Frenchman nodded his head quickly in salute and
went over to the Jaguar.

A torch light illuminated the three of them from the
shoreline and a French accented voice in English called
out.

"Over here. We will take you to your boat."

The three of them trod carefully across the pebbled
beach in the darkness, almost staring in desperation at
each footstep lest they save themselves of the
Frenchmen laughing at them if they lost their balance.
Tossing their suitcases into the boat and clambering on
board, they noticed the same two operatives who had
picked them up.

"Good job gentlemen. We thank you so much!" and the
youngest one shook their hands in the boat as they
settled for the quick row out to their awaiting fishing
boat. Stitch murmured, "Vive La France," which made
the two French operatives smile.

Before they knew it, the old white-haired fisherman who
had taken them over was chugging the boat back to
Dungeness where, yet again, they were met by Rachel
in the bread van.

Without a word, Stitch and Archer got into the back of
the van but rather than sit on the sandbags that had
been used as makeshift seats on the initial journey to

the harbour, they lay on the floor and rested their heads on them instead.

Mercury opened the passenger door and settled himself on the passenger seat. Rachel with her hands on the steering wheel was smiling widely at him.

"Thank you boss, I knew you'd look after him."

Mercury sighed and rubbed his eyes in tiredness. He yawned and quietly replied, "Rachel, you would not believe how much that lad has grown. We didn't look after him, he looked after us."

She nodded, selected first gear and set off; gently releasing the clutch so as not to disturb their slumber and returned them to base.

When the van stopped with a squeal of the brakes, Archer and Stitch raised themselves slowly from the floor, groaning and rubbing their eyes. Mercury looked over his shoulder at them.

"Ok fellas. Off to bed. Briefing in the morning at zero eight hundred hours in the ops room."

Archer and Stitch through squinted eyes, nodded and slowly slid out of the back of the van with their suitcases. Before they closed the doors, Mercury called out, "Oh and fellas. Well done!"

Turning to Rachel, he held out his hand which she took and they shook gently.

"And thank you my dear for getting us there and back safely."

"Oh it was my pleasure." She smiled at him.

"I'm sure it was," he smiled back, knowing her particular interest in Archer.

Chapter 10: Leaving the nest.

Archer woke feeling fresh and very much alive. The joy of completing another task initially swept over him, but it was soon to be followed by a sense of grief. For some reason he couldn't fathom, he had taken quite a liking to Brusilov and had huge respect for the way he had accepted his death.

He washed, changed but being a little later than usual, he took a cup of tea and a couple of slices of toast to the operations room where, as was customary by this stage, he was greeted by Stitch as he opened the door to him. Archer, still chewing on a bit of the toast, acknowledged him, "Mmm…thanks comrade," he mumbled as he stepped through, spilling some of his tea on his foot again.

"Do come in," Stitch replied in his mock posh English accent again.

Mercury was already smiling at Archer from the other side of the table as Archer walked towards it. Stitch closed the door and joined Archer at the table as Mercury addressed them.

"Gentlemen. An excellent job. In fact, the best job I have ever been involved in and believe me gents, that's a lot of jobs. The French didn't have all the intelligence, that's for sure, especially about Brusilov's illness.

Nevertheless, they're delighted with the outcome and have tied up all the loose ends."

Archer continued to chew, noting that there was something different about the way Mercury was looking at him. There was almost a tinge of sadness in his eyes. "This is where we let you go my friend."

Archer stopped eating and paused. Swallowing the last piece of toast in his mouth, he looked at Stitch then Mercury.

"What do you mean?" he felt a certain panic rise in his stomach.

Stitch whispered to him, "I told you things were going to change after the French job."

Mercury continued, "Well, you can't stay here forever. This is just a training complex at the end of the day. You've completed a number of jobs successfully; we have absolute faith in your abilities and so it's time you became one of our many assets. We'll be setting you up with a house in a small market town called Devizes in Wiltshire and you will be tasked from there. A post office box will be allocated to you in the local post office where you will receive your instructions and also receive your pay. Check the box at least once a week. We'll telephone you for anything urgent. If you carry out a hit, we'll give you a post office box address where you are to send a sympathy card with the targets' name written inside. We will also give you the address of a local farmer who will provide you access to one of his barns which doubles up as a training complex, very much like this one only smaller, where you can practice your skills. He's on our payroll so he's secure but don't worry, we will be keeping you sharp with lots of work!"

Archer was lost for words and he looked pleadingly at Stitch then Mercury.

"But, but, will I ever work with you two again?"

It was Stitch who answered that one.

"No mate. You're an asset now and you're more than capable of working alone."

Mercury added, "I'll be in touch from time to time, just to make sure you're ok. Other than that, you integrate into life as normal as you can. Get to know your community and remember to keep any cover story you have as tight as you can. Travelling salesman is a good one and works well with the need for a post office box," he smiled and winked at him.

Archer was stunned. Stitch sniggered at him when he saw that the toast he was holding had started to droop. Archer felt lost for words. He knew this day would eventually come, but it all seemed so fast, so sudden and almost like he was coming of age. When he had composed himself, he blurted.

"Well, what can I say? Delighted that I've made the grade, but gutted I have to leave you two. You've both been a large part of my life."

"But now you're on your own my dear fellow," Mercury finished.

Stitch grabbed his right shoulder and gave it a friendly squeeze, "Well.....take care Archer. This is where I sod off to prepare for the next recruit. Keep up the good work mate," and at that, Stitch held out his hand and Archer took it firmly, trying desperately to hold back tears. They shook hands without saying a word. Stitch's eyes said it all; there was a compassion for Archer and a proudness of a job well done. He smiled warmly, released his grip and stepped out of the operations room leaving Archer and Mercury to have one last word. Archer turned to face Mercury, "Are you sure I'm ready?" he pleaded.

"Oh yes. Definitely."

He paused for a few seconds and sighed deeply.

"You know, it's a terrible, dirty business we're in. We deal with the scum of the earth in order to protect the masses and to the innocent eye what we do is cruel, ruthless, calculating and final. Our pay doesn't reflect the bigger picture, but it allows us to live handsomely as you've found out. At the end of the day, death comes to us all, so we may as well make the most of the rewards."

Archer raised his eyebrows and nodded.

"I know you pray, lad. Stitch told me. Don't let that go will you? We deal in blood and death and some would ask why we think we're above the law."

Archer immediately remembered Sandra's words before she walked out of the door.

"But, as you know, sometimes the law just can't catch the people we are tasked against. Now without allowing your head to grow, I have to tell you that the department is mighty impressed with you. They've never seen a man with such ability and neither have I. From the moment I met you, I knew you were going to be special."

"And so here we are," Archer proudly announced.

"Here we are," Mercury smiled at him, like a father who was proud of his son.

"Right. Rachel is going to transport you to your new home. She'll have all the details of your tasking arrangement; your training complex and she'll tell you how to integrate into society. She'll have documentation for you, such as passports, a national insurance number and so on so that you can prove who you are to banks, utilities et cetera. If you have any problems, write to the post office box that we'll set you up with."

"Ok thanks."

Mercury slowly walked around the desk and approached Archer, holding out his hand. Archer took it and felt the warmth flowing between them. To Archer, Mercury was the father he never had.

"Ok, bugger off now. Rachel is waiting outside. Grab your stuff and go and join her."

Archer smiled, turned and walked towards the door. He paused and turned to Mercury.

"Just one more thing before I go...."

Mercury waited for his question, a sarcastic grin appearing on his face as he prepared himself for whatever was coming next.

"What IS your name?"

Mercury laughed, snapping his head backwards, "What did I tell you?"

Archer nodded and grinned as he stepped out of the door, "I know, I know, names aren't important. Yeah, yeah I get it!" and as he walked out of the door, he could still hear Mercury laughing.

Archer walked out of the barn complex for the very last time. As he crossed the forecourt to the house, he saw Rachel sitting in the driving seat of the Vauxhall Viva that he had become accustomed to her driving. She waved quickly to which he returned in kind and entered the farmhouse to pack his belongings away along with his pistol, buried deep inside the suitcase.

He walked out of the bedroom but turned in the doorway to take one last look at the home he knew was only to be temporary, his heart felt heavy and he quickly walked away to the waiting car.

After placing his suitcase into the boot, he opened the passenger door and sat in the seat with a sigh, looking through the windscreen and not making eye contact with Rachel. Noting that for this last drive, he didn't have to wear a blindfold.

"You alright Adrian?" she asked.

"Yeah. I'll be fine. Got to leave the nest eventually, haven't I?"

"Well yes, but that's a good thing," she tried to reassure him.

"I know, I know. But I'm going to miss those two."

"They'll miss you too, especially Mercury, he's taken a real shine to you."

Archer pretended not to react and looked down at his lap.

"We'd better be off then," she said as she drove off away from the farm complex.

Archer glanced at the car's wing mirror and just managed to catch a glimpse of Mercury, standing outside the barn watching them leave.

They drove for a couple of hours, with conversation mainly centred on how Archer would live. Rachel waxed lyrical about the market town of Devizes.

199

"I used to live there. Oh, it's lovely! They have a market in the town centre and the countryside is gorgeous. There's everything you need there."

Archer was beginning to feel much better about himself and the split from the training complex as Rachel talked on about what was to become his normal life.

They arrived in Devizes and drove through it to the outskirts of the town, where Rachel pulled into the concrete drive of a small two storey red brick house that looked to be decades old. The drive was to the right-hand side of a small but well cared for front lawn, which had a rose border and Archer saw a large wooden shed with two large front doors that obviously doubled up as a garage at the end of the drive to the side of the house. Rachel turned the engine off and held up a set of keys.

"These are yours, good sir," she reached behind her to the back seat and took two large brown envelopes, passing them to Archer.

"One is your pay for the French job and the other is an information pack to get you started in your new life."

Archer peered inside his pay envelope and opened his eyes in surprise.

"Wow! That'll keep me going for a while," he smiled at her.

Rachel acknowledged his smile with a smile of her own, she adjusted herself in her seat and stammered,

"I...I...er....well, I wondered if you thought about getting yourself a girlfriend? I mean...well...I really like you Adrian. Would I have a chance at being your girl?"

Archer couldn't help himself from blushing and looked Rachel square in the eye.

"I can't Rachel. I've already lost someone I had fallen deeply in love with and I'm not going through that again. Ever. Out of respect for her and because of our work, I can't allow myself to be involved again."

Rachel pleaded with him, "But no man is an island, Adrian. You can't live the rest of your life alone, surely?"

"Rachel, that's something I can live with. I don't have friends back at home, I'm used to being on my own. Besides that, I just know I could never love anyone else the way I did with Sandra. It wouldn't be fair."

Rachel began to cry and sobbed gently, "I've fallen in love with you."

"Sweet Rachel."

Archer felt the compassion rise in his chest for her as he took her hand, "I have great admiration for you, the way you've been there for me and the others. I'm sure you can understand."

He didn't say anything else as he allowed Rachel to compose herself before they departed. When she had stopped crying and the sobs turned to heavy breathing, he smiled at her tear swollen face and she smiled back.

"I know you're right Adrian, but you can't blame me for trying."

Archer laughed and squeezed her hand briefly.

"Got to go," he smiled at her and got out of the car. Balancing the envelopes in his arms, he took his suitcase out of the boot with the same hand he had the keys in. He walked to the front door and placed his suitcase down as Rachel reversed the car out of the drive and onto the main road. She pointed the car in the direction from where they had come and looked at

Archer, the tears still gently rolling down her cheeks. She smiled and blew him a kiss. Archer smiled back and held his hand to his heart and watched as Rachel drove off, leaving him alone with his thoughts and his new home. When she was no longer in sight, he turned on his heels and took a look at his new home from the roof line down.

"Home sweet home then," he muttered to himself and inserted the key in the lock.

Chapter 11: Retford, Present day.

Archer had returned to his home in Retford from Italy in the usual convoluted way. He packed his meagre belongings and pistol into his suitcase in Lucca, got a taxi to the railway station and made his way through France by rail. He never forgot his counter surveillance skills, even though he had zig zagged his way through France to meet his fishing boat on the coast. A lifetime of carrying out this task meant it was second nature to him now. He still used the old trick of pretending to stumble at the step into the train carriage to see if anyone was watching him board, or not board as the case may be. There were many occasions when he felt uneasy about a certain passenger, so sometimes he would let them board the train then abstain from boarding it in order to catch a later one.

His method of transmitting an operation's success, so that his transport could be arranged, hadn't changed. Morse code is no longer used by any military, but his profession was separate from those government departments and was also utterly reliable. Archer hated the modern digital way of communicating which was open to cyber-attacks despite assurances from the providing companies, so when he was introduced to new techniques, he refused. The department obviously thought for some time and eventually agreed to make allowances to their best operative. Even at his age.

Archer finally arrived at Kings Cross railway station in order to catch the train to Leeds, stopping off at his home town of Retford. It was a journey he had taken hundreds, if not thousands of times over the decades and still he carried out the same checks to keep himself safe. When he took a suitable seat, close to an exit, facing the rest of the seats so that he could see who was ahead of him, he couldn't help the feeling of relief as he travelled closer to Retford. Archer still carried out his exercises each morning, keeping himself strong, but even at the age of seventy-seven, he had to fight the increasing tiredness as his body rocked gently to the motion of the train.

When he eventually arrived at Retford, he made his way to his family house and still smiled as he located his door key, slid it into the lock and made his way inside. As he opened the door, the familiar smells of the interior wafted over him and he immediately thought of the memories of his mother in the early days of his career. He longed to hear her calling out when she knew he had returned home and heard the key in the lock and the opening of the door. Longed to smell the aroma of her cooking and singing to herself as she did so. Despite his age, he always felt like the teenage Adrian whenever he returned home and also always felt the guilt of having lied to her for the rest of her life about his chosen profession. He also instantly thought about Sandra and still, to this day, had to fight back the tears of losing his one and only love. The pain.

He took a few steps into the hallway, left the keys in his coat pocket which he hung behind the door on the coat hooks and made his way to the kitchen. Slowly he made himself a strong cup of tea and sat at the kitchen table, which had never been replaced with its wooden chairs; cushions being the only thing that had been added to them.

"Well Mercury you old sod, that's another one. God rest you my friend," and he raised his cup in salute before taking a long sip and remembering his long dead friend. He remembered how as he had settled into life in Devizes, Wiltshire, he received a knock on the door after a couple of years of living there and had carried out a few operations for the department in between.

When he opened the door, he was delighted and bemused at seeing Stitch.

"Stitch! I didn't think I would see you again?!"

He held out his hand to which Stitch gripped it firmly, as a friend.

"Archer, great to see you again lad!" he smiled his usual crinkly smile, "But I don't come with good news I'm afraid."

"Come on in my friend, I'll put a pot on."

Stitch entered and took a look around the house from his position in the hallway as he wiped his shoes on a doormat. Archer closed the door and moved past him and into the kitchen.

"Wow Archer. Nice place, but not a single picture or photograph anywhere. We trained you well."

Archer replied from the kitchen as he filled the kettle with water, "Ha! That you did, that you did. Come on through mate."

Stitch made his way into the kitchen, still observing how little Archer had made any additions to the house. They had trained him not to display anything personal; anything that can be used by an enemy agent that would leave him open to bribery, blackmail or leave a friend or family member open to kidnap. Archer was happy with his memories anyway, so this was a simple task for him.

Stitch pulled a chair out from the kitchen table and waited for Archer to make the pot of tea.

Archer reached into a kitchen cupboard on the wall, grabbed two cups with saucers and placed them on the table. He made a pot of tea and then placed that in the middle of the table along with milk from the fridge. He then sat and poured out a cup for Stitch first, followed by himself.

"Impeccable manners," Stitch smiled at him.

"Mother did well," Archer replied as they both took a sip in unison, the sounds of slurping echoing around the kitchen.

"I've bad news," Stitch started.

"Oh…."

"It's Mercury. He's in hospital. I'm not going to beat about the bush here mate, he's dying."

Archer felt the thump of shock in his stomach.

"Shit! What's wrong?"

"Cancer. He had been complaining of a sore stomach, so our doctors got involved and it turns out he's riddled with it."

Archer was overwhelmed with the news and couldn't hide his worry from Stitch. He shifted uneasily in his chair and fought against the feeling of sheer panic in his body.

"Jesus Stitch. Where is he?"

"He's in the RAF Wroughton military hospital. It's just down the road from here. Archer, he's been asking for you, so I'm here today mate."

"Are you taking me to him?"

"Yes, when you're ready. Take your time, get that tea into you."

Archer sat and finished his tea; his mind was racing at the news and he had to prepare himself to be strong when he saw Mercury.

When Archer had finished his tea, long after Stitch who sat patiently, he placed his cup on its saucer and looked at Stitch.

"Right. Come on, let's go," he slapped his thighs in confidence as he stood.

"My car awaits," Stitch replied as he stood and together, they walked out of the house, Archer locking it behind him and Stitch drove them to the military hospital. They both carried out their usual checks as he drove. Archer took the wing mirror on his side and manoeuvred it so that he could see behind them.

They soon arrived at the hospital and Stitch led the way to a private wing, through a maze of corridors for which there were no route signs. The smell of detergent, the gleaming floors and the way doctors and nurses bustled about only added to Archer's distaste of the establishments.

Finally, they arrived at the ward that held Mercury, a set of locked double doors with a keypad the only obstacle that held them back. Stitch swiftly entered the numerical code on the push buttons and opened the door where they were both greeted by a nurse receptionist on the left-hand side behind a chest height desk.

"Hello gentlemen, who are you here to see?"

"Mercury," Stitch quickly answered.

"Code?" She smiled at him, raising her eyebrows in question.

"Sergei."

Archer raised his eyebrows in surprise at the choice of codeword.

The receptionist smiled, bowed her head to examine paperwork then looked at them both.

"Go right ahead. Second door on the right."

As they walked towards the door, Archer asked Stitch, "Have you seen him before today?"

"No mate. But I've been here plenty of times before."

The anticipation and worry of what he was about to see rose in Archer's stomach as they got closer to the door. Stitch entered first and Archer's view was blocked slightly by him as all he could see was a pair of feet sticking up from under a thick blue blanket. As he approached the bed, he looked into the eyes of Mercury and tried hard to stop himself from reeling in shock. Archer couldn't tell if the eyes had sunk into their sockets at his illness or whether it was because the skin on his face was so taught that it accentuated them. He was thin, so thin. His neck seemed to be the thickness of a drainpipe; the veins clearly visible running up to his head. The blanket covered most of Mercury's body up to the collar bones, but Archer could see that Mercury looked like he had been starved for over a month. The muscle on his shoulders and biceps had all but vanished, leaving tight skin over what was left of any mass. Bone protruded to the surface of the skin everywhere and Archer could only imagine what the rest of Mercury looked like. This shell of a man was far different to the tall, lithe, confident and extremely fit individual that Archer was used to.

Mercury, panting, smiled as best he could at the two of them as they walked to his bedside.

"Stitch! Archer!" he panted.

"Hiya boss," Stitch replied, trying to force a smile.

Archer couldn't help himself. He rushed past Stitch and tried his best to hug Mercury, without feeling like he was breaking him. His clumsy attempt was acknowledged by Mercury who gently laughed.

"Oh Archer you big softy," he patted Archer's arm as he held the hug for a few seconds.

Mercury smiled at Stitch, gently mocking Archer's compassion.

Archer released himself and stood back, fighting tears.

"Jesus Merc. I don't know what to say."

"It's ok son," Mercury whispered, "It comes to us all, remember?"

"How long have you known? Are you getting treatment?"

Mercury panted a few times to prepare an answer.

"Known for about six months. On morphine for the pain, but I'm finished."

Stitch looked at him and asked, "Finished?" looking for clarification, but knowing what Mercury was about to say.

"Finished treatment. Finished life."

Archer felt the first tear burning down his right cheek, which Mercury noticed.

"No tears my friend. It's been a good life."

"Good God Mercury, I can't help it. You've been like a father to me," Archer blurted, mucus running from his nose as he tried to control himself.

Mercury rasped out a small laugh, his lungs fighting for more oxygen, "Some father, eh?"

Stitch chuckled but it was more out of compassion.

Mercury continued, "Now. Keep doing the good work, keep looking after yourself and be proud of what you are doing. Both of you," he said, also looking at Stitch.

As Mercury struggled to breath, Stitch interjected.

"Oh....sorry boss by the way. We didn't bring any grapes!"

They all laughed. Like a small band of comrades and ultimately, warriors, they laughed.

After a few seconds, Mercury closed his eyes and his breathing started to steady itself as he fell into sleep.

Stitch and Archer found a couple of chairs and sat at his side for a few minutes, studying the man as he slumbered.

"How long has he got?" Archer whispered to Stitch.

"Don't know mate, but it's really not long."

Archer looked at Mercury as he peacefully slept and felt safe enough to cry.

Half an hour crept by as they sat in silence, reflecting on their own memories of Mercury when he awoke from his slumber. He gradually focussed on the two of them and smiled slightly.

"Right then, bugger off," his smile grew.

Stitch and Archer both smiled back at the remark and stood, looking at Mercury in their final act of respect.

"Don't let your guard down," Mercury managed to add and tried to raise his hand to salute them.

Stitch rested his left hand on Mercury's right shoulder and held it there, "Goodbye boss," he whispered.

When Stitch removed his hand, Archer moved forward, his face streaming with tears as he sniffed like a scolded child.

He bowed forward, trying once again to hug Mercury and whispered, "Farewell my good friend. I will never forget you," as he held the hug for a few seconds more. Mercury relaxed his hard emotionless exterior and allowed Archer to feel the closeness of their bond.

"Goodbye son. Be good."

Stitch hooked Archer's elbow gently and pulled him away slowly. Archer stood, looking down at Mercury for a few seconds unable to control his tears and sobs as Mercury looked back at him. Stitch gently turned Archer by the elbow and they walked towards the door. Stitch walked through but Archer turned in the doorway to take one last look at Mercury. As he stood and looked at him, still panting for breath, Mercury smiled one last time........and winked. Archer nodded and smiled with utter compassion and respect, saluted in his usual sloppy style and turned to walk through the door where Stitch was waiting for him.

Stitch drove back to Archer's house and the two of them sat in silence. Every now and then, Stitch looked across at him to see him sitting with his head bowed in reflection.

"He won't see the morning," Archer suddenly announced as Stitch parked up outside his house.

"I don't think so mate. You know, he was so proud to find you, he knew you were something special and we all knew he saw you as the son he never had."

Archer placed his face in his hands and cried even more.

"It's a funny world we live in, Stitch."

Stitch gave a little laugh at that, "Yep. We care about each other, but care very little about our targets," he looked across at Archer, smiling.

"I never did find out his name," Archer laughed through his sobs and tears.

"Ha! None of us did. Remember, names aren't important."

Archer composed himself, looked out of the car window to his new home and invited Stitch in for a while longer with a cup of tea.

"No thanks lad, I'd better be going. I've got a job on," Stitch smiled his usual wisened smile at Archer and tapped the side of his nose to signify the secrecy of the job. Archer reached across and they shook hands, holding each other's hands for a few seconds extra.

"Good to see you again comrade, Archer mocked in a Russian accent.

Stitch laughed, "Da! Dasvidaniya comrade!"

Archer stepped out of the car, turned and leaned in to see Stitch then raised his hand in farewell. Stitch returned with a quick wave and a crinkly smile before driving off, never to be seen again.

Chapter 12: The past returns.

Archer woke at his kitchen table, looked at his watch and realised he had fallen asleep for an hour which explained why his neck was aching.

He rose slowly from his chair and moved down the hallway where he picked up his suitcase and took it upstairs to his bedroom. He had moved into his mother's room a long time ago after buying the house, because it was larger, but there were still objects left in his childhood bedroom that he kept. His move back to the family home had been sanctioned by the department many years ago. As much as he enjoyed living in Devizes, it felt like a natural thing to return.

He sat at the edge of his bed with a groan, rubbed his neck and started to unpack. Placing his clothes in the wardrobe at the foot of the bed, the last thing he came to was his pistol. It was looking well worn, with rub marks here and there from handling but as he disassembled it yet again, he smiled to himself as the internals gleamed back at him. The barrel was perfect, the slide and action that chambered bullets were so well meshed that he had become so used to its reliability and had total confidence in it.

That evening he was feeling awake enough to treat himself to a meal out, so he walked his way through the town to his favourite restaurant in Cannon Square where he was a known customer. Come what may, they always gave him a table and this was no exception at

Frank's restaurant as he was greeted with the usual charm by the manager.

"Ah mister Archer! Do come in. Would you like your preferred table sir?" the manager asked. He was charming but Archer knew he was giving a performance and nodded a smile at the offer of his usual table. The manager, a tall, thin, bald-headed man, wearing black rimmed national health glasses walked over to the table with a menu, pulled out a chair and held his hand over it, inviting Archer to sit. He sat and smirked at the real reason it was his favourite table. There were only two chairs and he always sat on the chair with his back to the rear wall of the restaurant, close to the kitchen and fire exits as he had always been trained. If an enemy agent were to burst into the restaurant, Archer could make a quick escape through the kitchen, where he could also have access to weapons. The chef's knives would be razor sharp and very worthy of wielding at a determined opponent if they chased him that far. The restaurant only had a few customers which, being midweek, was normal.

Archer ordered his favourite meal of salmon, potatoes and long stem broccoli with a homemade Hollandaise sauce, followed by the chef's very own apple pie and whipped cream. He washed it all down simply with water, not wanting to relax with wine until a few weeks had passed since his operation in Italy. He needed to stay alert for that length of time and even then, he would resist the urge to relax completely. When he had eaten, he paid using cash, leaving a very healthy tip which always excited the manager who wished him a pleasant evening and, "Do come back soon, we're always delighted to receive you."

Archer returned home and as he entered his family home; he felt the usual overwhelming loneliness when the dark rooms and the stillness welcomed him. Even at his late stage in life, his memories of Sandra were still very real and he walked slowly up the stairs using the handrail as a balance, the sadness washing over him. He always wondered what life would have been like if Sandra had been in his life. He wondered if they would have gotten married and had children and tried to have some kind of normality to their lives, but then he totally understood her reason for leaving him. Not once did he blame his career choice; he believed in it totally.

He slid into bed, crying a little at his feeling of loneliness and drifted into a deep sleep.

The following morning, Archer took a long hot bath, changed into a v-neck blue jumper, white shirt and grey tie, dark grey trousers and black shoes then slipped his pistol into the small of his back, inside his trouser belt after having checked it again. He walked out of the house, locking the door behind him, in order to take a walk into town where he could check his post office box. He hoped, as he always did, that he would find a letter to say his services were no longer required by the department, especially at his age, but he knew it was unlikely for now. It suited his masters to have assets of all ages and he knew that men and women of his age group would certainly be overlooked by their targets by being stereotypically assessed as unable to perform the task in hand.

It was another beautiful, sunny day with a slight breeze and not overly warm. He had walked down the row of houses to his street and was about to turn left to head for the direction of the town, when he was aware of a young woman on the other side of the road. She was wearing blue jeans with a pink, long sleeved cotton top and brown walking boots. She was trim and Archer could tell she looked after herself as her athletic frame was visible despite the clothing. Her hair had been dyed blonde as he could see dark roots and was tied back in a ponytail. To the normal eye, she was just an attractive young lady, but to Archer there was something extra about her and it made him feel uneasy. She looked at him as he walked, albeit very briefly, but Archer noticed it and continued to walk on. As he slowly walked towards the town centre, he became calmly aware that he could see her matching his pace on the opposite side and felt the hair stand on the back of his neck from the feeling of being observed. Archer walked on. He decided to abandon his plans and started to take a route that would take him out of the town, towards Eaton and the spot where he had killed his father all those years ago. If she was an enemy agent, he would have the opportunity in such a rural spot to be able to take her on and dispatch her. As he planned the assassination, he tried to work out who she could be. He wondered if his most recent job in Lucca had borne consequences. Had Ricci noticed Archer and had tasked his own team to follow him before he assassinated him? Had other agents from previous jobs somehow found out about him and managed to track him to Retford? Archer knew he and the department had been absolutely meticulous with his counter surveillance skills and his identity had been hidden with every overseas operation. The worry began to eat at him.

As he walked, he decided to deploy an old trick and stopped in his tracks to look down at his laces. He immediately squatted down to pretend to re-tie his laces and as he stooped, he quickly looked over his right shoulder to the other side of the road. The woman had vanished. He stood, looked over to where she had been, then looked back down the road from where they had walked, but could see no sign of her.

"Shit," he whispered to himself.

He returned to the centre of Retford, his senses at full alert as he got closer to the post office. Ducking into shop entrances and looking back a few seconds later, checking window reflections, changing direction and all the other movements he took didn't reveal the young lady. He checked his post office box and only found his payment for the Ricci job, which he stuffed into his coat inside pocket. There was no other envelope and so the department didn't have an operation for him, yet.

He returned home, took his coat off and stood in the living room at the front of the house, standing back in the shadows to observe the street from the bay window. He stood for about fifteen minutes, hoping he would see the woman again to confirm she was following him, but she didn't appear. The department had a contact number, should he need to use it, if he felt compromised and the wheels would be set into motion to keep him safe. He decided against it though and resolved himself to accept that this could be his last job. It wouldn't be sanctioned by his masters, but it would be acceptable to them. He'd had many years to master his skills, so he was more than confident he could complete this task himself.

He took one last look and turned to go to the kitchen for a cup of tea and as he did so, he looked at the battered sofa that replaced the one his father used to throw abuse, smoke cigarettes and drink himself to a stupor from. Looking at it with disdain, he went to his bedroom to safely dispose of his pistol.

Archer spent the rest of the day reading an old book in the kitchen, listening to the radio and thinking about his new adversary. He made his evening meal, all the while thinking about the new dynamic in his life and he smiled at the challenge. Before he knew it, he was in bed, late at night and drifted into a deep sleep.

When he woke in the morning, he washed, changed and headed downstairs and slowly crept into the living room. He quickly pulled back the bay window curtains and stepped back into the semi darkness thrown into the room by the net curtain beneath. He checked all the angles he could but couldn't see the woman at first glance. He waited long enough to make sure she wasn't there then moved into the kitchen to make his usual toast and tea for breakfast. He settled into a kitchen chair and started to chew on his toast, the radio tuned into BBC radio 4 so that he could hear the political debate and find out what is going on in the world. He instantly stopped eating when he heard three soft knocks on the door. Nobody called for him, nobody, so the surprise at hearing these knocks hit home. He waited to see if he could hear voices, stood from the table and looked down the hallway to the front door. The slight gap at the bottom of the door showed the shadow of only one set of legs, which seemed to be shifting weight from one foot to the other as the shadow waited for his response. He quietly removed a small kitchen knife, which he kept razor sharp, from its block on the kitchen worktop and stalked down the hallway. Three soft knocks sounded again as he got halfway down and holding the knife behind his back, he unlocked the door and peered around the gap. His breath almost left him as the young woman from yesterday appeared before him. He gripped the knife, ready to swing it into action, focusing on her neck which would be his primary target. She still wore her brown walking boots and blue jeans but was wearing a light blue jumper under a green Barbour jacket and carrying a large black handbag. He looked into her eyes, noticing how grey and incredibly pretty she was but didn't notice any malice in her. He guessed her age to be about thirty or early thirties at the maximum.

"Oh hello…." she leaned in a little, "I'm really sorry to trouble you and drop in on you completely out of the blue like this," she raised her eyebrows in apology. Archer still gripped the knife, knowing this was a good distraction technique.

"Yes, can I help you?" he croaked.

"Well. I don't know. I am actually tracing my family tree, which has led me to this address and I'm trying to trace the former occupants."

Archer feigned confusion, "Well, I'm sorry, I don't know how I can help you?"

"This may sound weird," she continued, "But my grandmother worked with a lady who lived here...Claire Archer?"

Archer was stunned. He felt his knees weaken but his grip on the door kept him upright. He had to think fast, but his mind was lost in the memories at the sound of his mother's name. He relaxed the grip on the knife. He knew so much about people's body language that he could tell this woman was genuine, so he took a leap of faith.

"Would you like to come in?" he asked.

"I don't want to intrude, but if I could have a moment of your time, I would really appreciate it."

"Yes, do come in, young lady."

He opened the door in the same movement of placing the knife in his pocket.

She stepped in, almost bowing her gratitude to him, "Oh thank you so much."

"Come through to the kitchen, I'll make us a pot of tea."

As she breezed past Archer, he could smell the same perfume he had smelt on Sandra all those years ago and again his knees felt weak. There was something about this lady that was familiar yet didn't sit right with him. She walked in front of him towards the kitchen and as Archer approached the living room door, he took the knife out of his pocket and threw it onto the sofa: a movement and sound she didn't see nor hear.

She entered the kitchen and waited for Archer. She looked around at the sparse walls and the lack of personal items that Archer didn't have.

"Wow! This is like stepping back in time!"

He laughed a little, "I live on my own. Always have, so I don't bother with things like that. Don't even put up Christmas decorations," he smiled at her.

"Don't blame you. Such a fuss."

"Please," he beckoned towards a kitchen chair, "Take a seat."

She thanked him and sat down with a straight back, smiling and watching as Archer made a pot of tea.

"I'm really sorry to drop in out of the blue like this," she repeated sheepishly.

Archer placed the pot of tea, milk, cups and saucers in front of her and his place at the table and poured for her then him when he had sat down.

"Thank you," she smiled. She lifted her cup after adding a bit of milk, took a sip and carefully placed it back in the saucer.

Archer took a sip, studying her eyes. Placing his cup carefully back down, he asked, "Did I see you yesterday?"

"Yes," she said, "I'm so sorry. I couldn't pluck up the courage to approach you, so I went home and thought about it."

"Ah!" Archer smirked at how that simple action may well have saved her life.

"So….you want to know about Claire Archer?"

"Yes. My name is Sally Clements and like I said, I'm tracing my family tree and there's a gap here."

She brought out a laptop and unfolded it on the kitchen table. When the laptop was running, she opened the files she had that traced her tree.

Archer's heart started to race for a reason he couldn't believe and was almost too frightened to comprehend as he studied the information on the laptop.

She showed him the lines of the family tree on the screen and pointed to her grandmother.

"That's my grandma. Sandra Walker."

She pointed to an old black and white photograph of Sandra, exactly the way Archer remembered her. Archer sat back in his chair, his heart pounding, the weakness from his knees suddenly enveloped his whole body and he started to shake with adrenaline.

"She's…your…grandmother?" he asked, this time his eyebrows were raised in wild questioning.

"Yes. Now, she married my step granddad, Richard Wilcox when my own mother, Julie Wilcox, was five years old, but she never spoke a word about my biological grandfather. My mother married Andrew Clements and had a daughter. Me! I asked about my biological grandfather when I was old enough and curious enough and my grandmother, Sandra, said they split under bad circumstances and never wanted to talk about it."

Archer was lost for words as he looked at the names on the laptop screen and couldn't find anything to say.

"So, I know she talked about her work in the factory and how she was great friends with Claire Archer. Apparently after my grandma split with the boyfriend, she maintained her friendship with Claire right up until she passed away ten years ago."

Archer couldn't help the emotion welling up inside him, his heart pounded so much that he felt like it was going to burst through his chest.

"When we were clearing up her effects, we found this old photograph of my grandma and I scanned it into my family tree."

"Sandra married a man who took on the role of father. Did your mother ever know who her real father was?"

"No. That's the thing. It was just not talked about. I've been trying to trace this Claire Archer and it has led me to this house."

Archer rubbed his eyes and stood from the table. He walked over to the kitchen window and held himself up at the sink in front of it. Bowing his head, he couldn't help the tears streaming down his cheeks. The pain of losing Sandra was matched with knowing that she was dead and before him was his granddaughter. She had had a daughter that he obviously never knew about and the sadness mixed with joy utterly confused him. He had never felt emotions like this, not even from Mercury's death.

"Are you ok?" she asked him, seeing that he was visibly shaken.

Archer took time to compose himself, controlling the flow of tears and coughing his throat clear. He turned to look at her.

"I'm ok. I can fill the gaps in for you," he croaked.

"Oh! Great!" she shifted with excitement in her chair.

Archer sat back down and touched the photograph of Sandra on the screen with his fingertip, stroking her face.

"I knew Sandra. Claire Archer was my mother," he smiled at her with reddened eyes.

"Your mother!? I knew she lived here, but I thought the house would have been sold on by now?" she asked, her eyes wider at the realisation that they were related.

"My name is Adrian Archer. When I was earning enough money, I bought the house with cash I had saved up and it's my name on the deeds. My father didn't leave a penny to mum when he died, but mum stayed on here, even after my father's death and lived happily ever after, so to speak. She passed away very peacefully twelve years ago in Bassetlaw Hospital and I've always lived here, so it felt right to keep it in the family name."

"Soooo, you're telling me that YOU are my biological grandfather?"

"It would seem so," he nodded at her, the tears flowing down his cheeks as he smiled warmly at her, "I can't believe it, after all these years. I never knew Sandra had a daughter. Our daughter."

He looked into Sandra's eyes in the photograph.

"Oh God, I loved her so much."

Sally reached into a pocket of the laptop bag and with her forefinger and thumb she slowly pulled out a photograph of a young Archer, smiling at the camera with a large oak tree and rhododendron bush behind him.

"My God, this is you," she said softly, smiling at Archer with fondness.

Archer took it from her gently and remembered their day in Clumber Park, then cried more; his chest bursting from the memories.

"My Sandra. My love. My only love."

Sally allowed him to reflect for a while. She smiled at her newly found grandfather and studied his face. She realised they had features which were the same. The same shaped nose and eyebrows and she felt a closeness at having closed a chapter in her family tree with Archer.

"You never married?" she asked.

"No," Archer replied, not keeping his eyes off Sandra's photograph, "I couldn't after Sandra." he added.

"Oh wow! Sandra must have felt she needed the security of her husband. I doubt she ever lost the love for you."

Sally tried to console him. She felt sad for his lifetime of loneliness.

"Well, we had to split, unfortunately. But I never stopped loving her. She was the only love I had or wanted. Nothing would have compared."

Sally's curiosity heightened and she felt compelled to ask, "Why did you two split up?"

"I had to travel a lot for work and it didn't sit well with her. That's all I can say Sally."

"Oh that's terrible. I'm so sorry for you."

She looked at the photograph of Archer and she touched his forearm, "You were such a handsome chap too," she smiled at him.

Archer laughed quietly, "Sandra was beautiful," as he stroked the photograph one more time.

He sat back and looked at Sally, realising too that they had similar features and she had Sandra's figure. He felt a sudden sense of pride for Sally, mixed with the emotion of a rekindled love for Sandra.

"Well, that's completed that part of the tree," she shrugged her shoulders in glee.

They sat and drank more tea as Archer tried to grasp the situation he suddenly found himself in. From nowhere, he was now a grandfather to Sally and she was obviously delighted.

They talked and drank for some time later when Sally checked her watch.

"Oh goodness, is that the time, I really must get home."

"Do you need to be home for your husband or something?" Archer quizzed.

"No, my dog Chippy. I'm a bit like you, I live on my own, but it's way past his dinner and walk time."

"Chippy?" Archer enquired.

"Yes, the name of my dog. Everyone loves a Chippy don't they?" she smiled, referring to the traditional English meal of fish and chips which made Archer laugh.

She closed the lid of the laptop, slid it back inside the bag and stood. Archer stood out of politeness and also to see her out of the door.

"Well Sally, I suppose I was the last piece of the puzzle?"

"Definitely. Wow..." she paused, "I know this is a bit sudden for you, but could we meet again? I'd really like to get to know you."

Archer was delighted and his eyes lit up as he smiled at her, "Yes definitely!"

"Well, how about I buy you lunch tomorrow?" Sally asked.

"That would be lovely."

"Ok good. I'll call here for one o'clock if that suits?"

"Certainly does," and they walked slowly down the hallway and got to the front door.

Archer opened the door and as she got halfway through, she turned and kissed him on the cheek.

"See you tomorrow grandad," she smiled cheekily at him.

Archer felt the glow of warmth from someone he now knew was family and allowed the excitement of this knowledge to sweep over him.

"Ok granddaughter, I'll see you tomorrow," and he watched her walk down the street towards her parked car. The funny thing was, as she approached her car, she gave a quick wave to him that was exactly the same way Sandra used to wave to him when she left to tend to her grandmother. He reeled in surprise and waved back. When she had driven off, he closed the door and returned to the kitchen. He finished off the pot of tea in silent reflection as his memories of Sandra washed over him.

Chapter 13: The new family.

Archer's mind was busy with memories of Sandra as he bustled about the house the next day and was aware of the growing excitement of meeting Sally. There was a sense of his life being complete, knowing that he had family; a blood line, someone he could bequeath his fortune to and the family house. All of these thoughts cascaded in his mind as he washed, shaved with his traditional straight razor and tidied himself up. He changed into his dark grey trousers, grey shirt, dark blue tie, dark brown jumper and his well-worn, but well-kept black shoes. His newspaper delivery was on time as usual, so he sat at his kitchen table reading the paper, eating his toast and drinking his usual pot of English tea. As he read the newspaper, he was aware he couldn't stop himself smiling. He was also aware of the little voice in the back of his head.

"Don't drop your guard!"

He chuckled at the voice and muttered, "Relax Mercury. All is in hand."

As he sat thinking of Sandra and his mother and keeping the pot of tea topped up, he had lost all track of time when he heard three soft knocks on the front door. In a flash, the rush of adrenaline shot through his body and for a fleeting moment, he was the young Archer from all those decades ago reacting to the same soft door knocks Sandra used to do. He checked his watch; it was quarter to one, then he checked the gap of light at the bottom of the front door to see the shadow of one pair of legs. Still, he couldn't take the chance and he walked into the living room so that he had a view of who was at the front door from the side of the bay window and instantly relaxed as he saw Sally standing, waiting for him to answer the door. He paused for a few seconds as he studied her, noting the similarities they had and the mannerisms she shared with Sandra. She was wearing a lovely purple polo neck jumper under a light brown wool coat, blue jeans and thick heeled brown boots. He walked into the hallway and opened the door to her, subtly checking the background as he greeted her.

"Ah granddaughter! Come in, come in," he smiled at her.

"Thanks granddad!" she smiled at him as she stepped into the hallway.

"So, we have a lot to talk about. Let me grab my coat and we'll head out. I left it upstairs, two ticks," he said Sally waited, looking around the sparse hallway as Archer made his way upstairs and into his bedroom. He had left his coat on his bed on purpose; he was deciding all morning as to whether he should trust Sally and not take his pistol or trust the voice in the back of his head. He looked to the drawer where he kept his pistol amongst his socks and decided to relax and not take the weapon. He grabbed his coat and headed downstairs to a smiling, patient Sally.

"Ready?" she asked.

"Yep, come on then. I'll take you to Frank's."

They exited the house and took the usual route Archer took to Frank's restaurant, all the while chatting small talk, leaving the important stuff to chat about over their lunch.

The manager greeted Archer in his usual pleasant way and enquired as to who the enchanting lady was accompanying him.

"This Frank, believe it or not, is my granddaughter."

Sally smiled and held out her hand, "Pleased to meet you."

"Oh, the pleasure is mine. Please, let me show you to an adequate table. I never knew you had a granddaughter Mr Archer; this is wonderful."

Archer knew he was saying that because it added an extra mouth to the final bill but smiled in politeness.

They were shown to a table, close to the wall and a few metres from the window. Not Archer's usual safe spot, but he went with it anyway.

When they had perused the menu and made their orders, Sally opened the ever-important conversation.

"So how did you and Sandra meet?"

Archer swallowed hard as he was thrown back in time and the memories came through. He felt disappointed with himself that he would have to lie to her, but knew he had no choice.

"Sandra was my first and last love. We met when I came home from a break in my engineer training and we hit it off immediately. She was the most beautiful woman I had ever seen."

"Was it love at first sight?" Sally beamed at him, her eyes wide in excitement.

"Yes....I believe it was, Sally."

"Gosh, it's so sad that you both split up. I can see she meant so much to you. And you never married?"

"No Sally. I guess I'm old school. I couldn't see myself with anybody else and as much as we split up, I still felt a deep love for her that couldn't be replaced. I never really got over her."

"Do you think she knew that?"

Archer thought about the way Sandra had left the house and held his reply for a few seconds, hoping it wouldn't sound boastful.

"I think she did. Even after our blazing argument, I think we still loved each other."

"But you never saw her again?"

"No. The damage had been done. My mother, Claire, was upset but she understood. I had said things in the heat of the moment, but there was no going back and so I concentrated on my work."

"For the rest of your life," Sally continued his sentence.

"Yes," Archer replied and looked down at the table in sadness.

"So…" Archer looked at her, "Tell me about your family. What do your mother and father do?"

"Dad is a businessman. He's in sales, but I'm not quite sure what. I think it's financial products like life insurance or something like it. He's fifty-five and looking forward to retirement. Mum is a housewife because dad provides very well for us. She's fifty-three and happy enough."

"A housewife? Now THAT is old school," Archer laughed.

Sally laughed along with him, "Some things are best done the old school way! Mum is happy enough."

"Have you got any photographs of them?" he asked.

Sally took her mobile phone off the table that she had placed there, upside down and thumbed through it, stopping at a suitable photograph.

"Yes, here. This is us, last Christmas in our living room," she said, turning the phone round to him.

Archer studied the photograph, noticing that Sally's smile was the same as her fathers. He was a stocky man with a bald head and a pock marked right cheek from old acne scars, making him very distinctive. Her mother even looked very happy, with long wavy hair, high cheekbones and perfect make up.

"Do you get to see them much?" he asked.

"Well dad is away sometimes, so he'll call me and we meet up for lunch and I see mum every week."

"What about you? What do you do to keep your dog fed?"

She smiled at the realisation that Archer had remembered she kept a dog, "Well I'm in I.T. That's Information Technology for you old school types. You know? Computers and stuff?"

Archer coughed a laugh, "Yes I'm fully aware of all that stuff, but I just don't use it. Even though I'm retired…." he lied, "….I prefer to pick up a good book and listen to the radio."

"You prefer the simple life then?" she asked.

"You could say that."

Their meals were presented and they talked as they ate. Archer felt very relaxed in Sally's company and the feeling was entirely mutual.

Archer finished eating as did Sally, so they continued to talk.

"Anyone special in your life Sally? Any plans for marriage? Children?"

Sally wiped the side of her mouth with her napkin, "Ooh no. I'm thirty, but I've no plans for anything like that at the moment. My work and the dog are keeping me more than occupied."

"Where do you live? We haven't discussed that."

"Just outside Mansfield, down the road really."

"Oh, so you're nearby, that's great!" Archer said with excitement.

"Indeed!" She smiled a beautiful smile at him, which really warmed Archer, "I'm so lucky to have found you." she added.

"The feeling is mutual."

They continued to talk and before long, Sally saw the time and announced that she had to leave.

Archer paid the bill despite Sally's protests and they walked back to his house. Sally was entirely comfortable talking about the private details of her life with him and she too couldn't help the smile that seemed to be permanently there as she got to know her long lost grandfather. They arrived at the house, Archer constantly checking their background, never dropping his guard and he was delighted to hear Sally say, "Grandad, can I keep in touch? Maybe see you each week and treat you to lunch?"

"Of course my dear, yes, of course. I would love that, thank you."

"Oh, I have something for you…" she said as she located her purse in her handbag by her side. She brought out the photograph of Sandra that she had scanned on her laptop and presented it to Archer.

"I thought you might like that."

He took the photograph and studied it, holding it and trying hard to stop his hand from shaking. She was beautiful and the sadness of missing her rose from his stomach. Fighting the tears of joy of receiving this gift, he managed to splutter, "Thank you. Thank you so much."

Seeing his bloodshot eyes, she leaned forward and gave him a puckered kiss on his cheek and Archer felt humbled. She squeezed his arm in sympathy, turned and walked down the street to her parked car and as she opened the door to enter it, she turned and gave Archer the trademark quick wave.

Archer felt his heart thump hard; she looked so much like Sandra when she waved at him and he stood to watch her leave, waving gently to her.

Sally drove off and she waited until she had turned the corner from Whitehall Road before she burst into tears. She too had felt the sadness of a lost love that happened decades ago and felt overwhelming sympathy for her grandfather as she tried to focus on her driving. Her mind was a kaleidoscope of images of the young Archer and Sandra, who to all intents and purposes were very much enjoying life before their split. As much as she was curious to the details of their parting, she knew it wouldn't be helpful to enquire deeper. She also felt incredibly happy and grateful that she had managed to find him. She drove on, all the while thinking about her achievement and arrived back at her terraced house before she knew it.

She parked on the road outside it, blending into the long column of cars parked outside their respective houses and reached for her mobile phone. She called her mother and told her about the discovery of Archer.

"Darling, that's wonderful! You've found my real dad, well done! Have you told your father?"

"No not yet, you're the first one I've told mum."

"Well, give him a ring and let him know Sally. This is so exciting!"

Sally smiled, "I will mum. I'm so happy!"

"I bet and while you're talking to him, can you remind him that I'm still alive?"

Sally paused as she tried to figure out the emotion of that last statement, determining if she was joking or being serious.

"Aw mum, you know dad is a busy man."

"There's busy my dear and there's busy."

Sally laughed but didn't hear it returned, so they talked briefly about her dog and ended the conversation with a promise to see each other at the weekend.

Sally took a deep breath as she looked at her contacts list on her phone and scrolled down to her father. She selected his number and waited to hear him answer.

"Yes?" he sharply answered.

"Hi dad, how are you?" she asked with an excited tone to her voice, almost begging him to listen.

"Fine. What do you want?" he gruffed.

"You know I'm doing the family tree and there was a gap with my biological grandfather?"

"Oh, that shit, yeah go on."

Sally was instantly disappointed with his usual reaction to anything she did, "It's not shit dad, I found him."

"So?"

Sally paused for a few seconds, composing the response in her mind and she selected the only one she could give to his reaction.

"D'you know what dad? Fuck you. I'm sick of your shit. Nothing I do is of any interest to you, is it?!"

He started to laugh and replied with all sarcasm, "Oh no, please tell me. Please tell me who this long-lost old retard is. I'm dying to find out," he continued laughing as he ended his sentence.

Sally put venom into her voice, "He's mum's biological dad, my biological grandad and he's more of a man than you'll ever be!"

He laughed louder then lowered his voice to her, "Just remember one thing my dear. You were just an accident."

Sally screamed down the phone, "Mum sends her love too, but fuck knows why!"

"Yeah, yeah…" he calmly replied then abruptly ended the call.

Sally sat in her car with the emotion of finding Archer being overtaken with the hatred of her father. She leaned forwards, bowed her head and cried hard into her lap, smacking her mobile phone with her fingers as though it was her father's face. A passing man walking his dog knocked on the window, his face a picture of concern as she looked at him. He mouthed, "Are you alright?" to which Sally nodded and raised a hand in thanks. She couldn't focus on him because of the tears flooding her eyes, but she showed her gratitude to the figure.

After a few minutes, she composed herself, took a deep breath and entered her house to be greeted by her brown Springer Spaniel who wildly wagged his tail and bounced at her knees.

Sally bent down and hugged her dog who had instantly brought her out of her bad mood after talking to her father.

"Chippy, it'll be fine, all fine," she smiled as the dog licked at her face and she tried to avoid it.

"Dad must be busy, he'll come round to the idea of grandad."

Chapter 14: Bloodline.

A couple of weeks went by and Archer met Sally a few times during that period. He was as excited to learn about Sally's life and family as Sally was to find out about his life and the countries he had been to. He was relaxed in her company but not relaxed enough to expose his complete identity and his chosen line of work. There was no point; he didn't want to lose Sally in the same manner as losing Sandra and so he spoke in general terms about those countries.

Sally spoke politely about her father, hiding how she really felt about him and giving his attitude the excuse that he was a busy man and under a lot of pressure.

It was a lovely, sunny Thursday morning in June when he did his usual check of the post office box and as he gave a sloppy salute to the staff, he opened the box and pulled out his mail. Along with all the other bits and pieces, he recognised the thick A4 sized envelope from the department which meant he had an impending job. Someone, somewhere, at some time was going to lose their life at his hands and he sighed heavily when he saw it.

"Not again," he muttered, "I'm getting too old for this." He turned on his heels and headed straight back to his house to examine the documents that he placed inside his hessian shopping bag.

When he returned home, he made himself a cup of tea and spread all the mail out on the kitchen table. There was a couple of bills, some advertising leaflets and then the envelope which stared at him, waiting for him to open it. He sighed once more, grabbed the envelope and ripped it open. The first document he read was a handwritten letter from his superior or superiors, whoever they were, congratulating him on decades of service and informing him this was to be his last job before they officially considered him as retired. He felt a huge weight fall from his shoulders and was jubilant at the thought of living the rest of whatever years he had left, with his new family. A normal life.

There were six photographs of a man, followed by the usual written document detailing who he was, his address, his movements, accomplices and activities. He read the profile before looking at the photographs and grimaced as he read the details.

"So, we have a mister Chapman, a fifty-five-year-old paedophile, child murderer, rapist and illegal firearms dealer. Child murderer?" he muttered to himself, inquisitive as to what his target had done. He read down the document and almost shuddered with anger at the information in front of him.

"Chapman is responsible for child pornography," he read aloud to himself, "Smuggling children, mainly from Africa and releasing them to the ring of men who exploit them for which he is paid a large sum of money. A nine-year-old girl escaped from the makeshift film studio they use and he is widely believed to have recaptured her then killed her as a message to the others."

He thumbed through the rest of the documents, noting how many firearms he had smuggled in through many European countries and reading about all his activities. "If ever a man deserved me knocking on his door, this man is it," he said to himself.

He tidied the written documents together, placed them down on the table then lifted a photograph of Chapman to study his new target.

It was when he focussed on the photograph that the gravity of the situation he now found himself in hit him hard in the chest. The fifty-five-year-old man, known as Chapman, was the father of Sally. The tell-tale identifier being the deep, pock mark scars dotted around his cheek. But there was no mistaking the other features he remembered from Sally's photograph on her mobile phone.

"Oh my God!"

Suddenly his mind was racing with emotion tinged with panic. Did Sally know what her father was really up to? "No! Of course not Adrian!" he scowled.

"Chapman? Why Chapman and not Clements?" he pondered. He wondered why the department's intelligence had not included his real name, but then he wasn't surprised when he remembered the words from Mercury, "Names aren't important."

He wanted to contact the department to tell them of his emotional and family connection to this case, but he knew that would fall on deaf ears. He also remembered the other advice from Mercury all those years ago, "There's always a bigger picture."

And the advice, he knew, was entirely correct. Everything he said was perfectly correct. He thought about his plan for a while, then packed all the photographs away and took them upstairs to his bedroom, hiding them deep in the old suitcase filled with clothes where he also kept his pistol. Taking the pistol, he checked its operation again, "Time to carry out another act my friend," he said to himself, as he checked the tightness of the silencer screwed onto the muzzle of the barrel and replaced it in the suitcase.

He returned downstairs to the kitchen, made another pot of tea and sat, planning his final operation. He could take the harder path and finalise the intelligence file by adding his own surveillance, but he decided to make the parts fit by subtly asking others to do some of the work for him. If he could get the target to come to him rather than the other way around, his final hit could be his masterpiece.

A few days later, Sally arrived at his house bang on time for the two of them to take a walk into town and grab a bite to eat for lunch. Yet again, they entered Frank's to be greeted by the owner himself, making his patronising but friendly small talk which Archer tolerated and they were shown to their usual table as prescribed by Frank. As they made themselves comfortable, Archer started a serious conversation.

"Sally, I have something very important that I would like you to consider."

Sally was puzzled but she could see the seriousness in his face.

"Yes, ok, go ahead grandad."

"I've gone through life not knowing that I had a bloodline, but this is now a wonderful answer to a question which has followed me throughout my life. So, I need you, as my granddaughter, to consider my proposition very seriously," he paused to add dramatic effect.

"Yes, I promise I will. What's wrong?" Sally showed deep panic.

"Relax, it's a good thing," he said.

"I have a certain amount of money saved over the years and I'll never have it spent by the time I pass away," he smiled.

Sally relaxed and dropped her shoulders in relief, "Oh thank God. I thought you were going to tell me you are ill or something dreadful."

Archer laughed a little, "No, nothing like that. I'm fighting fit. But it would make me very happy if I could name you in my will as the sole benefactor to my estate. Please?"

"Grandad, I've really only just found you and, at the end of the day, mum is your biological daughter. Surely she should be named in your will?" she almost pleaded with him.

"I know, I know. But in reality, you are the one who found me, not your mother. She more than likely had her reasons for not tracking me down, but you're the one who did the work and found the courage to find me. You are my bloodline and this will help me as much as it will help you."

Sally smiled sweetly at him and sat back in humility. She thought for a few seconds, smiling at how sweet her grandad is to her.

"Yes of course, I agree. How can I disagree? You're right, you are blood so I suppose it's only natural. But I'm paying for lunch!" she laughed at him.

"Brilliant. It's a deal!" Archer laughed back at her.

They were served their meals and ate heartily. Even to Frank, the banter and chatting between the two of them gave the impression to the unknowing that they had known each other for a very long time.

Sally and Archer finished their meal; Sally paid as she requested and they walked slowly back to Archer's house. Sally had hooked her arm through her grandad's as they walked and talked. When they arrived at the house, Archer asked Sally to come inside for a minute extra.

"I have something for you....."

"Oh, ok," she sounded surprised.

Archer opened the front door and stood to one side out of chivalry. When Sally was in the hallway, Archer closed the door behind them and asked her into the kitchen.

They both moved into the kitchen, Sally first and she looked at the kitchen table to see a thick brown envelope.

Archer moved past her and took the envelope and turned to her, holding it out.

"Please consider this as a gift and my way of saying thank you for finding me. I can't tell you how much you mean to me, so I hope this will help you out."

Sally looked entirely bemused as she gently took the envelope out of his hand.

"What is this grandad?"

"Open it," he smiled at her.

Sally opened the envelope to find it filled with cash. Her eyes opened wide in surprise and her mouth fell open.

"There's ten thousand pounds in that."

Sally started to protest, but Archer was having none of it, raising a hand to stop her.

"Now, before you say anything else young lady, this is non-negotiable. It would please me greatly to know this is going to help you out. You're a very decent young woman with the world in front of you and a good head on your shoulders, so I know you won't use it frivolously."

She stammered, "I..I..don't know what to say? This is totally unexpected! I'm not here for money, I didn't know you had this, I'm here because I found you."

"I know all that and now you've found me, you've given me another purpose to life. So please, accept it and enjoy it."

Sally sighed, rushed forwards and wrapped her arms around him, crying.

"You're such a kind man....so kind," she cried into his shoulder.

Archer patted her forearm, not only because he felt pride but because she was starting to strangle him.

"Come now, stop the crying."

She released her grip and stood back, sobbing and looking at the envelope.

"If only my own father was like this," she whispered.

Archer didn't respond but knew there was something about her father that she was keeping from him, even though he knew the full horror of his activities.

"You know, it would be lovely to meet your parents sometime, just to say hello."

Sally nodded, controlling her tears, "Yes I think that's the next step. I'm sure they would love to meet you."

"No rush," Archer replied, "Now, get yourself off to Chippy. You could buy him a lovely raincoat with some of that," he pointed at the envelope and chuckled.

"I'll spoil him somehow grandad."

She rushed forwards again and gave him a quick hug.

"Thank you so much once again," she said with utter gratitude.

"You're very welcome my dear. Go on now, I'll see you to the door."

They walked down the hallway slowly, giving Sally time to compose herself before she stepped outside to her parked car. She turned around at the door to him, "I'll see you soon grandad. I'll speak to mum and dad."

She moved forwards and kissed him on the cheek and Archer opened the door for her. Once again, as she walked to her car, she turned and gave him a quick wave which filled Archer's heart with joy. Again, he saw the similarities between her and Sandra, waved back as he watched her leave then closed the front door and felt the tears welling up in his eyes.

"Sandra, why didn't you tell me? God, I loved you so much," he whispered aloud.

Sally sat in her car and looked at the envelope on her lap. She wiped away the last tear and felt a heavy heart at the thought of telling her father what had just happened. She thought about not telling him about her grandad, but he said he wanted to meet her parents, so she took it as a duty out of respect to Archer and resigned herself to the task. She drove off and returned to her house in Mansfield.

When she parked up, she retrieved her mobile phone from her handbag on the passenger seat in order to talk to her mother first, followed by her father. Phoning them from inside the house would be impossible with Chippy bouncing around with excitement at her arrival. She selected her mother's number and selected it with her thumb.

"Hello dear," her mother answered.

"Hi mum, how's tricks?"

"All good Sally, how are you?"

"Same here mum. In fact, I've met grandad again today."

She felt the happiness growing in her gut and fought back tears as she spoke, "Mum, he's such a nice man. You wouldn't believe what he's just done!"

"Go on, I'm listening."

"Well, we went for lunch today and he's going to change his will to have me as his main benefactor to his estate. Not only that, but he's just given me ten thousand pounds, just because he's so kind."

"That's wonderful Sally. What a lovely thing to do. What are you going to do?"

"It's opened up doors mum. I've been wanting to do a few things with the house, but it will also pay for a course I want to do in college to help my work. I can't believe it. I didn't think men like him existed anymore," she laughed.

"Yeah, he's old school. He's from the era when men looked after their nearest and dearest. Your father puts money into my account, don't get me wrong, but it's barely enough for a pair of shoes," she said sarcastically.

"Well, we'll have to go on a shopping trip with some of this too mum."

"That's not what I meant love. No, you spend that wisely on yourself. He gave that to you and you alone, so make the most of it. Are you going to tell your father?"

"Yes mum, I really have to. Grandad has expressed a wish to meet the two of you. Would you be ok with that?"

"Yes of course. That would be super. Whether your dad is there or not, I couldn't care, I'd love to meet him. At the end of the day, he's my long-lost biological father too."

Sally couldn't help the smile on her face and even as she ended the call with her mother, she still smiled through the thought of having to phone her father. She thumbed through the contact list on her mobile phone and hesitated before slapping her thumb on his number. The phone rang a few times before he snapped his answer.

"Yes?" he quickly said.

"Dad. I know you don't care about grandad, but I just need you to listen. Just for a few seconds then I'll leave you to it."

He sighed heavily with impatience, "Go on."

"I met him today and he's given me ten thousand pounds and he's putting me down as the main benefactor to his estate. Just like that. He is such a kind and gentle man."

For once her father didn't make any kind of sarcastic, cutting remark.

"Ten thousand pounds?"

"Yep. He has money saved and thought he had no family to bequeath it to….until now."

Her father stayed quiet and she could tell he was thinking.

"Here's the bit you won't like, not that you like anything I say, but he has expressed a wish to see you and mum. Do you think you could act nice for an evening meal with him?"

"Yeah, sure, why not. When?"

Sally was somewhat surprised and reared her head backwards in shock as she sat in her car talking to him.

"Oh! Good. Soon then. I'll let you know."

"Righto," he replied and hung up, quickly.

"Bastard," Sally mouthed at her phone and pretended to spit at it. She gathered herself, got out of the car and entered her house to an ever-excited Chippy who bestowed her with love. She smothered him with hugs and kissed the top of his head, then very quickly ran upstairs to her bedroom to hide the thick envelope of money.

She spent the rest of the day working on her laptop and planning how to invest her new and very sudden bump up in her finances. As she was doing so, she knew her next priority was to unite her parents with her grandad and complete the circle. She resolved to make the first move the next day.

Chapter 15: The final plan.

Archer woke the following day and hoped that the start of his plan was fitting into place. He washed, shaved and changed into grey trousers and light blue grandad collar shirt. His newspaper was waiting for him, half sticking out of the letter box as he made his way downstairs and he took it and walked into the kitchen to make his usual tea and toast. He turned his kitchen radio on after making his breakfast and sat to read the paper, muttering the forever doom and gloom headlines. As he turned a page, he heard three soft knocks on the front door and instantly recognised them as coming from Sally.

He was a little surprised but was equally pleased, not only at the surprise of seeing Sally again, but because he knew the plan was taking shape.

He quickly and quietly moved into the living room, peered around the side of the bay window and smiled when he saw Sally waiting for him to answer. He floated into the hallway and opened the door, then showed his surprise at seeing her.

"Sally! Come on in my dear, I've just put a pot of tea on."

"I won't be long grandad, I've got work to do."

She stepped inside and Archer closed the door behind her. They walked into the kitchen, but Sally stayed standing up.

"A quick cup of tea?" he asked her.

"Sorry grandad, no thanks. I'll be quick, mum and dad would love to meet you so I was wondering if you would like to have a meal with us all at Frank's on Saturday evening, say for eight o'clock?"

Archer smiled widely, "Yes that would be super. Wow!, this is all happening at once. I get to meet my long-lost daughter."

Sally smiled and felt incredibly proud of herself, "Brilliant. I'm sure you and mum have much to talk about."

"Indeed, we do. Your father will be able to fill in a few blanks for me too, I'm sure."

"Well. I'm sure all will be revealed. It'll be good grandad; I'm so looking forward to it."

"That's settled then. Obviously if there's any changes, you can let me know."

Sally moved forwards and gave him a kiss on the cheek. "I'll see myself out grandad. Sorry for the rushed visit, but I'll arrange Saturday evening and see you there."

She trotted quickly down the hallway and as she started to open the door, she turned and called down the hallway to him.

"Thank you again grandad, I can't tell you enough how much you've done for me. Saturday is on me, ok?"

Archer laughed and called out to her as she was halfway through the door, "Ok my dear. Drive carefully now."

She closed the door, stepping out to another beautiful summer's day and really noticed the birdsong for a change. She almost felt like skipping to her car but kept her dignity and composure as she entered it and drove off back to her house.

When she arrived, she walked back into her house and took her mobile phone, which she had left charging and made the necessary calls. She knew the call to her mother would be easy enough and that she would agree to Saturday evening, but she dreaded the call to her father. Again, she selected his number and exhaled a deep breath to calm herself. He answered with the usual greeting to his daughter.

"Yes?"

"Dad, I'll be quick. Frank's this Saturday evening for eight o'clock. Can you make it?"

He exhaled the usual lack of patience for his daughter, "Fucks sake. I have fucking things to do on Saturday!"

"Do this one thing for us all, then we won't bother you after that. Please dad?"

He paused for a few seconds, sighing his distaste whilst Sally waited.

"Fuck it alright then. Yeah I'll meet the old bastard, I'm sure I can pretend to be all nicey nicey for a couple of hours."

Before Sally could say her thanks, he had already ended the call without any other word.

She listened to the few bleeps on her phone which signified the end of the call and stared at it, half in disbelief that he could be so callous. She tried to quell the rage rising in her stomach and resisted the urge to violently throw the phone against the living room wall. It was Chippy, quietly standing at her feet looking up at her with his tail softly wagging, which brought her round to quickly forgetting about the call to her father.

"Come on Chippy. A quick walk, then back to work." She looked at her phone again and searched for the phone number for Frank's restaurant and dialled it. A young male voice answered.

"Hello Frank's restaurant."

"Hello, could I book a table for four this Saturday evening at eight o'clock please?"

"One moment madam…." Sally heard the sound of turning pages in a book, "Yes madam that's available. What name shall I book it under?"

"Archer," she replied, "Sally Archer."

"That's fine, I have that booked for you and we'll look forward to seeing you all then."

"Thank yoooouuu," she replied and ended the call. She looked down at Chippy who was patiently waiting.

"Come on then, let's go."

Chapter 16: Family meeting.

Saturday morning and Archer woke, carried out his strength exercises for an hour and enjoyed a long, hot bath. For his age, he was incredibly strong and fit. To the casual observer, he looked like the stereotypical slow and aged man which suited his purposes beautifully. He changed and whittled the morning away by reading the paper, drinking tea and maintaining his pistol. He also took the intelligence file out again and re-read the contents regarding the man he knew as Chapman, but everyone else knew him as Clements. As he read, he tutted aloud, whispering, "Bad man. Bad, bad man."

He carefully oiled the pistol, making sure that it had just the right amount to keep the moving parts flowing freely and yet not too much that the oil gummed up with the dust present in the atmosphere.

He decided to take lunch in Frank's and stepped out to a rainy day, grabbing his Blackthorn walking stick as he exited the house to walk into the centre of Retford wearing his long coat and a flat cap.

Entering Frank's, he was greeted again by the owner. "Ah mister Archer. How are you today?"

"I'm fine Frank, just fine."

"I see we are welcoming you and more of your family this evening? Miss Sally Archer phoned a couple of days ago to book a table for four."

Archer smiled at the mention of Sally's name. She had booked it under the surname Archer, dropping her birth surname of Clements and he felt the pride rise in him. It also gave away how she really felt about her father.

"Are you ok?" Frank asked, looking at the walking stick.

"Oh yes, I'm fine. My arthritis plays up a bit when it rains," he smiled.

Frank took his coat and hat and showed Archer to his usual table at the back of the restaurant.

Archer ate a small lunch, studied the other customers as they sat, ate and talked and felt a very sudden peace wash over him as he thought about Sandra and his mother. It was a peculiar feeling; he couldn't feel sadness or joy, it was just a feeling of mutual peace. Like he knew they were resting well. He almost felt Sandra smiling at him now that he knew about their daughter and granddaughter, whom he had become very close to.

He left the restaurant and returned home, spending the rest of the day listening to the radio, reading his book and taking gentle short naps on his bed.

When he woke from one of those naps in the evening, he looked at his watch and saw that the time was seven o'clock. He washed and changed into dark grey trousers, white shirt and dark blue tie with a light brown wool jumper. When he moved downstairs, he took a look out of the living room bay window at the weather and was pleased to see the rain had cleared. There was the odd dark cloud that was spilling a bit of rain in the distance, but it heartened him to know he would be dry on arrival at Frank's. He took the walking stick propped up at the side of the front door and left the house, slowly making his way to the restaurant.

When he arrived, he entered to be greeted by Frank again. Frank had dressed in a suit this time and Archer knew it was out of respect to his best customer who was dining with a new found family.

"Ah there you are mister Archer. We have your table prepared, you're the first to arrive. How are you now? I worried about you earlier."

"I'm fine Frank, just fine. It plays up every now and then, but I rested this afternoon and took my medication so it's all good."

"Excellent. This way please." Frank escorted him to a table in front of his usual lunchtime table, close to the wall and pulled out a chair for Archer to sit. He had worked out by now how Archer liked to sit, facing the entrance and had selected the perfect chair for him.

"Thank you Frank," Archer said and slowly sat to await his new family, placing the walking stick on the floor close to the wall.

He had only sat for a few minutes, again studying the other customers when he saw Sally enter the restaurant. She looked beautiful, wearing a dark blue dress with a thin white belt around the waist and he smiled at the natural similarities between her and Sandra as the memories of what she used to wear came flooding back to him. Sally was greeted by Frank and he could see him greeting her with open arms and upturned palms as he complimented her on how she looked. As Sally took a few steps further forward, Archer saw Chapman and his wife enter. Chapman looked exactly like his photograph, the marks on his right cheek the most prominent feature, but he had put on a little bit of weight as the white shirt he was wearing was bursting at the buttons. Archer then saw his daughter but had to check his emotions. She was wearing a white blouse with black trousers and black high heels. She looked different to Sally, strangely it was Sally who reminded him more of Sandra and he stood to greet them.

Sally rushed forwards with excitement as her parents walked behind her and Archer opened his arms to hug her in a greeting.

She squealed as she got to within a few feet of him, "Grandad!" and wrapped her arms around him. Archer almost lost his balance as he hugged her back and laughed, "Hello my dear," and they squeezed each other.

"Grandad, this is my mother, your long-lost daughter Julie."

She stepped to one side to reveal her. Julie smiled politely, moved forwards and held out her hand which Archer took and shook gently.

Julie looked lost for words and uttered, "Hello…."

"It's ok. You don't have to call me "dad"," he replied to her, easing her discomfort.

She looked down at her feet and smiled when her husband barged forwards, holding out his hand.

"I'm Andrew. Andrew Clements," he said, without a smile on his face, his cold eyes burning through Archer.

"Pleased to meet you, Andrew," and they firmly shook hands.

Archer faced Sally and said to her parents, "Your daughter does you credit. You've brought her up to be a fine young lady."

Her father huffed a little and pulled out a chair and sat down. Sally pulled out a chair next to him and allowed her mother to sit, awkwardly, then Archer pulled out a chair between him and Julie allowing her to sit.

Archer sat and started the conversation as the waiter presented them with menus.

"So, Julie. You must have plenty of questions?"

She blushed and looked out of the corner of her eye to her husband who sat looking at his menu, not even smiling once.

"Well not really. I know you and mum split up for a reason, but when she met my dad, I just saw him as my real dad. I'm so sorry. I never traced you because that's how I grew up. Sally did all the work, she's really into studying the family tree."

Archer felt saddened by her obvious lack of interest and he could tell that she was suppressing her feelings because of the presence of her husband for whom Archer could only feel revulsion for. He studied her and realised they had the same shaped eyebrows and nose, but that was all. The rest was Sandra and he felt sad, so sad that she had been born without knowing who he really was. But then, even his own mother never knew who he really was.

"That's fine, I understand," he said reassuringly, then turned to Andrew.

"And you sir. What does Sally's father do for a living?"

Clements looked surprised at being asked and said, "I'm in logistics. I transport all sorts of goods around Europe and other parts of the world," he said as he returned to looking at the menu.

"That must keep you very busy then?" Archer asked.

Julie replied before he could say a word, "Yes, he spends a lot of time away from home."

"Well….it's better to be busy than being bored, I always say," he laughed a little.

Sally laughed too as did Julie, but Andrew didn't even flicker an emotion.

"Shall we order?" Sally announced and Archer beckoned over a waiter.

They ordered and tried to talk small talk as they dined, but the atmosphere was very difficult between the ladies and the man across the table who Archer was pretending so hard not to show any hatred for. When their meals were presented, they ate almost in silence and when they finished, Julie made her excuses to use the bathroom and Sally added, "I'll come too."

Archer stood in respect of the ladies leaving the table, but Clements sat, not even acknowledging their temporary departure.

Archer sat, looked across at Clements and asked, "Do you specialise in anything with your line of work?"

Clements looked at him, leaned forward and laced his fingers together with his elbows on the table.

"You listen to me, you old arthritic bastard. I don't know you; I don't fucking want to know you. I'm here out of curiosity and to tell you something. Are you fucking listening?"

Archer held half a smile and sat back, awaiting Clements's next vile words.

"Yes. I hear you."

"Good. I know you've become very close to my pathetic daughter and I know you've got money. If you want to see that fucking woman again, you better cough up. Do you understand?"

Archer pretended to be vulnerable and placed a hand on his chest, feigning shock.

"Please, I meant no harm with that money and I don't ask for harm in return," he pleaded.

Clements growled, "Shut the fuck up. You cough up twenty grand and you'll have all the access you want to Sally and I'll fuck off forever. Do you get me?"

"Yes….yes. Please, I don't want to lose Sally. She's only just found me."

"Right then, old man. You get me the money and I'll leave it there. If not, you'll never see her again and believe me, I'll make sure of that."

Archer so wanted to take a fork from the table and shove it through his eye, then use a spoon to take out the other one and he felt the bile rise in his stomach, but he held it all back.

"I agree, yes, ok. Please….I can have that for you tomorrow night."

"Thought you might, you old bastard."

"Yes alright, I get it. Could you come round to my house tomorrow evening at seven o'clock and I'll have it for you?"

Archer gave him the address and Clements took out his mobile phone, tapping it into the maps application he had. He rose from his seat and murmured to Archer, "I'll see you tomorrow," then turned, pretended to dial out on his mobile phone and walked out of the restaurant.

When he had left, Archer checked his surroundings to see if anyone was looking at him. When he realised no one was, he allowed himself to smile. His plan was taking shape beautifully and the trap had been set.

A couple of minutes passed and the ladies returned to the table and took their seats. Sally immediately noticed her father's empty chair.

"Where's dad?" she asked Archer.

He shrugged his shoulders and replied, "He had a phone call which he said he had to take, then gave his apologies and said an urgent matter had turned up at work and he needed to go. Such a shame, I was getting on well with him when you two were in the bathroom."

Sally looked surprised, "Really?"

"Yes. Lovely chap," Archer smiled at her.

Julie was not surprised in the least and apologised to Archer and Sally in turn.

"I'm sorry Adrian, he is a busy man with a very important job. We don't see much of each other. I'm sorry Sally, that's dad for you. You know what he's like. Would you mind giving me a lift home? Your father will obviously have taken the car."

Sally looked concerned for her and nodded, "Yes of course mum. No problem."

Archer looked over at the waiter and motioned a writing movement with his hands for the bill. The waiter nodded and brought it over to them.

"Sally, I know you said this is on you tonight, but please let me pay. Julie, I know and understand you don't want any contact with me...."

Julie interrupted him, "Please don't take any offence at that. I just don't see you as dad and I know you split from mum with bad feelings. It's nothing personal."

Archer raised a hand, "It's fine, honestly. But as a parting gift, just let me pay?"

She smiled, looked at Sally and replied with sincerity, "Ok then."

They rose from the table and Archer took his walking stick then paid, leaving a handsome tip as usual and they were bid a good night by a very grateful Frank who held the door open for them.

When they got outside, they walked to Sally's car and he opened the passenger door for Julie. She thanked him and when Archer closed the door behind her, he walked around to the driver's side and stopped Sally just as her hand was on the door handle.

"Sally, I have a little something for you tomorrow evening. Could you come round at half past seven please?"

"Oh grandad, you don't need to give me anything you know. You've already done enough," she presumed.

Archer laughed a little, "No, money isn't involved this time, but I do have an important matter for us both. I can't tell you yet, just come round tomorrow."

She smiled at him and gave him a kiss on the cheek and as she opened the door she said, "Yes of course, that's fine. I'll see you tomorrow."

Archer closed the door behind her and waved at them both as Sally drove off. He stood, smiling and watched them as the car disappeared through the streets. He was smiling at the thought of his plan being in place, but he was also worried that Sally wouldn't ruin it. He turned and made his way back to his house where he washed, slipped into his pyjamas and slid into bed. He could make his preparations tomorrow.

Chapter 17: The final act.

He woke to the most beautiful sound of birdsong on a summer's morning and realising it was still early, he lay in bed with his thoughts to entertain him. He reminisced about his life a little and remembered Sandra. He had propped up the photograph of her on his bedside cabinet and he lay on his side looking at it.

"You were so beautiful Sandra. How I wish you could have forgiven me," he whispered to the smiling photograph of her.

"Perhaps you will, when it comes to my passing and I see you again my love."

He lay in his bed for a couple of hours more, listening to the birdsong followed by the sounds of human activity as car engines were started, children screamed and laughed and mothers chatted together as they walked their children to school. Then he raised himself out of bed, carried out his strength exercises, stretched his body and decided to take a hot bath before breakfast. He walked downstairs with the intelligence file of Clements, or Chapman as the file had named him and spread it out over the kitchen table. He did his usual breakfast of tea and marmalade on toast, glancing over the profile that had been written about his last target. He felt utterly calm. Even though Clements had been aggressive towards him, he was used to such behaviour and didn't feel intimidated. Over breakfast, he read his

newspaper and listened to the radio and stayed there
until lunchtime.

Lunch, once again, was taken in Frank's and once again
it was eaten at his usual table. He ate, paid and as he
was leaving, he turned to Frank who was smiling at him
from the counter.

"Frank my friend, I always get a good meal here and I'm
very grateful to you. We all enjoyed a superb meal last
night, so thank you once again."

Frank noticed the change in Archer's voice and dropped
his usual patronising manner as he replied.

"You're very welcome mister Archer, you've always
been very good to us too. I'm glad your granddaughter
found you and I hope we see you all again. The young
lady seemed so delighted to see you, it warms the heart
sir."

Archer smiled and noticed how Frank hadn't mentioned
Andrew and Julie. Archer gave him a sloppy salute and
exited, walking out of the restaurant feeling somewhat
proud of himself.

He took a detour to the shops as he walked home and
went into the card shop on Carolgate and bought a
sympathy card.

When he returned, he climbed upstairs to his bedroom
and fetched his pistol. Checking its operation one more
time and making sure the silencer was firmly in place,
he took it downstairs and into the living room. Sitting in
the armchair to the right of the living room door, facing
the bay window, he slid the pistol down the side of the
chair cushion making sure it was in line with his hand as
he stood up then sat back down again. He practised

sitting down and locating the pistol over and over again, making sure the arm and hand movement seemed natural to a pretend observer sitting on the sofa opposite him. The same sofa his loathsome father used to hurl abuse from and drink himself into a drunken stupor. When he was satisfied, he returned to the kitchen and wrote out the sympathy card and addressed it to the post office box he usually wrote to in order to signify a successful kill. Then he took to reading his book and listening to the radio. Now it was just a waiting game. As the hours passed, he was aware of the sun falling for the evening and he made himself a couple of slices of cheese on toast to keep his strength up. When he finished, he washed his plate and cutlery and tidied them away. As he did so, he was almost startled when two quick and loud knocks sounded on the front door. He looked at his watch and saw that it was five minutes to seven o'clock.

"Time for the final act," he told himself and looked for the shadow of a pair of legs in the daylight through the thin gap at the bottom of the door. He swiftly and quietly moved into the living room and peered slowly around the window frame of the bay window. He smiled when he recognised Chapman, standing and looking around him as he waited for an answer. He viciously knocked twice more. Archer quietly moved into the hallway and stooped his back a little, pretending to look frail as he opened the door. Before the door was even halfway open, Chapman barged in, his face red with anger.

"You fucker. You left me hanging there!"

Archer stood back and took a couple of quick steps backwards to open the door fully.

"Sorry. Come in. Through to the living room on the left there."

Chapman stared at him briefly then rushed into the living room, standing in front of the fireplace and waiting for Archer to close the front door and join him.

Archer walked slowly into the room and held out a hand over the sofa.

"Take a seat."

"Where's the fucking money old man?"

"Sit, sit, please. It's here, I just need to compose myself. This is very stressful."

As Chapman bent down to sit on the edge of the sofa, Archer made the same movement at the same time and lowered himself into his armchair, sliding his right hand down the side and locating the pistol.

Chapman sat with his elbows on his knees and an expectant look on his face as he stared at Archer.

Archer pretended to be gasping for air and trying to compose himself.

"You better hurry up you old shit. Look at you for fucks sake! Fit for fuck all…"

But before Chapman could say another vile word, Archer swooped the pistol out and fired two bullets. Both of them tore into Chapman's right kneecap, burrowing deep into the bone and depriving him instantly of the ability to stand and attack Archer. As Chapman started to scream, Archer flew out of his chair and moved forward to him as he clutched at his right knee with both hands, the blood flowing freely down his shin, soaking his trouser leg. Archer gripped his neck with his left hand and squeezed it as hard as a vice, then slowly slid the silenced end of the pistol inside Chapman's mouth.

"Ssshhhh now. No more screaming mister Chapman or I'll end it now!" Archer whispered with venom at him. Chapman stared back at him; eyes wide open at the realisation that Archer knew his pseudonym.

"When I take this pistol out of your filthy mouth, you better just take the pain like a man. If you scream, I'll end you right now. Are you listening?"

Chapman nodded small, quick nods with the pistol in his mouth.

"Excellent," Archer hissed and slowly took the silencer out of his mouth, then gradually released his grip, stepping backwards to his armchair, all the while keeping the pistol trained on Chapman.

Chapman sat back on the sofa and raised his knee, the agony wrapped across his face as he tried not to move his leg, clutching the damage with his hands.

"Not quite the old fucker then. Who are you?" he growled through clenched teeth.

"The name is real; the retired frail old man is not. I've been a nightmare for many, many people like you."

"How do you know my other name?"

"You're not the only one with connections, you idiot. Did you really think you could get away with that kind of vile activity and escape the notice of powerful people?"

Chapman didn't react. He carried on grimacing at the pain and clutching his knee.

"I have a question for you, Chapman."

"Ask then for fucks sake!"

"Did you kill that young girl?"

Chapman closed his eyes in agony for a few seconds, rocking backwards at the pain in his knee, studying Archer then answered.

"Yes. Absolutely. She fucking deserved it and it was a message to the rest of the little bitches!"

Archer realised Chapman knew there was no point in lying. Archer probably already knew, so he might as well reveal his true character.

Archer felt nothing but pure rage for his target, but he needed to bide his time. The final piece of the plan would soon take shape and he was so sickened with Chapman that he couldn't find the words to show how much he felt hatred for him.

Archer sat, staring at him, emotionless and unconcerned about Chapman's condition as the blood had trickled from his knee, down his shin and started to drip onto the floor.

Chapman was clutching at his knee and gasped the odd, "Ah!" in pain as any slight movement released a new shooting pang of agony, when Archer heard three soft knocks on the front door. He rose from the armchair, keeping the pistol pointed at Chapman and quietly closed the living room door. He moved to the bay window and peered around the side to see Sally standing at the front door. With the pistol pointed towards his target and out of view, he tapped on the window, drawing Sally's attention who smiled in recognition and beckoned her in. He moved back into the room, standing in front of the fireplace with the pistol still on Chapman, listening for the front door to open then close.

Sally stepped inside and called out, "Grandad?"

"I'm in the living room dear. Go into the kitchen please."

Sally was a little bemused but thought that this was part of the "little something" that her grandad had for her. She walked into the kitchen to find the table strewn with photographs and documents. As she moved closer to the table, slowly, she began to realise the photographs were of her father.

"What the.....?" she whispered to herself. She picked up the photographs and then began to read the dossier about her father. After a few minutes of reading, she rushed to the nearest receptacle, being the kitchen sink and vomited violently. She wanted to scream with anger and hate, but she knew that would only attract attention. She was equally bemused at her grandad and how he had received these documents and a thousand questions flowed through her mind. So many questions, so much emotion that she almost felt dizzy.

She walked down the hallway and opened the living room door where she was immediately greeted with the sight of her grandad, standing in front of the fireplace with a gun. She looked in the direction of where the gun was pointing, turned to her left at the sofa and saw her father, clutching at his knee and obviously in pain. Her father didn't say a word.

"Grandad? What the fuck is going on? Why have you got a gun?"

"Please my dear, there is something you need to know and understand."

She stood in the doorway, waiting for an answer.

"I'm not the frail old man everyone takes me for. My split from your grandmother was because of this. It was because of what I do. I'm an assassin to the worst kind of people and Sandra couldn't accept it."

"You….you've been doing this all your life?" she raised her eyebrows in utter surprise.

"Yes…and now I have to deal with your father."

She looked down at him and stared at him with complete revulsion.

"He's not my father. He never really was."

She turned to address him.

"Look at you now. LOOK AT YOU NOW!" she hissed at him, leaning into his face.

She slapped him as hard as she could, but Chapman just looked at her and a smile grew on his face as he started to chuckle. She slapped him hard again, but the smile just grew.

Sally looked at her grandad and felt an overwhelming rush of emotion for him. She understood. She couldn't help herself and rushed over to Archer and held out her arms to hug him. Archer saw her speed and diverted his attention to her and as she got closer, he stepped back a half step, his foot clipping the hearth of the fireplace and he momentarily lost his balance as he raised his left hand to stop her and regain his balance.

He called out, "No Sally!" as she moved forwards, distracting him and it was just enough time for Chapman to play his trump card.

Archer saw Chapman's right hand slip inside his coat pocket and very swiftly produced his own pistol with a short silencer and pointed it towards Archer.

Archer, despite his loss of balance and subsequent tumble, was able to fire off two shots at his target just as Chapman fired two shots at Archer.

Archer's shots were not as accurate this time. One bullet tore into Chapman's upper right arm, the other bullet struck him in the side of his neck, blood splattering on the wall behind him. Chapman dropped his pistol, the power in his right arm lost to the bullet within it. The whole movement had accentuated the pain in his knee and he growled at the amount of agony he was in.

At the same time, Archer felt the hammer blow of the two bullets fired by Chapman slamming into his chest. His knees instantly collapsed from the hydrostatic shock cascading through his body and the strength immediately left him, his pistol clattering onto the hearth. He managed to hear Sally screaming, "NO!" as he fell to the ground.

He lay in front of the hearth and felt the searing, excruciating pain in his chest and he fought hard for breath. Gasping he looked up to see Sally standing over him, the look of worry etched across her face.

"GRANDAD!" she called out and she knelt next to him and panicked at the sheer amount of blood pumping out of his chest. Her hands shook as she didn't know what to do, but Archer calmed her. Looking up at her, he smiled as he gasped for air.

"It's ok, it's ok…." he whispered, "Calm yourself."

He laboured for air, trying desperately to stay awake, fighting the urge to drift into a very deep sleep.

"I'm so sorry Sally," he gasped, "Forgive me."

Sally burst into tears as she realised her grandad was slipping away, "Oh grandad. Of course, there's nothing to forgive."

Archer smiled as he stared into her eyes, "That's my girl….thank you."

He breathed deeply a few times, his lungs rattling and the sound reverberated in his words, "Sally…..send the card. The card…."

Sally watched him, trying to comfort him and held his left hand and she nodded to him through the tears, stroking the side of his face.

Archer felt the pain disappearing and his breathing became shallow as thoughts and memories cascaded in his mind. As his eyesight became blurred and flowed into darkness, he saw Mercury's face, smiling at him. He saw his mother and then as the last breath was exiting his lungs the darkness gave way to a brilliant white light. He looked into it and gradually saw a figure approaching him. He could only feel love now, there was no pain. He wasn't even in the living room anymore; he didn't know where he was and yet he felt an overwhelming sense of belonging. As the figure approached him and he began to recognise it, he no longer felt alone. As Sandra came into his vision, she held out her hand and smiled at him, mouthing the words, "I love you."

Archer held out his hand and took hers.

Sally watched him as he passed away. The heavy breathing, the struggle for air gradually weakened as his eyelids began to close and she heard him whisper, "Sandra.....Sandra."

She cried like she had never cried before as she watched his chest, no longer rising and falling from his body demanding oxygen to live. She looked at his still face and his final act was a small tear which welled up in his right eye, then overflowed and trickled slowly down his cheek. She smiled at him through her own tears and said a prayer as she wished him farewell.

"Dear lord, please accept this kind soul into your kingdom." she whispered, "Judge him with your sweetest mercy and allow him to rest with loved ones."

As she sobbed over his body, she whispered to her grandmother.

"Sandra, he's back with you now. Please forgive him."

As she grieved over Archer, her father spoke up.

"You stupid bitch. Can't you see he baited you?"

He was gasping in panic as he held the wound in his neck with his left hand, the blood trickling through his fingers. Sally looked over at him with hatred and he continued.

"He gave you ten grand because he knew you would tell me and I would end up here."

"He was more of a father as well as a grandfather to me in the short time that I knew him!"

"Don't be so fucking stupid," he blurted, blood mixing with his saliva as it flew in droplets out of his mouth.

"He's a fucking assassin. He didn't know kindness."

"AND YOU'RE A FUCKING CHILD MURDERER AND MOLESTER!" she croaked at him.

"Ha! Business is business," he said, dismissing her.

Sally saw Archer's pistol lying to the side of the hearth and she knew what had to be done. She leaned across Archer's body and took it in her right hand and stood up, pointing the pistol at Chapman. Her chest was heavy with sadness and loathing at the same time.

Chapman saw the change in her expression and started to panic.

"Don't be stupid Sally. Get me an ambulance. My phone is in my left pocket. Get me an ambulance."

Sally didn't even hesitate and fired a shot at him. The bullet tore into his right cheek, bulging the eye and snapping his head back in shock. She saw that the first bullet didn't do the job and kept pulling the trigger, the sound of the brass bullet shells echoing around the room as they landed on the floor. The bullets entered his face, bursting his eyes, tearing holes in his flesh and shattering teeth as they drilled through him. Eventually the pistol stopped firing as it had run out of bullets and she lowered it, sobbing as she surveyed the body.

Despite the mess she had created, she felt nothing but satisfaction that her monster of a father was finally gone.

"Not much of an accident now am I dad?" she whispered to the body.

Sally looked at Archer, knelt next to him again and kissed him on the forehead.

"Goodnight grandad," she whispered as she stroked his hair, "It's finally over for you now."

She stayed a few seconds with him, then felt a sense of urgency move over her as the realisation of the situation she was in, dawned on her. The police would have to be called and she knew the scene would be forensically examined, so she wiped the pistol clean of her fingerprints with Archer's jumper and carefully placed it in his hand. She squeezed his index fingertip onto the trigger, so that if the pistol was examined it was only his prints on the gun. If the trigger had been kept clean, questions would be asked as to how he fired it. She decided to leave the rest of the room as it was. It didn't matter that her DNA would be around the room, as she had made many visits to him and it would be dismissed as so. Or at least, that's what she hoped. She took the mobile phone out of Chapman's pocket and dialled 999, then wiped it clean with his clothing and placed it in his hand.

Sally moved out of the living room and quickly went to the kitchen, where she left the intelligence file but took the sympathy card in order to post it to who knows where. When she got to the front door, she took a mental check of everything, ensuring she had done her best to hide her tracks then exited the house. She kept her head pointed downwards, lest a passer-by saw her reddened eyes from crying and made her way back to her car. As she drove home to Mansfield, she stopped at a post box and dropped the sympathy card into it. She continued to drive and she thought about her grandad and how proud of him she felt. She tried hard to explain in her mind, how she could feel the way she felt about this old assassin being her grandfather, but she eventually gave in to the feeling. Only God could judge her now.

She arrived at her house and fought the tears as she walked to her front door, trying to keep her composure and look normal to those nosey enough to view her. When she entered the door and slowly closed it behind her, Chippy came bouncing down the hall to greet her in his usual enthusiastic way. She bent down and hugged him and smothered him with love as he licked at her face.

She spent the rest of the night in a dark living room, lost in her thoughts and emotions and as she went to her bed in tears, she wished Archer a goodnight.

Chapter 18: The road continues.

A few days passed by and Sally wondered why she hadn't seen the report about Archer and her father on the television. Every time she left her house, she expected to be swooped upon by hidden police officers, but nothing happened.

On the fourth evening, she sat in her living room with the television on, which she was paying no attention to as she carried out internet searches on various websites with her laptop, when she heard three loud and quick knocks on the door. The sudden rush of adrenaline at hearing the knocks put her into a panic and she exited her living room to open the door.

The street was in a semi darkness as the sun was setting and she looked at the source of the knocks to see a wide shouldered, middle-aged man, dressed in a dark grey three-piece suit, black shoes and wearing a long coat. He had a chiselled jawline and dark brown eyes which showed very little emotion.

"Yes?" she asked.

"Good evening. Sally Clements?" asked the man.

"Er, yes."

"Police madam. May I come inside?"

Sally stepped to one side and replied, "Oh. Yes. Come in," the panic rising in her stomach.

The man entered the hallway as she closed the door behind him.

"Don't do that again," he said as he led the way into the living room with a confidence Sally had never seen before and she felt compelled to follow.

"Sorry? Do what?"

"I said I was from the police and you never thought to check my identity."

"Oh. Yes, you're right but you're so well dressed I just automatically assumed you are who you say you are."

The man raised a finger, "Never assume. Always check."

"Ok then. So, who are you?"

"Names aren't important Sally, but I come from a government department that nobody knows exists. You are not in any trouble and I have a proposition for you that you will not be able to resist. We need people like you."

Sally was instantly confused. It gradually dawned on her that this man was not in her home to question and arrest her about the killings in Retford.

The man continued, "Sally, we know Archer is dead and we know what really happened. We monitored police radios and so we took over the scene. You slipped up a bit."

Sally was utterly bemused by now and crossing her arms she asked, "What the hell do you mean?"

The man smiled at her knowingly, "How could Archer post the sympathy card if he was dead? Our operatives only post those cards when their jobs are complete."

He waited for her response, but Sally was lost for words.

"We know your bloodline; we know what you did to your so-called father and so we want you to become an employee. You will be handsomely paid my dear!"
Sally felt a sense of relief and yet a sense of worry about her future. She thought quickly after looking around her, taking in her life so far.
She nodded to him, taking the ultimate chance.
"Ok then, who are you?"
The man straightened himself, she could see he was proud of his discovery as he smiled more at her.
"You will know me as Mercury."